IMPACT

IMPACT

Alice Reeves

iUniverse, Inc.
New York   Bloomington

Impact

This is a work of fiction. All of the characters, names, incidents, organizations, and dialogue in this novel are either the products of the author's imagination or are used fictitiously.

iUniverse books may be ordered through booksellers or by contacting:

iUniverse
1663 Liberty Drive
Bloomington, IN 47403
www.iuniverse.com
1-800-Authors (1-800-288-4677)

ISBN: 978-1-4401-9207-4 (pbk)
ISBN: 978-1-4401-9208-1 (ebk)

Printed in the United States of America

iUniverse rev. date: 12/02/2009

One

October 22, 1997

Houston, Texas

As Marianne Mavin stepped out of La Parisian where she worked, pulled the door closed and keyed the deadbolt in place, she noticed that the newly hired janitor had not replaced the burned-out light bulb teetering above the door. She shrugged. Not my problem.

With the door securely locked behind her, she turned and squinted toward a small fuzzy-white puddle. The boxes, she thought, shivering at the grotesque shapes darkness had given familiar objects.

I ought to just get in the car and go. Forget the boxes. The kids would never know. For a moment, she hesitated. A sense of guilt raced through her. "But I would," she whispered, then pulled in a steadying breath. Don't be silly, she thought. Anyway, there's no one here but me and that old brindle cat. I'll just throw the boxes in the trunk and go. It'll only take a minute or two.

An intuitive sense of foreboding suddenly shot through her. A chill ran down her spine. She hesitated briefly, then pushed the feeling aside and started toward the containers. This really was a stupid idea. But I have no choice, now.

Lights from a passing car flicked eerily over the area.

Cans clattered.

Her heart leaped. "Who's there?" she called.

"Meow," came from the dark.

Relief sped through her, then the unmistakable scrape of a footstep sounded.

Gasping, she whirled around. "Who's there?" she again cried.

1

A bulk tore itself from the side of the building and loomed before her.

Her throat closed.

The heavy scent of garlic filled her nostrils. Her heart pounded.

She gripped the keys with fingers gone suddenly sweaty. "Who are you?" she asked, commanding her voice to firmness. "What do you want?"

Her mind whirled frantically. If I can get to the car, I'll be safe. Forcing her fright-numbed legs to motion, she edged toward her car.

A flash of passing car lights brushed a narrow face.

She relaxed a bit as she recognized him. "Oh," she said, breathing easier. "What are you doing here?"

He stepped closer. "Waiting for you, Missy."

Alarmed, she shrank back, turned and bolted for the car. A string of obscenities poured from him as he stuck out a foot and tripped her. Her head snapped back. The keys flew from her hand. A kaleidoscope of images whirled and danced before her eyes. An arm crumpled beneath her. Grit bit into her face. Hands gripped her. A knee rammed into her back. She fought for breath. "No," she wheezed. Hands tightened. Swearing, he rolled her to her back. She struggled. Clawed at his face. Missed it. Her fingers landed on a button, clutched it. She felt it tear free.

Swearing, he rolled her face down. Caught her wrists. Tied them together. Again flipped her to her back. Straddled her. "Help," she screamed. "Bitch," he muttered. A fist slammed into her face. Again. Something sharp bit into the flesh beneath her chin. "Holler again and you're dead." he threatened. A vise-like grip caught her jaws. Squeezed. Her mouth popped open. He jammed a rag into it. She gagged. Fought for breath. Her mind swung crazily. Oh, God, what can I do? What can I do? Hands clutched the neckline of her dress. Tore it open. The feel of cold metal slid between her breasts. Her bra fell aside. He bent. Bit a nipple. Pain. Pain. She moaned. Blood, hot to her cold flesh, spread over her breast. Blood. Blood. Her panties were off. Her legs forced apart. A zipper whispered. He was inside her, pounding, hammering, ripping, tearing. Blood. Blood. Blood. Searing pain raced through her. Fired her brain. Bloody images spun.

Two

Marianne, her right arm in a cast from armpit to finger-tips, her head cris-crossed with bandages and her birth canal packed with yards of sterile gauze, lay on a narrow hospital bed fighting her way up through layers of thick, clinging anesthesia. Impersonal faces bent over her. Snatches of remembered talk now and then penetrated the encompassing fogginess. Questions. Sympathy. Small gaps where no words existed, where for a time she retreated into the restful comfort of emptiness, remembering nothing. But only for a time.

As she struggled closer and closer to the surface of her mind, she cringed from the hurtful, invading awareness. A tear crawled slowly past her temple and disappeared as if never `formed into the edge of the soft cotton bandage covering her head. Whimpering, she sought to return to forgetfulness where no pain existed.

A green-capped nurse fussing around her bed looked down at her. "Well, you're back with us," she whispered, her voice friendly.

Marianne groaned and mumbled through stiff, parched lips? "Did?"

"Doctor Shaw will want to know you're awake," the woman interrupted, turning away.

To forget the snippets of horror tumbling through her mind, Marianne silently prayed as she drifted back to that hushed, tranquil reservoir of darkness. Minutes later, Doctor Shaw stood beside her and lifted her hand. She roused. "Glad to see you're awake," he said, feeling for her pulse. "They'll get you to a room shortly."

Marianne woke, "Is?"

Gently, he patted her hand. "Everything's fine, dear," he said, turning away. "We'll talk later."

"But, but . . . " Marianne said, watching his white head disappear through the door.

3:30 that same morning.

At the pound of heavy footsteps, Marianne struggled up from the last gossamer wisp of forgetfulness and saw Len, guilt written across his face, hurry into the room, the tail of his half-buttoned shirt flopping. With a modicum of maturity now settled across his rugged features, he was even more handsome than six years earlier, when, as Freedom High's heroic quarterback, he had first approached her for a date. He fell to his knees beside her bed. "My God, Marianne, what happened?" he asked. "Was you in a wreck?"

The scent of cigarette smoke, stale beer, and an illusive suggestion of perfume that clung to the rich plaid shirt he wore, assailed her nostrils.

He lifted her free hand, kissed it, and stared at her swollen, lacerated face, her bandaged head, the bloodied slits through which she looked.

Unaccountable feelings of shame coursed through her. She closed her eyes. "Raped," she mumbled, her lips feeling like slabs of splintered wood.

His deeply-tanned face stiffened into an unreadable mask. His entire being seemed to withdraw. "Raped?" he cried, dropping her hand. "Son of a bitch," He stared at her through eyes grown suddenly hard, rose to his six-foot-four, bent, reached as if to take her hand again, then apparently changing his mind, quickly pocketed his own. "Son of a bitch. Who? Who?" His lips curled in distaste. Revulsion filled his voice. "Raped." Hastily, he stepped back and stood silent a moment. "Sorry Marianne, but I, I gotta get outta here," he muttered. He shook his head as if stunned, abruptly turned away, and without a backward glance stalked out the door.

Feeble morning light had brightened the sky when Doctor Shaw, with a nurse in tow, entered Marianne's room. "Good morning, young lady," he said. On reaching her bed, he lifted her hand and smiled at her. "You feel a little better this morning?" He released her hand, folded the covers back, and began to examine the cuts, bruises and abrasions that covered her body. "Ummmm, looking better," he murmured. He glanced up at her. "They ever get hold of Len?"

Remembering the distaste she'd seen on Len's face, Marianne cleared her throat and blinked back tears. "Yes," she whispered, avoiding eye contact.

He drew the covers in place, straightened his lean frame and dismissed the nurse, then walked to the window and stood gazing out. At last, he sighed heavily and turned back to Marianne. "Mrs. Mavin . . . Marianne, there's no easy way to say this, but . . . you lost your baby, and . . . you'll never carry another."

Denial sprang to her lips as she shut out the hateful, invading words. She grasped the covers with her free hand, threw them aside, placed her hand on the gentle curve of her abdomen and glared at him. "That's not true. Look. Look, I'm pregnant." Her voice broke on tears.

Quietly, Dr. Shaw approached her bed, stood a few moments, then sighed and patted her foot. "Get some rest, dear," he said, turning toward the door. "We'll talk tonight."

Thoughts of the past crowded in. Anxious for an interruption in her menstrual cycle, she had at last given up on nature intervening, and months before had begun her campaign. After weeks of daily harping for the two of them to go to a fertility clinic, Len had finally given in. When thorough examinations and tests were completed, time was needed for Doctor Shaw to collect a large enough bank of Len's sperm to insure fertilization. Days that seemed like weeks dragged past as they waited for her to ovulate, then additional time to get the results. When, at last, a test determined that she was pregnant, she was ecstatic.

Remembering, she folded her arm around a clutch of blanket, rubbed a bandaged cheek against it and stared out the window. Against the bleak, wintry sky, pictures of her assailant, castrated and sprawled in a puddle of his own blood, spread their guile before her.

She closed her eyes, and as she drifted off, memories of the previous night crowded in.

For the last thirty minutes she had questioned Bertha's sanity for staying open so late. It doesn't make sense, she thought. Other stores along the strip close hours earlier.

And tonight of all nights, when unexpected circumstances had left her alone in the store, a young Hispanic couple, the woman about her own age, had drifted in. Apparently coming from the restaurant at the end of the strip, they had delayed her closing.

Apprehensive, Marianne had watched them leisurely browse, the man absently rolling a toothpick between his teeth, the woman removing every maternity dress La Belle carried, holding them against her swollen body and turning toward the man for his smile of approval or frown of disapproval, then carelessly cramming the clothes back on the rack.

Making small talk, Marianne joined them and followed the woman, hand-brushing and smoothing the discarded garments and carefully replacing them to their accustomed spot. Finally, they thanked her and left.

Irritated, she glanced at the clock as she hurried behind them and locked the door. Fifteen minutes late already, she thought. And on the very night I'd planned Len's favorite meal. If he bothers to come home on time. After calling home several times and leaving a message each time, she had given up when the couple walked in. Maybe he'll call back, she thought as her mind turned to the past weeks. A sense of hopelessness surged through her. Get real, Marianne, she told herself. Since when did a meal lure any man away from his favorite watering hole? Len loves to eat, but expecting mere food to work magic is foolish. She sighed.

She dismissed the unhappy thoughts and reached to turn off the strong, overhead lights as a police cruiser passed. They flashed their lights and waved. It was a comfort to know that every hour, on the hour, they drove past. She chuckled. Ordinarily, I could set my watch by them, she thought. Every night but tonight. Keys in hand, she hurried towards the back of the store.

Sobbing, Marianne struggled up from the bottomless abyss into which sleep had taken her. Her eyes snapped open just as a nurse entered the room carrying a tray which held a paper cup and a hypodermic syringe.

Seeking oblivion, Marianne swallowed the contents of the cup and turned her hip for the blessed relief the hypo would bring.

As Marianne woke from the drugged sleep, truth began to filter into her consciousness; the painful wrenching of her back; the gut-deep cramping in her pelvis; how quickly she'd been shunted out of emergency; the compassion on Doctor Shaw's face as he told her the bad news. It's true, she thought. It's all true. I can't hide from it any longer.

Resignation settled on her, weighted her down. The constant chatter in her head subsided as depression set in. A sense of guilt claimed her thoughts. If only I hadn't pinned so much importance on those boxes, she thought. But that wouldn't have changed anything. He would still have been out there waiting to grab me.

The watery October sky had deepened to night when the unmistakable pound of Len's heavy footsteps again sounded.

"Well, they got the son of a bitch," he said on entering the room. Reaching her bed, he hesitantly lifted her hand, bent and lightly brushed her cheek with his lips.

Relief poured through the haze of grief enveloping Marianne. "Thank God," she whispered. "But, Len . . . Len I lost the baby." The words rushed out. Her voice thinned. "And I can't ever have another. Not ever."

He dropped her hand. His mouth gaped open. "You what? You mean after all I went through to get you pregnant? Why'n you tell me that last night?"

Tears, just beneath the surface, spilled over. "I didn't know."

Staring at her, as if at a stranger, he plopped into a chair and sat silent as sobs wracked her. At last, refusing to meet her eyes, he glanced at his watch, shuffled his feet and rose. "Look, " he mumbled, "I, I'm sorry 'bout everything, Marianne, but maybe it's for the best. Maybe we're not s'posed to have children . . ." He stood silent for a moment, then turned away. "I better go."

Feelings of total desertion washed over Marianne. "Please call Bertha and the church."

Stony-faced, he nodded. "Okay," he said.

Three days later, Dr. Shaw, and a nurse wheeling a towel-draped cart, entered Marianne's room. "Going to remove the packing this morning," Dr. Shaw said. "See how you're coming along."

Ten minutes later, with the slight bulge of her lower abdomen lessened, hard reality became even clearer to Marianne.

Three

Three days later, Marianne, slumped in a wheelchair, absentmindedly responded to the hospital volunteer's attempt at small talk, then with pain raging in her heart, she lowered her chin to her chest and retreated to the place in her mind where her baby still lived.

At last, Len's heavy footsteps sounded. Sticking his head in the door only long enough to announce he'd be waiting out front, he closed the door and left. Thoughts of the excuses he'd used to avoid going to see her, again ran through Marianne's mind. Tears stung her eyes.

As the attendant wheeled the chair into the hall, she saw Len leave the building almost at a run. By the time she and the volunteer reached the door, he had pulled her Toyota into the driveway and was waiting.

As Marianne got in and settled into the passenger seat, Len drummed his fingers on the steering wheel. Barely giving the attendant time to close the car door and step back, he jammed the accelerator to the floor and tore out of the driveway.

Marianne groaned. "Len," she cried.

He glanced at her from the corner of his eye. "Sorry. Didn't mean to hurt you. I just gotta get to work! *We had another explosion at the plant last night.*"

As Marianne's pain subsided, she studied him, his narrowed eyes staring straight ahead, his jaw clamping and relaxing, his body pushing against the car door as if trying to get as far from her as the interior of the car allowed. Why wasn't it all over the news this morning? she wondered. What's going on? Puzzled, she looked away and frowned. "I didn't hear anything about it on the news," she said.

He flared. "You sayin' I'm lyin'?"

"No, Len. It just seems that with so many people living near the plant, the TV stations would have announced it. They always have, in case there's another explosion."

Silently, he stared straight ahead and ground his teeth.

Moments later, some hundred feet ahead of them, a traffic light turned red.

Waiting until the last second to slam on the brakes, the car jolted to a stop, only inches from an elderly woman, who, with the aid of a cane, was moving slowly across the street. Marianne, again thrown against the seat back, groaned.

"Sorry," Len said.

Startled, the woman blanched and stopped short, then with eyes stretched wide, watched him as she continued on.

When the light changed, giving the woman barely time to clear his bumper, he floor-boarded the pedal and lurched ahead.

"Len!" Marianne cried in alarm.

Exasperation filled his voice. "Damned old woman can't walk she oughta stay home," he muttered. "I gotta get to work."

Leaning as little as possible on Len, Marianne entered their duplex and dropped, exhausted, into a recliner.

"Whacha wanna eat?" he asked.

"Tortilla soup and crackers," she said." Lots of crackers," she added.

"Another damn stop."

"I'm sorry. Forget it. I'll just–"

His face reddened. *"Sorry,"* he muttered. "Like I tol' you, I jus' gotta get to work. Anything else?"

Wordlessly, Marianne shook her head.

Thirty minutes later, Len returned. He placed a box of saltines and a quart container on the kitchen counter, turned toward her and lightly brushed her forehead with his lips. "I'll prob'ly be gettin' home late," he said on his way out the door.

As the days crept by, Marianne, sleeping in snatches, only picked at the food Len brought in. With his claim of working weekends and his coming home later and later on other nights, their relationship quickly deteriorated to little more than mutters and grunts. Resentfully, she watched him come and go.

Since that horrid night she tried to push from her mind, the thought of leaving the safety of her home held nothing but terror for her. The only place she felt totally safe was behind the double-locked doors. With her ears keenly tuned to every sound, even the ring of the phone or the emptying of the ice-maker was enough to send her heart racing, yet the time for her first post-hospital visit to the doctor was coming up. A sigh trembled up as she thought of it.

Four

With her stomach in knots, Marianne clenched her icy hands and shifted her gaze from the streets they were traveling to the back of the driver's head.

"You all right, Miss?" the cabbie asked, catching her eye in the mirror.

Marianne pushed harder into the corner of the seat, held her breath and nodded. "Yes," she said.

Twenty minutes later, she exited the cab, stood a moment wrapping herself in courage, then pulled in a shaky breath and approached the door to the fertility clinic. Blinking sunlight from her eyes, she entered and glanced around.

Women in all stages of pregnancy sat about the waiting room leafing through ragged pages of months-old magazines, waiting to see if the womb-encompassed babies they carried were alive and growing as expected.

Bitterly, she laid a hand on her stomach as grim reality again settled in.

Thirty minutes later, she was weighed, her vitals taken and was shown to an examination room. Hands clammy, legs clamped tightly together, she settled into a chair and waited.

Doctor Shaw entered, smiled and held out a hand. "How are you today, young lady? You're looking good," he said.

Marianne shrugged and forced a smile. "Okay."

Laying her chart on the examination table, he studied it, then straightened and turned to her. "I see you've lost a few pounds." A teasing note entered his voice. "What's wrong? Isn't that husband of yours feeding you?"

Tears sprang to Marianne's eyes. She sniffed and groped in her purse.

Face still, eyes watchful, Doctor Shaw looked at her. "Sorry, dear," he said, averting his eyes and handing her a box of tissues. "Losing or gaining weight is normal for a woman who's been raped . . . uh . . . are you getting out any?"

Not trusting herself to speak, Marianne shook her head.

"That would help you get through these first weeks." His voice was kind.

She looked down at her clenched hands. "I know, but . . . but there's nowhere I want to go,"

"Len come with you today?"

Fighting the need to tell all, Marianne swallowed hard and shook her head. "I took a cab," she said. Pushing a wheeled stool close, he sat down, soberly looked at her and frowned. "Have you two talked about any of this?"

Marianne blinked rapidly and again shook her head. "No," she blurted. "I've tried and tried, but he won't talk about it. I know what I did was stupid, but once I'd parked my car back there, what else could I do?" Her voice thinned. Tears stung her eyes. "He's always angry. He, he acts like it was all planned . . . like I knew that man would be out there waiting for me. Like, in some way, I had lured him."

Silently, the physician shook his head.

Marianne's heart wrenched. She dabbed her eyes and blew her nose. " Len began to change that night," she blurted. "He's always mad about something and he claims he's working all the time, but he's lying. I know he's lying, and, and . . ."

Doctor Shaw patted her shoulder, stood up and pushed the stool aside. "We'd better see how you're doing," he said, opening the door. Virginia," he called. "Get Mrs. Mavin ready for a pelvic."

Twenty minutes later, Marianne faced the physician across his desk. "The Apasine will have you feeling better in no time," he said, handing her two prescriptions. " And don't try skipping a dose because you begin to feel a little better. It usually takes about six weeks for the Prozac to kick in, but as I said, the Apasine should begin acting in a day or two. Just follow the directions and take one of each, every morning and remember, to get the results you need, don't forget to take them. Just follow the directions and you'll shortly begin to feel better. Just don't forget. One of each, every morning." He raised his brows and smiled. "Okay? "

Marianne nodded.

" If you don't have a favorite pharmacy, the one next door can fill them. And I want you to see one of these counselors," he said, writing on a sheet of paper. "It doesn't matter which of these you go to. They're both good, and whoever you choose will help you over the rough spots in the weeks and months ahead." He laid his pen down, handed the paper to her, then leaned back in his chair and sighed. "Marianne, you need to get out of the house. Be around people. I can't stress how important that is. Find somewhere to go. If nothing else, go walking, go to a mall, go shopping. Anything. But get out. You can't hide from people forever. I know it's cold and I know you're afraid, but . . ." He shrugged. "Get a friend to go with you, or carry a can of pepper spray and use it if you think anyone who approaches you is dangerous. Or do both if it'll make you feel any safer. But get out of the house. Please dear, get out of the house."　　.

Wordless, Marianne rose and turned toward the door.

"See you next week, dear, and don't forget to tell Len to call me."

Len will never call you, Dr. Shaw, Marianne thought as she waited for a cab. And he'll never go to a counselor.

The following morning, Marianne, spatula in hand, walked to the door of the bedroom and looked at Len sprawled fully clothed beneath the covers. Thank God, something's working, she thought. "Len. Len, get up," she said. "Breakfast is ready. How many eggs do you want?"

Lifting his head, he squinted at her through red-streaked eyes. "Damn. You don't mean you're cooking again."

She eyed her cast-encased right arm and forced a laugh. "I felt like I could at least manage breakfast this morning. Now, come on . . . get up. We need to talk."

"Ain't nothing to talk about," he muttered. Rolling out of bed, he headed for the bathroom. "Anyway, all I want's coffee."

"Grits and bacon are ready. All I have to do is fry the eggs and. . ." Her shoulders sagged. "Oh, very well."

Minutes later, he entered the kitchen scowling, and plopped into a chair.

Marianne poured coffee into mugs she'd carefully placed on the table, pulled in a quick breath and pushed a slip of paper towards him. "Len," she said, swallowing hard to control the suddenly watery sound of her voice. "Doctor Shaw gave me the names of a couple of counselors who --"

Len glared, picked up the paper, ripped it to pieces and threw the shreds to the floor. His voice rose to a shout. " I told you I ain't talkin' to no damn counselor 'bout all that shit, Marianne," he said. "Not now. Not ever."

"But--"

He slammed a fist to the table. The cups danced. Coffee sloshed. "Shut up Marianne and listen to me. There ain't no buts. I don't give a shit what old man Shaw says, I ain't goin' to no damn counselor. What's wrong with you? Cain't you get that through your thick head?"

Anger, too long withheld, raced through Marianne. Her face grew hot. "You shut up, Len," she cried, tossing a dishtowel onto the spilled coffee. "Listen to yourself . . . Your filthy language, your grammar, your hostility. Where's all that coming from?" She glared at him. "Sounds like you need to see a counselor." Tears sprang to her eyes, ran down her cheeks.

Len's chair clattered to the floor as he leaped to his feet. "Plenty uh room you got to fine fault wi' me after what you done," he raged, kicking the offending chair out of his way. Grabbing his jacket, he headed for the door, yanked it open and stomped out.

For days, Marianne brooded about whether to go to one of the recommended counselors alone or forget it and try to overcome the life-robbing feelings of hopelessness that twisted their way through her mind night and day. Maybe Len's right. Maybe he doesn't need to go to a psychologist. Maybe, I don't need professional help, either. Maybe I can overcome these awful feelings without anyone's help, she would think one minute. In the next, doubt and apprehension would again take over.

For days, the battle raged within her, until at last her mind cleared, she quit fighting, chose the female adviser, and phoned for an appointment.

Now, here she was one month later, nervous and filled with doubt, riding skyward.

After leaving the elevator on the twenty-fourth floor of a towering office building in downtown Houston, Marianne located Suite 2415, stood a moment gathering courage, then sucked in a deep breath and with her heart racing opened the door and approached a desk where a blue-clad blonde wearing a headset sat keyboarding. Fighting to control her qualms, she approached the desk and cleared her throat.

Startled, the receptionist looked up and smiled.

"I know I'm running late, but I have, or did have, a nine-thirty appointment with Doctor Rubin. I'm Marianne Mavin."

The brown-eyed receptionist picked up a yellow marker and drew a line through a name on a book lying open on the desk. "No problem, Mrs. Mavin ," she said. "Doctor Rubin's running a little behind today, too, so you're on time. Please have a seat," she said, lifting a ringing phone to her ear.

Berating herself for what she considered a weakness, Marianne picked up a magazine and sauntered to a chair, then quickly glanced at her surroundings. The room was done in pale yellow, white wicker and greens. Towering Ficus, spreading Schefflera and giant ferns stood in clusters about the polished wood floor. Shafts of soft light sifted through shiny black vertical blinds, and about the walls hung an artist's conception of gleaming-white beaches edging life-like shades of green and blue waters that in the distance grew to an intense blue that stretched beyond towering palms where the beach curved. A sense of peace settled over her. All morning, doubt had dogged her and she had vacillated about whether or not to keep the appointment. Now, she relaxed and put aside the doubts she'd earlier harbored. I know this is right for me, she thought. Surreptitiously, she glanced at the girl at the desk.

Uncalled, the attack and its consequences, now weeks past, again claimed her mind as she blindly thumbed her way through the slick pages. Twenty minutes later a door to her left opened and a woman, inches taller than Marianne, dressed in a black pin-striped suit, her darkhair arranged to form a heavy bun laying low on the back of her neck, approached Marianne. She smiled and held out her hand. "Mrs.

Mavin, it's so nice to meet you," she said."I'm Louise Rubin. Please come in."

Marianne rose and followed the doctor to a room where tall vases of fresh flowers sat on polished wooden pedestals. She sighed, sat in the chair the doctor indicated, and stared at her clenched hands lying in her lap. "I shouldn't be here, Doctor Rubin. I feel foolish in coming."

Doctor Rubin smiled. "Are the medicines Doctor Shaw prescribed working?"

Marianne nodded. "Yes. I'm feeling much better, except for the people at the rape-crisis center that I attend constantly telling me that I'd get over our loss easier if I"d give up the things I'd bought for our little angel. But I can't . . . " She raised her head, looked into the counselor's eyes and clenched her jaws. "I'm not getting rid of them."

The psychologist studied Marianne's clenched jaws, her defiant demeanor, and shrugged. "Your choice," she said, her voice soft. "If they bring you comfort, by all means keep them. At least, for a time." She paused, then continued. "Doctor Shaw tells me that you're still nursing the illusion that you're pregnant. Is that right? "

Pleasure shone from Marianne's eyes. She nodded. "Yes, sometimes I do," she said. She blinked rapidly and shook her head. Her voice grew watery. "No. No. I do all the time." she corrected herself. "How can I forget that I'll never hold a baby of my own in my arms? That I'll never be a mother? Only the week before . . . before I was raped, Doctor Shaw took a sonogram and said it's a girl. A baby girl." A hint of a smile moved across her face. Her voice lifted. Her smile widened. "A girl. I couldn't believe our luck and could hardly wait to feel life within me. I felt that God had truly blessed us. Then . . . " Her smile faded as hard reality pushed her happiness aside. Her shoulders sagged. Her voice weakened. She lowered her head. "Was a girl," she mumbled. Tears she could no longer control poured from her eyes. Sobs wracked her.

Dr. Rubin sat quietly until Marianne's crying lessened, then coughed and spoke, her voice soft. "I'll need to see you twice a week until we can get you back to normal," she said. She cleared her throat and studied Marianne, who sat, her face buried in her hands.

Marianne nodded, groped at a box of tissues the doctor had placed on the desk top and mopped her tears.

Five

Five weeks later, on leaving the orthopedic's office for the last time, Marianne ignoring the emerging signs of Christmas wherever she looked, sat on the edge of the seat and watched the cabbie skillfully weave through Houston's midday traffic. As the housing complex came into view, excitement filled her. Minutes later, she tossed $40.00 over the seat to the driver, leapt from the cab and hurried into her home.

Flinging her keys and purse into a chair she passed, dropped her clothes as she walked, by the time she reached the bathroom, she was naked.

Thank God, at last I can take a real bath, she thought, gathering wash cloths and towels. She stepped into the shower and reached for the shampoo. Once she felt that her head was clean, she scrubbed her pale, withered arm, liberally soaped a second heavy washcloth and scoured her body to a bright pink, luxuriating in the feel of water flowing over her. After drying off, she tossed the towel atop a stack of others lying on the floor near the overflowing clothes hamper.

I must get the wash done before Len gets home, she thought, remembering the tantrum he had thrown the previous week when she had used the last of the sheet towels he claimed as his.

"I'm sorry, Len." she had apologized. "I didn't realize I was using the last one." Her voice dropped a notch. "I just needed to, to take a bath, and . . . and I feel so dirty all the time. Maybe when this cast comes off and I can take a real shower- -"

Len snorted. His voice dropped to a mumble. "You feel dirty?" His lips twisted in a sneer. "Hell, it'll take a damn sight more'n soap and water to clean you up!"

She gasped. Her face burned. "How dare you. What do you mean by that?" she cried.

"If you ain't smart enough to figger it out, well . . . And Hell. Look at all that damned food in the icebox. Why don't you eat it, 'stead of walkin' 'round here lookin' like a scarecrow reject?"

Marianne's temper flared. "What difference does it make to you how I look? You're never home."

He narrowed his eyes, dropped his shorts, stepped into the shower and slammed the door as if to cut off her response with a noisy stream of water.

The memory, along with her excitement, vanished. Listlessly, she looked in the mirror. With six weeks growth now hiding the lacerations on her scalp, she looked forward to the time when the blond thatch would again reach her shoulders.

She leaned into the mirror and ran a fingertip down the thin livid scar that emerged from just inside her hairline, slanted down her forehead, snicked through her eyebrow and came to a stop midway her left eyelid. Thank God I didn't lose my eye, she thought, bringing her attention back to the present.

Dragging in a braving breath, she turned to the full-length mirror she'd avoided since her hospital stay and studied her body: her breasts, now shrunk to near-flatness, her once-shapely legs, stick-thin, her arms, her neck. I guess I do look like a scarecrow reject, at that, she decided. She twisted around and brought her left buttock into view, then another twist and the right one was reflected.

A smile crossed her face as she remembered the day the butterfly was needled into her skin. Her spirits lifted.

During her first two weeks of college, her time had been so devoured by selecting courses, familiarizing herself with the location of, and the fastest route to, classrooms scattered from one end of the huge campus to the other, that she had made few friends.

Then, one night following a Friday afternoon football game, a handful of pajama-clad girls crowded into the room she and Frances Barnes shared and invited the two to join them on a trip to downtown Austin the following day.

Janie Williams grinned. "Dottie's getting a tattoo like mine on her butt." she said, yanking up a pajama sleeve.

Marianne stared at the redbird blazoned high on Janie's arm. How daring, she thought. Even Len hasn't bought into that yet. "Do your parents know?" she blurted, instantly wishing she'd kept her mouth shut.

Janie shrugged and for a moment looked forlorn. "They don't care what I do," she said. "Long as I don't cause them any trouble or interrupt their trips to Tahoe or the Riviera, or . . . " For a moment she fell silent, then looked at Dorothy. A wistful note crept into her voice. "But I guess Dottie's folks are different. She had to ask their permission."

A knock at the door sounded.

"Enter," Francis called.

The housemother, Mrs. Loquist, swung the door wide, glanced around the group, and smiled. "Glad to see y'all getting acquainted, girls, but lights out in ten minutes."

Slowly, Janie rose, stretched, and yawned, then turning her back to Mrs. Loquist, she winked at Marianne and mouthed, 'We'll be back.' "All I've got to do is fall in." she said, joining the others scurrying out the door.

Twenty minutes later, after Marianne had dismissed Janie's promise and was dozing, the door creaked open, and one by one the girls crowded into the darkened room. Whispering and laughing, one dug a candle from the pocket of her robe and lit it from a cigarette lighter Janie extracted from hers, then secured it to an ashtray yet another girl carried.

Early the following morning, the group rode into the city, browsed through a mall, gorged on egg rolls, rice and 'moo goo gai pan', took in a movie, then went to the tattoo parlor where Janie's arm had been decorated.

After intently studying the pictures on display, Marianne, shushing any qualms, chose an image, bared her rear-end, and minutes later had walked out with the red, yellow and green butterfly adorning her buttock.

Returning to the present, Marianne smoothed a hand over her hip and again faced the mirror. Len's scowling face rose before her. If I'd known then what I know now, how different my life would be, she thought.

In the weeks that followed, Marianne fell into habits that brought little islands of peace into her life. Rising early from the recliner that had become her bed, she quickly bathed and was out of the house before Len woke.

After buying the Houston Chronicle off a news rack, she'd go to the neighborhood Burger King, McDonald's, or IHOP, order breakfast, choose a back booth where she wouldn't be disturbed and read as she ate.

By nine o'clock, she was off to a Mall where she walked laps, where the sights and sounds of Christmas wrenched tears from her eyes and wrung her near-bursting heart dry. Where she could escape Len's sharp tongue. Some might call me cowardly, she'd tell herself. But I can't take any more of Len's tantrums and the longer it takes for the trial to begin, the worse he becomes. It's better if I'm not around when he's home. But why is he always so mad? Is it me or . . . if there is another reason, what is it . . . or who is it?

As the nightmares came less often and months of counseling inched by, Marianne came to accept the fact that she had lost the only child her now-barren body would ever hold. On this, her last day, she sat across the desk from the psychologist, listening to last-minute advice.

"Marianne, unless a person walks around wearing blinders, avoiding children is impossible." Dr. Rubin said. "You know that. They're everywhere, and at this point, as we Texans like to say, it's time to climb back on the horse that threw you. If you haven't thought about returning to La Belle's, perhaps you should." She tilted her chair back.

Marianne bit her lip and lowered her eyes. Her breath fluttered in her throat. The hated face of her rapist rose before her inner eye. The remembered smell of the restaurant garbage again filled her nostrils. She cringed. "I have thought about it," she said. "But . . . I'm not ready to go back." Hope filled her heart. Her voice lightened. "And now that the cast is off, I thought I'd volunteer to work in the nursery at one of the hospitals. What do you think?"

Dr. Rubin brought her chair down with a thump. Incredulity raised her voice. "Work in a nursery at a hospital?" She shook her head. "Marianne, I can't believe you. What can you be thinking? No. Definitely not. You're far too vulnerable for that . . . and it wouldn't be good for the babies, either. Within minutes of being born, you'd become attached to one of them, then a day or so later it would be gone. Then another would claim your affection and be gone, then another, and another, and soon the progress we've made would be wiped out. Do you see what I'm saying?"

A fresh stream of tears flowed down Marianne's cheeks. She nodded. "I do. But, but I need someone to love more than anything on earth. Someone to love and hold close to my heart, to watch her first attempts at crawling and walking . . ." Her voice broke. "And, and do all the funny things that babies—"

"I know, Mariannne. But you're wishing for the impossible. Those are the actions an infant does as he or she grows. You know that, and you know that the only way you'll ever experience watching a baby grow from birth to adulthood, is by adoption." Not where you'd be caught up in the throes of losing a baby, day after day."

"Len will never agree to adoption. He wouldn't before, and I know he'll be the same now."

Dr. Rubin sighed and sat back in her chair. "Marianne, I wish I could offer more encouragement, but I'm afraid I can't. I'm being honest with you. If you pursue hospital nursery work, even if one of the hospitals would hire you, there's always the likely risk that you'd be worse off than when Dr. Shaw sent you to me."

"But why?" Marianne asked. "How? How can anything be worse than living an empty, childless, unfulfilled life?"

"The why is that by taking a chance at working with infants you could relapse and never recover, and, in time have to be instituted."

"Instituted? Instituted for what? You mean like losing my mind?"

Dr. Rubin nodded. "It could be called that."

"But . . ."

"Marianne, I have a good clientele made up of both men and women. Mostly women however, and unfortunately, many of them have experienced the same heartbreak you're going through. For one reason or another, they've lost their first baby, and a few have even been left barren, as have you. The difference is that after reaching the stage of healing you've reached, and they're well enough to continue their lives, a few of them decide to open a day nursery for working mothers."

Marianne brightened, sat straighter. "What a wonderful idea. I could . . ."

Not so wonderful", Dr.Rubin said. "Wait until you hear the rest of the story."

Marianne smiled and shrugged. "Okay, but I don't want to open a nursery. I just want to work with ba . . ."

Dr. Rubin continued. "I know, dear. But these women, after struggling through the loss of their first baby and graduating from my care, ignored all opposing advice either I or their physician gave them, opened a nursery, and within weeks began to slide downhill, until they reached a point where they had to be hospitalized, and sadly, in time some had to be institutionalized."

Marianne's eyes widened as she listened, her mind gripping every word the doctor said.

Dr. Rubin's eyes moistened. Her voice dropped. "Sadly, three of these women have been institutionalized for years and will be for the rest of their lives. Psychology can only help them so far." She relaxed, breathed deeply, leaned back in her chair and lifted her eyes to Marianne's.

"If you simply must work with children, Marianne, I beg you, go back to The Haven. The risk there is nothing compared to what you're suggesting."

Six

January, 1999

Homer Graham, a widowed, seventy-six-year-old retired bookkeeper, wearing a loose- fitting brown leather jacket and a knitted cap pulled over his ears, clutched a paper bag and slowed his already-slow footsteps to a crawl as he approached the intersection of Main and Warner's Lane.

When he gained the corner, he glanced down Main and shook his head in disgust. "*Stupid fool*," he scolded himself as he paused and from a pocket, pulled out a gold, heavily-embossed watch that was anchored to a belt loop of his immaculate khakis by a long gold chain. Narrowing his eyes against the bright sunlight of early morning, he squinted at the timepiece. Better hurry up and get here, Joe, he thought. Besides missing one of the best parts of this whole damn trial, you're gonna get left this morning, cause I'm not going to miss any of it. Not long as I can help it, anyway. And I can help it. He chuckled at his thoughts, waited a couple more minutes, then resumed his walk, again paused, and looked down the street, glanced at the watch that had once belonged to his father, sighed, and dropped it back into his watch pocket. Irritation surged through him. "Damn fool," he again chided himself. "You know better than to wait on him. He's always scaring up one excuse or another for being late, and time after time you stand here and wait for him. You could've been seated by now." He sighed, dismissed all thoughts of his new-found friend and turned toward the courthouse looming two blocks away. He chuckled as remembered faces of the lawyers rose before his inner eye. It ought to be fun, today, watching them pick the jury, he thought, and I'm not going to miss a word of it. As he placed a brown, polished shoe on the first step of the long climb, Joe's voice, strained and breathless, broke into his thoughts.

"Hey, Homer, wait up a minute. What'cha in such a hurry for? I was late getting up this morning, but . . . Anyway, I just finished breakfast."

"Yeah. Yeah, I know," Homer said, remembering the dry toast he'd washed down with the dark brew he called coffee. He smothered a cough. "I waited a couple of minutes on you, but when you didn't show up, I just couldn't wait any longer. We've waited a whole year for this so-called man to be tried, and I don't want to miss any of it, now that it's finally going to happen." A smile broke his pallid face into a network of fine lines and wrinkles." His smile widened as he and Joe began the climb. "As you know, they pick the jury today and I really want to see who they choose. See if I know any of 'em that'll help decide that rapist's future. I expect the D.A. would like to load the jury box with women, but I don't believe Anderson will let that happen. Not if he can help it, anyway. He can really be wishy-washy at times, but as we know, when he gets on a roll, he's hell on wheels. Of course, how much of that he can get away with depends on who's the judge."

Seventy-three year old Joe, steadily climbing, breathing hard from the exertion, grunted in agreement.

At the door to the courtroom, Lesley Crowley, a guard who, over a period of years, Homer and Joe considered a friend, greeted them with a wide smile and an extended hand."Good morning, Gents. Good thing you fellows made it early, or you'd've had a tough time getting a good seat today. Even then, it won't be the best in the house." He turned and pointed. "The roped off section where you usually sit is for the jury pool, but the seats right behind them ought to give you a good view of what's happening." He shrugged and smiled. "Sorry, but that's the best we can do today. Hope you enjoy yourselves."

Homer and Joe smiled. "Thank you, Les," they said in unison, as if rehearsed. "We will." then hurried down the aisle.

Clutching a paper bag that held a fried- egg sandwich and a bottle of water, Joe slid past Homer, who had taken the aisle seat, and dropped to the hard wooden pew They sure as hell don't make it comfortable or anybody to come to these things, he thought, chastising himself for forgetting the pillow he usually brought. Why in hell don't they use some of our tax money and buy cushions for these damn hard benches?

Waiting for the day ahead, he closed his eyes and began to rotate his head in an attempt to relieve the recurring pain in his neck. Guess I should've gone back to that old sawbones, Clark, before now, but what's the use? That dope he prescribed don't help me all that much, and all he'll do is give me something else that ain't gonna help much either. Heart heavy, his thoughts leaped back to his younger years, to the time when his muscles were strong and flexible, when handling an eighteen-wheeler nourished his ego, made him feel more manly, when pain was a rare experience he easily brushed aside, and when, after months of passionate begging and Agnes's constant refusal, she had finally agreed to marry him. Tears he quickly blinked away, surfaced. If you was still here, you'd've stayed on my case till I went back to him, he thought, remembering what she called teasing, he called nagging. His thoughts turned to the intense anguish her death had brought thirteen months earlier when her heart had simply given up its struggle of keeping her alive, how humongous their king-sized bed had grown overnight, how thoughts of her haunted him daily. With you gone, what've I got to live for? Nothing. Nothing. No children. No friends. No nobody 'cept Homer . . . all the rest of 'em either up and died or moved away. He swallowed the lump that had risen to his throat, dropped his head and stared at his scuffed, rundown shoes, his thoughts still on Agnes. You know I ain't religious, Agnes. Never claimed to be, but I did always hope that God, if there is a God, would take me first, but . . . He blinked against threatening tears. I guess we're not the ones who sets that timetable. Guess that sounds selfish, like I wuz wishin' you uz sittin' here 'stead uv me, but I don't wish that. You know I don't. It's just that since you left, 'cept for Homer and these trials we come watch, my life is empty. Empty, empty, empty. He inhaled a shaky breath and sighed it out.

In the hall, the clang of an elevator sounded as it shuddered to a stop. The thump of walking sticks and the grinding squeak of ungreased walker wheels, accompanied voices as retirees made their way into the courtroom and sought spots as close to the bench as they could get. Hearing-aids squawked and squealed as they were adjusted to as fine a pitch as the owners could tune them.

"All rise," the bailiff called, as a diminutive man in a black robe, his thinning white hair standing in wisps around his head, entered the courtroom through a door directly behind a raised platform where an eye-catching leather chair sat. "Your Honor, Judge Coley F. Jackson"

Judge Jackson climbed to his chair, reached for his wooden mallet and banged it on the dias. "Order. Order," he shouted as he took in the confusion around the room. "Order."

As the crowd quieted, he continued. "Ladies and gentlemen, because of the sensitive nature of this case, selection of the jury will be held in my private quarters, therefore it's not open to the public. Sorry to disappoint you, but the trial, which is set for one week from today will be open to anyone who wants to come. All of you come back . . . you'll be welcomed then, and bring a friend" He motioned a guard forward. "Mr. Collier, if you'll clear the room of everyone but those in the jury pool, and Mr. Kane, if you'll give me ten minutes before you send the first person in, we'll get on with today's business."

Annoyed, Joe followed Homer into the crowded aisle. "Where in hell did that judge come up with all that privacy stuff?" he growled. " Hell, pickin' a jury for a murderer's trial don't get all that kinda special treatment. What's so special about this one? What kind of questions can they ask that's gonna embarrass anybody?"

Homer shrugged and headed for a restroom with Joe close on his heels.

"It's a damn good thing I ain't in that jury pool," Joe said, making his way to Homer's side, "'cause if I wuz, and they picked me, they'd really be unhappy cause I'd give 'em hell when it come to deciding if Loper's guilty or not. Wha'choo think about all that crap about keepin' us waitin' a whole week before they start the trial? Damn fool judge! Why'nt he just go on and get it over with and start the damn trial tomorrow, 'stead of keepin' us waitin' another whole damn week?"

Homer pulled the restroom door open and again shrugged. "I don't know, but I 'll tell you what I do know," he said. "When I get out of here. I'm going to that little park down the road and eat my peanut- butter and jelly sandwich, then I'm going to go home and take a nap."

"Yeah. Yeah, I guess I'll do that, too. Ain't nothin' else to do. I guess I just need a little excitement in my life every once in a while, an' these trials always get me kinda revved-up. Least for awhile."

Seven

As the door closed behind the judge, Carmine watched the clock that hung behind his chair move slowly through minutes that seemed like hours. At last, the court clerk rose and turned to the pool of prospective jurors.

"When your name is called, please stand, repeat your name and follow the bailiff."

"Carmine Lassiter," he called.

Tense, Carmine did as instructed and followed the bailiff through the door the judge had taken and down a narrow hall to a door that opened to the judge's private quarters. Quickly, she took in the furnishings. Except for several folding chairs closed and propped against the back wall, two rectangular tables placed in front of a desk that sat on a raised portion of the floor, two large green filing cabinets and shelf after shelf of books she assumed were law books, the room was bare. Behind one of the tables sat a woman, behind the other, a man, each seemingly involved in papers spread before them and each table positioned so they faced Judge Jackson who sat at the desk. A uniformed guard stood in back of the judge, his holstered revolver in plain view. A roomy, old-fashioned chair sat empty beside the big desk. That's where I'll sit, I guess, she thought, as a shiver of fear skittered through her. I've always hated guns. The woman looked up and smiled.

The bailiff led Carmine to the sturdy, old-fashioned chair, then turned to her. "If you'll sit here, Miss."

As Carmine settled into the seat, the judge spoke. "All right, let's get on with it." He looked down at Carmine and smiled. "Please relax, Miss. Despite what you might have heard, we really don't bite in here."

His smile broadened as he nodded at the woman who sat at one of the tables. " Mrs. Perkins?"

Perkins rose. "Thank you, Your Honor," she said, as she approached the chair where Carmine sat.

She smiled. "Please state your name," she said.

"Carmine Lassiter."

"Is that Miss or Mrs. Lassiter?"

"Mrs."

"Mrs. Lassiter," Perkins said, avoiding eye contact with Carmine. "Did you come to a decision about the guilt or innocence of Mr. Loper before you arrived here today?"

Carmine shook her head. "At the time the crime happened, I might have, but that was over a year ago." She shrugged. " If I'm chosen to serve, I want to hear all the evidence before I make a decision."

"Very wise. Mrs. Lassiter. Have you and I ever met, or have you had occasion to go to the District Attorney's office at any time, for any reason?"

"No. I've never met you." She shrugged. "And I've never had a reason to go to the District Attorney's office."

"Thank you. Did you see the picture of the prisoner in yesterday's Houaton Chronicle, or see him in a news broadcast?"

Carmine nodded. "Yes."

"Which?"

"Both."

"Did you know him? If not from the picture, perhaps by name? "

A chill ran down Carmine's spine. She shook her head and blinked back tears. "No."

"Do you know or have you ever known anyone who had been beaten and raped, or miscarried a baby for any reason?"

Carmine blinked hard to fight back tears. " Yes. Myself. I wasn't beaten or raped, but I lost my first baby because I was young and foolish and fell off a step-ladder I had climbed on to get a can of peaches I was craving."

"How far along were you in your pregnancy?"

"Three months."

"And that was your first baby?"

"Yes."

"Then you later had other children?"

Carmine sat straighter, taller, "Yes. I have two boys and a girl. I always regretted that I'd been so foolish when I was young, but I finally decided that if I live to be a hundred, I still won't be perfect. But I'm not alone . . . neither is anyone else perfect. They say that everyone makes mistakes of some kind so I finally decided to forgive myself." She spread her hands in a gesture of surrender.

"Have you ever known anyone who had been beaten and raped and talked with you about it?"

Carmine's voice lowered. She nodded. "Yes I have. A childhood friend."

"Did she overcome the experience?"

"I don't know. When my husband and I moved here to Houston, she and I gradually lost touch . The last I heard anything about her, she still didn't have any children and she told Betty, a mutual friend , that she didn't want any. "

"With the notice of the trial appearing in the local paper, along with the complete story of the rape and its consequences again making headlines, have you discussed Mrs. Mavin's experience with anyone?"

"No."

"Thank you, Mrs. Lassiter. That's all. Mr. Anderson?"

Anderson rose and turned to Carmine.

"If I understood you right, Mrs. Lassiter, you first read about Mrs. Mavin's experience in the Chronicle the day after the alleged rape occurred. Am I correct?"

Carmine nodded. She swallowed noisily. "Yes."

"And that same day, you saw a newscast that carried the story. Local? National? Do you remember which one N.B.C. C.B. S., A.B.C., Fox? Which? Any of them, or all of them?"

" F. O. X."

"And that was over a year ago? Was that a morning or an evening broadcast?"

"Both, I think. On the morning broadcast the newsman told about the rape and its ensuing results as part of the local news, but they didn't linger on it. The evening news, however, covered the entire happening along with other national news."

"Let's turn our attention to the evening news. Was your husband present?"

"Yes."

"Did you and your husband discuss it?"

She nodded. "Yes. Briefly. The children were present, so we didn't say much about it. With him working eight to five, Mondays through Fridays, on a high-pressure job, and me wrestling with the children all day, after getting them fed, bathed, and off to bed, we're usually so tired all either of us want to do is get some rest. We do little talking."

"I see. How old were your children, Mrs. Lassiter?"

"Six years, four years, and a baby, seven months at the time."

"So all three were home all day, every day?"

"Oh, no. No. Freddy was in school until two in the afternoon."

"Did you and your husband later find time to discuss it?"

Carmine shook her head. "As I said, we just wanted to rest."

"To bring things up to date, have you discussed Mrs. Mavin's experience with anyone since the announcement was made that the trial would begin today? Friends? Neighbors? Anyone?"

"Yes, several friends and I did discuss it briefly. It was just something to talk about."

"Thank you, Mrs. Lassiter," Anderson said as he turned toward his seat.

Judge Jackson looked at Carmine and smiled "Discussing something like Mrs. Mavin's experience would be a great temptation for many women to vent their feelings about men in general."

Carmine smiled. "Yes sir, I agree. And ordinarily, my friends and I would have done that, but usually the group has so many personal issues . . . I should say so many personal health issues, to talk about that by the time we get them all hashed out and turn to our husbands, kids and recipes, we're all talked out and ready to go home."

"Thank you, Mrs. Lassiter," Judge Jackson said.. "We'll see you here at 7:30 Monday morning."

Eight

Feeling as bleak and dismal as the distant sky looked, Marianne sat stiff and silent beside Len. She shivered. Maybe when this trial is over, the tension between us will end, she thought. Closing her eyes, she lifted her hands and massaged her temples where nights of sleeplessness throbbed. The time has come to again face Loper, she thought, as his image rose before her. Her stomach tightened. Bile lurched to her throat. Swallowing hard, she waited while Len pulled into the parking lot and cut the motor, then drawing in a trembling breath, she opened the door, stepped out of the car and turned toward him. "You ready?" she asked.

"No," he growled, staring straight ahead. "You go on."

Apprehension filled Marianne. "Len, you know Ms. Perkins said it's imperative that we present a --"

"I know what she said, Marianne. I'll be there."

Tightening her coat about her, Marianne bit her lip and turned toward the courthouse. As she climbed the wide marble steps, she paused and looked back to see Len, hunched against the cold, sauntering slowly towards the building. Her thoughts turned to the past year. Confused, she stared at him. It's almost as if he's ashamed to be seen with me. Do others look at me the way he does? Why? Do they think I'm guilty of flirting with Loper? Of leading him on? That I deserved to be raped? What? She shrugged as thoughts of the night of their anniversary pushed in.

Leonard waiting impatiently beside the apartment door, had gritted his teeth and glared as Marianne entered the living room. "I guess you know you ain't going nowhere with me in that rag," he had said.

Marianne looked down at the navy-blue dress bagging from her shoulders and felt heat suffuse her face. "I, I'm sorry," she stammered, remembering the fear that filled her as she had driven to The Galleria. How numb her legs had felt beneath her, as constantly glancing from left to right, she entered the giant structure. How brave when she bought a palm-sized gun. "It's new. I thought you'd like it."

"Why in hell would'ja think I'd like it?" His voice rose. "You look like a whore in it. Lookit how them little tits ya got left, stick out."

She blinked away a rush of tears. "I'm sorry," she whispered. "I never seem to do anything right anymore."

"If you had any sense in that thick head of yours, you'd know the damned thing's not right, or them little mosquito bites you got left wouldn't show."

Marianne ignored the slur. "That's not true," she said. "They don't show. My breasts are not . . . I have on a brassiere and it's too big for me right now. Maybe you're seeing a fold of cloth. Anyway, what more can I do? Bind myself?" She gathered a handful of blue at her waist and held it out. "This dress fits like a tent. That's why I thought you'd like it."

Eyes blazing, he thrust his head toward her. "Think what you want to, but I say it's not right."

"Please, Len . . . let's not quarrel." Her voice quivered. "I'll change. It's our anniversary."

"Anniversary, hell," he sneered. "What've we got to celebrate? Five years of happiness?"

A whiff of anger shot through Marianne. "Five years of marriage I thought of as happiness. That's what we've got. Why don't you just say what you're thinking?" she taunted. "Say the rape was my fault." She propped her hands on her hips and leaned toward him. "Say it Leonard. Say it. Say that I flirted with him. That I asked for it. That is what you believe, isn't it?"

Leonard narrowed his eyes and stared at her. "I always heard it takes two to screw."

Her mouth dropped open. Tears spilled down her cheeks. "How can you think that? You know I didn't do anything to cause Loper to rape me."

"What I know, Little Miss Innocent, is that you're just like your old preacher paw. You never do nothing wrong."

Marianne fired back. "Daddy might have been pious, but at least he didn't . . . "

Leonard's face twisted into a snarling mask. He raised a hand and took a step toward her. "You leave my daddy out of this," he bellowed.

Marianne's heart pounded as she stood her ground. "You're the one who brought the subject up."

Lowering his arm, he stalked to the door, then spun around to face her. "You twist everything I say. Quit trying to put me on a guilt trip."

"Put you on a guilt trip? What do you think you're doing?" she cried. Her anger fled as quickly as it had risen. "Len, why can't we pretend these past months never happened?"

"Not when another bird's been in my nest," he jeered. He yanked the door open and bolted through it.

Marianne hurried behind him and followed him through the foyer. "Len . . . wait," she called. "Len. Len."

Ignoring her plea, he strode to his pickup, got in, ground it to life and roared out the driveway.

Why does he treat me like this, she asked herself, re-entering the apartment. Tears spotted the front of her dress. Like a wildly-grinning-jack-in-the-box, a thought leapt into her mind. Maybe there's someone else. The well of tears suddenly ran dry. Questions she had refused to ask herself filled her mind. Why did it take so long for the police to find him the night I was attacked? Where was he? Who was he with? Why does he resent me so?

Numbly, she reached for a handful of tissues and wiped her face as her heart flayed against her chest wall. Falling onto the couch, she had lifted a hand to her dress-front and absent-mindedly scrubbed at the wet splotches.

Shaking off the memory, she lifted her chin, squared her shoulders, entered the cold, impersonal building, and hurried down the hall to a room from which a hum of feminine voices emanated. Doesn't matter, anyway, she thought, entering the crowded courtroom.

Assistant Prosecutor, Isabel Perkins, apparently watching for Marianne's arrival, hurriedly rose and met her halfway down the aisle. She smiled. "Well, here you are," she said, grasping Marianne's hands. "Gee, you look great. Are you feeling a little more comfortable about testifying?"

Marianne shrugged and dropped into the chair the lawyer led her to. "I guess," she said.

Perkins chuckled. "As I told you, you don't have to. We've got him nailed."

"I know . . . but I want to."

Perkins smiled her approval. "You're sure?"

Marianne nodded. "I'm sure."

"Okay. Before this is over, we'll send that scum-bag to Huntsville." Her face sobered. "A word of warning, though. Anderson's good. Very good. Don't let him rattle you."

At eight o'clock sharp, a door behind the bench opened and the judge, followed by the bailiff and the jury, stalked out.

"All rise," the bailiff called. "Your Honor, Judge Coley F. Jackson."

"Be seated," Judge Jackson said as he took in the confusion around the room. Seating himself head and shoulders above the crowd, he shouted, "Order." and banged on the dais with his wooden mallet. "Quiet. Quiet. If there's anyone here who can't refrain from talking, out you'll go." His voice rose. " Now, once more, QUIET."

Except for last-minute arrivals rushing in to find seats, the crowd silenced and turned their attention to the beardless prisoner, who, head shaved, handcuffed, shackled and dressed in a faded, orange jumpsuit and flip-flops, entered from a second door behind the judge accompanied by two armed deputies, who led him to the defense table where he sat down.

The Media, crowded into a darkened area down front, suddenly came to life. Pens and pencils were busy above slender writing pads. Artists began sketching likenesses of the judge, the jury, the lawyers and the prisoner.

"Looks like the rumor-mongers are here in full force," Joe whispered.

"Shhhhh, Of course the Media 's here, and I've asked you before to quit calling them rumor-mongers. They're just doing their job. Without them we'd never know what's going on in our own country, much less learn what's happening in the rest of the world. For a change, Joe, be quiet. Please be quiet. I want to hear what's going on, and I can't listen to you and the court."

Joe continued as if deaf. "This trial's gettin' more publicity than any I ever seen or heard about, 'cept maybe O.J.'s, or that queer out in California that kidnaped that little girl," he mumbled. "Looks like when that Mavin woman told the police that this guy raped her and made her lose her baby, and the Chronicle got hold of it, it spread like wildfire all over the country. Look at 'em. They're here from everywhere, like they believe her, but I damn well don't." Scorn entered his voice. " It's a good thing I ain't on that jury,'cause I'd damn shore give 'em hell.. She's lying. Just flat lying. You know she is. Hell, who's ever heard of a woman losing a baby just cause a man takes a little? Wha'choo think?"

Homer narrowed his eyes and glared at Joe. "I think you're wrong. Dead wrong. And I also think you're gonna get us kicked out of here if you don't shut up, he whispered.

Putting the judge's warning aside, Joe raised his whisper a notch."Ahhh, Homer," he muttered."You're crazy as a loon. How can you say that? From what I read in the paper, at least one woman in Houston hollers rape every night, but I sure as hell ain't ever read nothin' bout none of 'em losing a baby. That's just a bucket of crap they've hatched up. Them what's got husbands go to bed with 'em, whether they're knocked up or not, and the rest of 'em . . . well . . . Hell, all I know is I ain't never heard 'bout nothing like this before. Hell. How can you believe what she says?"

Homer shook his head in disgust and shrugged.

Judge Jackson scowled and again rapped on the podium as his eyes swept over the assembly and stopped on Joe. "This is my last warning," he said."Be quiet or out you'll go." Narrowing his eyes and emphasizing each word with a quick nod, he stared at Joe. "Now, if that's fully understood?"

Joe clamped his jaw and turned his attention to the front of the room as the judge continued.

"Ladies and gentlemen," the judge said. " The case before us today is a criminal case, one in which the plaintiff, Mrs. Marianne Mavin, alleges that on the night of October 22, 1997, the defendant, Robert Loper, did attack, beat and rape her, thereby causing her to lose the baby she was carrying and leaving her barren."

" Mrs Mavin will be represented by Assistant District Attorney, Ms. Izabel Perkins, and Mr. William Anderson, the court-appointed lawyer, will represent Mr. Loper

"Let me remind you that during the course of this trial, I will not tolerate any excessive talking or emotional outbursts in my courtroom. Once more, if there is any, he or she will be immediately ejected. Now if that's clearly understood, we'll continue . . ."

The judge looked at Isabel Perkins and nodded. "Mrs. Perkins, do you have an opening statement?"

She rose from the table where Marianne sat and turned toward the jury."I do, Your Honor. We intend to prove that Mr. Loper willfully, mercilessly, and without cause, attacked, beat and raped Mrs. Mavin. In addition to her testimony, testimony from police who were on duty in that particular area the night the rape occurred, hospital personnel, a café worker, a scientist from Houston's police department, Dr. Alan Shaw, who was caring for Mrs. Mavin during her pregnancy, Dr. Andrew Jameson of the Oslo laboratories in Philadelphia, Pennsylvania, who is renouned for his expertise on the consequences many women suffer from rape, and Mr. Anthony Jerius from the F.B.I., who is globally known as an expert on D.N.A., which is a fairly new , but accurate method of identifying anyone, will prove beyond all doubt that Mr. Loper was the man who raped Mrs. Mavin. Material evidence will also be presented from the clothing Mr. Loper wore on that tragic night, all proving beyond all doubt that Mr. Loper is guilty as charged."

"Mr. Anderson?"

Anderson rose and turned to the gallery. "In addition to testifying in his own behalf, we have requested a friend of Mr. Loper 's to testify as to the character of Mr. Loper and to his movements on the night in question. Together, they will prove that Mr. Loper, despite any so-called proof, is innocent of the crime with which he's charged."

The judge knitted his brows and stared at Anderson. "Is that all, Mr. Anderson?"

"Yes sir."

Judge Jackson glanced at a clock on the wall opposite him and banged his gavel. *"Adjourned for thirty minute."* he called.

Joe stared at Marianne as she rose from her seat beside the lawyer. "'nother damn cry baby," he said. "When in hell are women gonna learn they're here to please men and have babies? Don't they know that they come from a man's rib and he's the boss?"

Without answering, Homer yawned, rose, stepped into the crowded aisle and joined others as they made their way to the doors.

Joe, sticking close to Homer, added his voice to the babble. "I didn't think that damned judge was ever gonna give us a pee break, but if I don't stretch and move around a little, that damn arthritis hurts like hell. I didn't get much sleep again last night. 'tween gettin' excited about this trial startin' today, and my damn back hurtin', I just couldn't sleep.. Yours bothering you ?"

Agitated, Homer heaved a sigh. "A little. Not much."

Nine

Lisa West, apologetically pushed past spectators in the last row of Courtroom Eight, eased into the one remaining seat against the wall and smiled at the woman next to her.

In answer, the stranger, her face like her body, ringed in bulging layers of fat, silently stated her position by shifting a foot farther into Lisa's territory and tenaciously gripping the arm rest between them.

Mentally, Lisa shrugged and fought to control her flaring temper. She narrowed her eyes. Bitch, she thought. You'd never get away with that in my part of town. Sucking in a deep breath, she laid a legal pad across her knees, dug in her bag for a pencil, and turned her attention to the front of the room.

Today, Marianne Mavin's rape trial began and Lisa wanted to capture every word of it. If she could turn Marianne's experience into a real heart-wrencher, surely she'd earn an A from her journalism professor.

Twenty minutes later, Lisa's thoughts were interrupted as the spectators stirred.

"All rise ," the bailiff called. "Court is now in session, the Honorable Coley F. Jackson presiding."

The judge rapped on the dais. "Be seated," he said. "Mrs Perkins, call your first witness."

"Margaret Baker."

Minutes later, the bailiff ushered in a slight, well-built brunette. Impatiently, Perkins tapped a foot as she waited for the witness to be sworn in and seated, then quickly rose and approached her. "Please tell us your name and occupation," she said.

"My name is Margaret Baker and I'm a nurse."

"Are you a private nurse or do you work in a hospital . . .or perhaps in a doctor's office?"

"I work at Ben Taub Hospital."

"Ben Taub. Houston's newest hospital. Which department do you work in?"

"The emergency room."

"Daytime or night?"

"Night."

Perkins lifted her brows and looked at her witness. "So you work nights in the emergency room. How often? Evey night?"

Baker shook her head." No. Thursdays though Tuesdays."

"Is that year-round?"

"Yes, except for vacation and sick days."

"What 's your position?"

"Head nurse."

"That must be very trying on you . . . on the entire staff, dealing with and treating, sick and traumatized people night after night. You must see some awful things."

The witness nodded. "I do. We do. But after awhile we learn to handle them by treating the ones who come in as impersonally as we can. Otherwise, we'd lose our minds."

"Did anyone who came to emergency on the night of October 22 of last year leave any lasting impression on you?"

Baker's face became still. She nodded. "Yes," she said. "The police brought in one woman whose condition left a vivid impression on all of us. It doesn't happen often, but that night when they brought in Mrs. Mavin, who had been beaten and raped, it affected all of us. Not that seeing victims of beatings and rape is all that uncommon . . . we see them almost every night. But that particular one was different. She was pregnant and was losing the baby she was carrying, even as I strove to retrieve any semen she might have retained."

"Then you personally examined her?"

"Yes, it's part of my job. As head nurse, I'm required to examine all rape victims. "

"And you found her pregnant and bleeding?"

Anderson leaped to his feet. "The prosecutor's putting words into the witnesses' mouth, Your Honor."

"Overruled," the judge said. "Please continue, Mrs. Perkins."

"Please answer the question, Ms. Baker," Perkins said. " Mrs. Mavin was pregnant and bleeding. Is that correct?

"Yes."

"And she lost her baby as a result of the rape?"

"Yes. I later learned that she had."

"Did you find any semen on examining her?"

"Yes."

"Do you know whether or not the semen you retrieved came from the defendant?"

"I have no idea. Once it leaves our hands, it ceases to be our business."

"Are you not allowed to follow up, or is that your personal choice?"

"Personal choice. However I did wonder how Mrs. Mavin was doing and what happened to the man who had done such an awful thing to her."

"Thank you, Mrs. Baker. That's all," Perkins said and returned to her seat.

The judge looked at Anderson. "Questions, Mr. Anderson?"

Anderson looked at the notebook he was holding and waved his hand. "None, sir. I pass."

Judge Jackson frowned, narrowed his eyes, then turned back to the prosecutor. "Next witness, Ms. Perkins."

"I'd like to call Officer Ricardo Hernandez."

Minutes later, a young, slender man wearing a policeman's uniform, followed the bailiff into the courtroom, was sworn in and seated.

"Mr. Hernandez, as a member of Houston's police department, were you on duty the night of October 22nd of last year . . . 1997?"

"Yes."

"What shift were you working?"

"Nine to five."

"That's nine in the morning until five in the afternoon. Is that right?"

"No. Just the opposite. I work from nine at night until five in the morning ."

" That must be awfully hard on your family. Do you always work those hours?"

"Yes, and it would be hard, if we had children, but right now, there's just my wife and I." A smile stretched across his face. "Until our baby is born."

Perkins smiled. "So, you're expecting a baby. When is it due?"

His smile widened. "The fourteenth of April."

"April, fourteenth. A spring baby. Will this be your first one?"

"Yes."

"At this stage of pregnancy, isn't being alone every night hard on your wife."

"No ma'am. Just the opposite. Julie is all right at night. No sickness. She sleeps well. During the day is when she has her problems . . . when she needs me." He looked pensive. "And thanks to Captain Pierce's understanding, I'm there."

"Wonderful. What were your duties on the night of October the 22nd of last year?"

Hernandez shrugged. "The same as always. Just patrol our area and see that all is well."

"What area is that?" Perkins asked.

"From Justice and Piedmont to Bailey and Piedmont. It's a large territory."

"Is that your regularly assigned route?"

Hernandez nodded. "It is. I've had it now for two years."

"Were you alone on the 22nd, or did you have a partner?"

"I had a partner. Because of any danger we might encounter, we always work in pairs."

"Thank you, Mr. Hernandez."

Judge Jackson raised his brows and looked at Anderson. "Cross, Mr. Anderson?"

Anderson looked at the notebook he was holding and waved his hand. "I pass."

The judge glanced at a clock on the opposite wall.

"Your next witness, Ms. Perkins."

" Michael Donovan."

"Detective Donovan," she said as a tall, rangy man settled into the chair and looked at her. "Please tell the court how it happened that you and Officer Hernandez found Mrs. Mavis on the night she was raped."

"Allegedly raped," Anderson said.

Perkins ignored the interruption. "On the night she was raped," she repeated.

Mike Donovan, his voice husky, cleared his throat and began to speak. "I was riding shotgun with Officer Hernandez that night to evaluate his job performance. It isn't often I do that, but . . ." He shrugged. " As we approached La Belles, Hernandez slowed the car to a crawl and flashed his spotlight along the sides of the building as he said he and his partner routinely did after the store closed each night. That's when we saw Mrs. Mavin's car was still parked out back where it had been an hour earlier. Except for the nightlight, the store was dark, so we decided we'd better investigate."

"Then riding with Officer Hernandez isn't part of your regular duties, Mister Donovan?"

Donovan smiled and shook his head. "No ma'am," he said, shifting in his seat. "I'm happy to say it isn't. Riding a patrol car's not that much fun, despite what kids think."

"Please continue."

"Well, when we drove around to the alley, we saw Mrs. Mavin on her knees, struggling to get to her feet. She was filthy, bloody, scared, crying, her clothes in rags. Her arms were bound and hung useless behind her. How she ever got to her knees was more than I could figure. She's some woman, in my book." Donovan paused to suck in a deep breath. "We immediately put in a call for an ambulance and removed the binding from her wrists, then spent the next fifteen minutes or so trying to convince her that we were the good guys, before she'd allow us to get close enough to wrap a jacket around her and get her into the patrol car."

Perkins waited a moment, then asked, "Do any more details come to mind?"

Donovan nodded. "Yes. She was holding on to a frayed scrap of cloth as if her life depended on it."

Perkins walked to the evidence table, picked up a small, clear plastic bag and returned to the witness. "Is this the cloth she was holding, detective?" she asked, handing him the package.

Donovan put on his glasses and looked at the contents. "Yes ma'am," he said. "That's it. Had a button on it." He pointed to a spot on the plastic. "And that's my mark."

"And was evidence found that conclusively identified this button as coming from Mr. Loper's clothing?"

"Yes ma'am. The lab found that it came from the shirt he had worn that day."

Holding the button, Perkins walked to the evidence table, picked up a larger clear plastic-wrapped package and turned to the jury. "As you can see, this button Mrs. Mavin tore off her assailant's clothing that night came from this shirt," she said. "Robert Loper's shirt. The shirt Detectives Tippin and Haney retrieved from Mr. Loper's home later that night."

She again turned to Donovan and smiled. "Thank you, Detective Donovan. Your witness, Mr. Anderson."

Anderson waved his hand. "No questions," he said.

"Do you have another witness before we break for lunch, Mrs. Perkins?" Judge Jackson asked.

"I do, Your Honor. Detective Haney."

Perkins sucked in a series of calming breaths as she waited for the witness, then quickly rose and approached Haney as he settled into the witness chair. "Detective Haney, did you and Detective Tippin obtain any evidence from the home of Mr. Loper on the night of October 22, 1997?"

"Yes, We found the shirt and pants that Mr. Loper had worn that night."

"And?

"We turned them over to the lab men."

"Do you know whether or not they found evidence of sexual fluids on the clothing you obtained?"

"I was told they did."

"Thank you, Detective Haney."

Judge Jackson looked at Anderson. "Questions, Mr. Anderson?"

Anderson rose and approached the witness. "You say you found Mr. Loper's clothing in his home."

"Yes."

"You and your partner, Tippin?"

"Yes."

"Was anyone else present?"

"Yes. His wife."

"Was he arrested at that time?"

"He was."

"Thank you, sir. That's all."

Judge rapped on the dais. "You folk have a good lunch," he said. "We will reconvene, in forty-five minutes."

Ten

Judge Jackson, proceeded into the room by the bailiff, climbed into his chair, looked out at the noisy gallery who were hurrying to their seats and rapped sharply on the dias. As the onlookers quieted, he looked from the prosecutor to Anderson. "Everybody ready?"

We are, Your Honor, " said Perkins.

Anderson looked up from the papers he was studying and nodded. "So are we," he said.

"Then call your next witness, Ms. Perkins."

"Mr. Leroy Couples from Houston's Police Laboratory."

Perkins smiled at Couples as he took the witness chair,. "This won't take long, Mr Couples, I promise. What, if anything, did you find when you examined the clothing Mr .Loper wore on the night Mrs. Mavin was raped?"

"We found the D.N.A of both the rapist and the victim."

"The D.N.A. of both him and the victim?"

"Yes."

"Are you an expert in the use of DNA?" Perkins asked.

"No ma'am. I don't know if I'll ever consider myself an expert, but the deeper I get into the study of it, the more I want to learn. It's an exciting new field. . .and it's absolutely foolproof," He smiled and shook his head. "Like I said, the more I learn, the more I want to learn," he repeated. He paused. "But, despite the fact that I don't consider myself totally accomplished, I am positive of our findings on Mr.Loper's clothing," he added.

Perkins smiled. "That's all, Mr. Couples and good luck with your ongoing career." She turned to her opponent. "Your witness, Mr. Anderson."

Anderson dismissed the opportunity with a wave of his hand.

Perkins paused a moment, then, with a notebook in her hand, again rose.

"My next witness is Franco Rivas," she said.

The bailiff left the room and returned minutes later with a short slender man who was sworn in and directed to the witness chair.

"Please state your name and occupation," Perkins said as she approached her witness.

"My name is Franco Rivas. and I'm a dishwasher at The Hotter, The Better."

"Please tell the court what The Hotter, The Better is."

"It's a restrunt that cooks really gooood Mexican food." He smiled. "That's why Mr.Garcia named it The Hotter, The Better. We Mexican folks like our food plenty hot, and when you eat there and you want it any hotter than they made it, they'll make it hotter for you. They'll put more peppers in it."

"Will you tell us where The Hotter The Better is located?"

"It's a building all by itself by the end of a little strip on Raven Street."

"What do you mean by a little strip?"

"It's a building that has some little stores strung out in it. You know, not very big, but it's kinda like a mall."

"What kind of stores are we talking about?"

He rolled his eyes upward like he was concentrating. "Well, the end what's closest to us is a laundry where some of the women that work at the restrunt take the tablecloths and dish towels and aprons an' things like that that we use, to wash and dry 'em, and uh . . . uh, there's a computer store right next to 'em, where they got a few TV's and computers and everything like that . . . and another one where people can buy cards to send somebody, and there's a couple more, but I don't remember what kind." He chuckled. " I know that La Parisian's on the other end of the strip, though, cause my wife goes there sometimes, so I know where it is. It's just a little strip. Ain't no big stores in it like Sears or Penneys or Dillard's like what's in a regular mall."

"How many hours a day do you work, Mr. Rivas?" Perkins asked.

"'bout eight."

"*I see. What are your hours?*"

"*I come in 'bout six and work till two,*" Rivas said.

"*I see. Is that mornings or evenings?*" Perkins asked.

"Morning."

"Do you often work the night shift?"

"Nome, I don't work the night shift very much"

"Then, ordinarily, you work mornings? Is that right?"

"Yessum, that's right," Rivas said.

"On the evening of October 22, 1997, how did it happen that you were working the night shift instead of the morning one?"

"Uh, I worked 'em both. I asked the boss how come when he asked me to work that night, too, but all he said wuz cause Juan got real sick an' had to go home." He smiled. "Course I made more money, but I didn't get my siesta."

"What are your duties?"

"'sides washing dishes an' pots an' pans, Mr. Garcia says that puttin' out the garbage is part of bein' a dishwasher, so I put it out."

"Did you put it out that night?"

"Yessum."

"Did you notice anything unusual that night?"

"Unusual?"

"Different."

"Oh, yessum. When I brought out the first load uh garbage cans an' turned 'round to go back in, I saw Mr. Loper 's truck parked in back of the restrunt, 'stead u up front where he mos'ly parks. An' somethin' else seemed peculiar. He wuz parked close as he could get to the restrunt, kinda like he was tryin' to hide the truck, but he wuz gone. I ask' myself why he would do somethin' like that, but it wuzzunt none of my bizzness, so I didn't keep after it. But like I say, he wuz gone."

"What do you mean when you say that he was gone? Wasn't he in the car?"

"Nome, he wuzzent in the car."

"How did you know that he wasn't?" Perkins asked.

"Cause I went and looked. I thought maybe he got sick like Juan did and wuzz layin' down on the back seat, but he wuzzunt in there. Then I thought maybe he forgot somethin' and went back in the restrunt to get it, but when I went back in to get the rest uh the cans, I 'specially looked for 'em, but he wuzzunt in there, either." He shrugged his shoulders. "I don't know where he went. I jus' know I didn't see him nowhere."

"Did anything else happen that night that you recall?"

"Yessum. I heard a girl holler one time, but nothin' else I know of."

"You say you heard a girl cry out. Could it have been a woman?"

"Yessum, I guess it could."

"Did she say anything, or just cry out?" Perkins asked.

"She said somethin'. She hollered help. At's all I heard . . .her hollerin' help jus' one time."

"Could you tell where it was coming from?"

"Nome," Rivas said. "You kin hear all kinds of noises out there at night. Cars goin' by. Kids in 'em screamin'and hollerin'. Some of 'em hollerin' help. Can't pay 'em no 'tention. " He smiled. "They always screamin' 'bout somethin', thinkin' they havin' fun." Again, he smiled. "You know, 'at kind of noise."

"So you were not aware that a woman was being beaten and raped in back of La Belle's that night?"

Rivas' voice dropped. He frowned and shook his head. "Oh nome. Nome. 'fide knew what was happenin', I'd uh tole Mr Leon so he coulda called the police, but I didn't know."

"That's Mr. Garcia?"

"Yessum."

"Do you have a record of any kind that shows you were working that night?"

"Yessum. I keeps all my work papers for taxes for the gov'ment an' it's in 'em. Kep 'em ever since I first come here. Got 'em since 1981." He sat a little straighter and smiled. "I'm uh citizen."

Perkins smiled. "We're glad to hear that you're a good, tax-paying citizen, Mr. Rivas. Do you have any other proof that you worked that night?"

49

" Yessum. Mr. Leon knows it. He's the boss."

"Thank you, Mr. Rivas." She turned to the defense attorney. "Mr Anderson?"

Anderson rose, and with a writing pad in hand, approached the witness. "Mr. Rivas, you said that the accused always parked out front. Is that true? Are there never any exceptions? Always can cover a large block of time."

"Yes sir, I know it can, but like I said, I don't recall ever seein' Mr. Loper park anywhere but out front, an' I been workin' there since a little after I come here from Mexico."

"Since you don't usually work later than two in the afternoon, is it possible that he parks in the back every night he goes to The Hotter, The Better?" Anderson asked.

Rivas shrugged. "Yes sir, I guess it is. I don't know. All I know is that his car wuzz back there that night. An' another reason I remember when it wuzz 'cause the next day the man on TV said a lady was beat up an' rape' back there."

Anderson was silent for a moment as he looked at the pad in his hand, then turned away from the witness. "Thank you, Mr. Rivas. That's all," he said and returned to his seat.

Judge Jackson looked at the clock, rapped on the dias, and looked out at the crowd. "Time for a break, folks. See you back here in twenty minutes."

Eleven

Twenty minutes later:

Judge Jackson, weariness clearly evident on his face, climbed into his chair, and with a rap of his wooden mallet, brought the noisy courtroom to attention. "Everyone's here and accounted for I see," he said, glancing around the room, then scowled and turned his attention to Joe. "I hope that all of you understand the necessity for my no-talking rule and follow it. If you don't, I suggest that you leave now, rather than embarrass yourself by having to be escorted out." He paused, then when no one rose to leave, he turned his attention to the lawyers.

" Mrs. Perkins, Mr. Anderson, are you ready?"

"I am, sir," Mrs Perkins said.

"Mr. Anderson?"

"Ready sir," Anderson said.

"Mrs. Perkins, you say you have additional witnesses. Is that right?

"Yes sir."

"Then let's get on with it." He rapped on the dias . "Quiet," he called. "Everyone quiet, and listen up. If you simply must talk, take it out of here. That applies to everyone. Now, once more, if that's clearly understood we'll get on with the trial."

A hush fell over the gallery, leaving only the quiet hum of the controlled- climate system. He waved a guard forward.

"Just as a reminder," the judge said, raising his voice and looking directly at Joe. "Anyone who forgets where he is and persists in creating a problem, Mr. Collier, here, will immediately escort that person out of my courtroom." He frowned. "I hope that's clearly understood."

Moments later, Collier, overlooking the room, stationed himself less than three feet from Joe. Homer clamped his jaws to keep from laughing. Guess that'll keep him quiet for awhile, he thought.

Again, the judge banged on the dias. "Mrs. Perkins, call your next witness."

"Doctor Alan Shaw," Perkins said.

Whispers from women circled the gallery as Doctor Shaw, a tall, lean, white-haired man entered the courtroom. "He's my daughter's doctor." "Mine, too." "It's almost like my Janie thinks he made a special trip from heaven just to help her through this last pregnancy. She had already lost two babies and was having an awful time carrying her third one until she went to him. Now, she's the mother of a fine baby boy, and my husband and I are grandparents for the first time." She expelled a light chuckle. " In her eyes, Doctor Shaw can do no wrong."

Judge Jackson swung his head from side to side as he surveyed the gallery, lifted his heavy gavel and pounded lightly on the podium. "Ladies," he said, as a smile he couldn't hide played over his face. "Dear ladies, I appreciate how you feel about the happiness Doctor Shaw has apparently brought into your lives and the lives of your children, but my no talking rule applies to you, too. Sorry, but you'll have to be quiet or leave."

He waited a moment, then turned to Perkins. "Seems everyone's ready to hear the rest of this case, Mrs. Perkin are you?"

"I am, Your Honor," Perkins said as she rose and walked toward the witness chair. "Doctor Shaw, will you tell us something about how Mrs. Mavin came to be pregnant and what you found on the night of October 22nd of last year when she was hospitalized after being raped?"

Doctor Shaw sat silent a moment as if gathering his thoughts before he began to speak. "When Mrs. Mavin came to me in mid-March of last year, she wanted to know if I could find out why she had been unable to get pregnant and what, if anything, I could do to help her conceive." He smiled. "I've never seen a woman who wanted a baby as badly as she did." He paused briefly as if lost in thought, then continued. "After thoroughly examining her and running a number of tests, I found there was no reason for her inability to get pregnant, therefore I suggested that her husband come in for a few tests. Two and one-half months later, he came in and two months after that, she was pregnant."

"What were your findings, Doctor?"

" The tests I ran showed that Mr. Mavin was very light on sperm."

"And you were able to correct that problem. Is that right?"

Doctor Shaw nodded. "Yes, but it took time. That's why she was only three months into her pregnancy when she lost her baby".

"Does this procedure have a name? And is it brand new?"

"It's called artificial insemination. The practice isn't brand new, but until a few years back, the procedure was used only on animals. Cattle, mostly. Now however, usage of the technique has advanced to a time when it is widely used on women who want a child, but cannot have one because her mate is short on semen"

"Will you explain how artificial insemination was used to impregnate Mrs. Mavin?"

Doctor Shaw hesitated a moment before answering. "After examination of Mr. Mavin and finding nothing other than a lack of enough sperm that would prevent his wife from getting pregnant, I began a series of withdrawing and freezing his testosterone until there was a large enough bank of the fluid to insure impregnating Mrs. Mavin. Then, it became just a matter of waiting for the proper time to thaw the fluid and inject it into her uterus, then another six weeks to ensure that her body had accepted it." He shuffled in his seat and spread his hands. "Six weeks later, examination proved she was indeed pregnant." He paused and shook his head. " What a happy woman she was. Simply exuberant. But then, of course, began the long wait to become a parent." A smile stretched across his face. "I've never seen a woman any happier than she." An expression of sadness replaced the smile. "It's too bad she'll never experience the joy of having a baby."

"Thank you, " Perkins said. "Now, if you'll tell us about what you found the night Mrs. Mavin was raped."

Doctor Shaw pulled in a deep breath before answering. "When I reached the hospital, I found Mrs. Mavin emotions were torn as badly as her body. She was weeping uncontrollably, her head and body were covered with blood, bruises were forming everywhere, and after closely examining her, I found that in addition to that, she was in the process of losing the baby she had so desperately wanted, and that despite all future efforts she would never again be pregnant . All I could do was mend as much as possible."

"Never?" Perkins asked.

"Never."

"Thank you, Doctor Shaw," Perkins said.

"Cross, Mr. Anderson?" Judge Jackson asked.

Anderson shook his head. "No, sir," he responded.

The judge looked at Perkins. "Next witness, Mrs. Perkins."

"Dr. Andrew Willis."

"Dr. Willis," Perkins said as a short, plump, white-haired man was sworn in and settled into the witness chair, " you are recognized the world over as an expert in the field of the consequences many women suffer after rape. Is that correct?

A faint smile relieved the lines in his face. " So I'm told."

"Will you share with us some of the problems you've witnessed."

"Of course." He pulled in a deep breath, released it and began. " Besides destroying a woman's self-respect, making her feel shamed, many times she is damaged psychically as well. And that's just the beginning. Many women . . .In fact, most women I have found, suffer from the loss of part, if not all, of their reproduction organs: their ovaries are damaged; their uterus; their tubes; and all that's left behind is a shell, both physically and emotionally."

"How do women overcome these emotional problems that arise out of rape? Or do they?"

Willis hung his head for a moment, then began to speak. "A few women overcome them, but most never do. They end up miserable wretches . . . cold, suspicious, fearful, trusting no man."

Even an occasional sniffing or the sharp in-drawing of breath from the gallery quieted, all staring at the man in the witness chair. All listening intently. All concentrating on his words.

"Have you spoken with Dr. Shaw about Mrs. Mavin's condition?"

"I have. Poor woman." His face reddened. "Rape and the storm it leaves in it's path, is the most heinous crime any man can commit against any woman . . . and if she's pregnant, killing her baby in the process is . . ." He paused, expelled his breath and shook his head. " unforgivable. Totally unforgivable."

"Thank you, Dr.Willis."

Judge Jackson, solemnly looked at Anderson. "Cross, Mr Anderson?"

Anderson shook his head. "*No, sir.*"

Judge Jackson looked at the witness. "Thank you for your testimony, Dr. Willis," he said. "That's all."

Except for muffled weeping, a stunned quietness filled the room as the doctor left the witness chair.

Twelve

Judge Jackson, his manner clearly revealing his thoughts, shifted his body, cleared his throat, and looked at Marianne who sat silently weeping, her face washed free of make-up by a steady stream of tears, then shifted his gaze to Perkins. "Any other witnesses, Mrs. Perkins?" he quietly asked.

"Yes, sir," Perkins replied.

"Very well . . . Let's take a break. Give everyone a chance to calm down, then we'll come back and finish up for the day," he said.

Perkins nodded. "Yes sir," she said.

"Mr. Anderson?" the judge asked.

Anderson shrugged. "Sounds good to me."

"Very well. So it is." He looked out at the gallery and rapped his mallet on the dias. "See everyone back here in fifteen minutes, " he said. "Sharp."

As the onlookers rose and began soberly inching their way to the doors, Marianne, hardly breathing, her eyes locked on the prisoner, sat immobile, and watched the guards wrench him to his feet and hustle him out, then released her breath and sat a moment longer as a slight dizziness assailed her, Then, exhausted, she rose and turned to Perkins.

"Are you okay?" the attorney said. "You don't look so good. What can I do? I know all this is very trying on you, but . . . Why don't I get a can of juice for you? Maybe it'll perk you up a little. Let's see, there's orange, grapefruit, a mixture of several fruits, and of course the ever delicious coke is always available. Which do you want? I'll pick up a snack, too. Do peanuts sound good?"

Marianne turned reddened eyes toward the lawyer. "Yes, and a coke please ."

"Back in a minute," Perkins said. "There's a restroom just outside the hall door if you need to . . . No, you'd better wait until I get back so I can go with you."

Eighteen minutes later, Judge Jackson climbed to his seat, rapped on the dias and brought the restless crowd to silence. "Mrs. Perkins, call your next witness."

Perkin's voice rang out. "Anthony Jerius."

The judge watched the witness as he followed the bailiff into the room, took the oath, and dropped into the witness chair.

Notebook in hand, Mrs. Perkins approached him. "Please tell us your name, who you work for and what position you hold."

"My name is Anthony Jerius, I work for all of you, and I head the D.N. A. branch of the F.B.I."

As if awakened from an after-meal nap, spectators in the gallery stirred, sat taller, stretched heads higher, straining to catch every word. "Please explain, Mr. Jarius."

"I work in the investigative branch of the F.B.I."

"Where?"

"Just about anywhere I'm needed, but mostly D.C."

"That's Washington, D.C.?"

"Yes ma'm."

"Do you, in your search, often find fingerprints on knives, guns or weapons of any kind?"

"Yes, but we're rarely asked to do so. My department is primarily focused on finding and analyzing DNA."

"DNA. That's a fairly new method of obtaining a more positive identification isn't it"

"Yes."

" Maybe even better than fingerprints?"

"No ma'am. Not maybe. It is better. It's a fairly new science, and it's been developed to the point where we can now trace a person's ancestry back to its roots by using bone fragments or hair from the deceased or even clothing they've worn if it hasn't been washed, and if nothing else is available. It's an exciting new tool for law enforcement."

"Did you find any evidence that definitely linked Mr. Loper to the rape of Mrs. Mavin?"

"We did. We found undeniable evidence that he was the man who raped Mrs. Mavin.."

"Did Mr. Loper cooperate in giving a sample of any kind to compare with your findings?"

Jarius shook his head and smiled. "No, we didn't ask him. He didn't need to. We had the clothing he wore that night and it gave us all the validation we needed. "

"Undeniable, irrefutable proof ?"

"Yes, undeniable, irrefutable proof. I have complete faith in it's accuracy. I've never seen it fail."

"You brought charts to show and explain just how this new tool works. Is that right?"

"Yes ma'am," Jerius said.

"Will you please explain it to us?"

"Yes," Jarius answered, then rose from the witness chair and walked to two large panels that had been set up during the break, and that were covered with sheets of heavy, cotton fabric. After removing the covering from the lined, color- coded boards, he began to explain how they arrive at their foolproof findings, then turned to the gallery. "Questions, anyone?" When no one raised a hand, he returned to the witness chair.

"Thank you, Mr .Jerius," Perkins said. "That's all."

Judge Jackson looked at Anderson. " Cross examine, Mr. Anderson?"

Anderson slumped deeper in his chair and waved a hand. "No, sir," he said.

The judge rapped on his desk and brought the fascinated on-lookers to attention. "Ten minute break," he said as he rose and turned toward the door behind him.

"'nother pee break, I guess," Joe remarked, as he joined Homer in the aisle "Looks like the good judge's got hisself a little kidney trouble there."

Homer grunted.

Thirteen

Ten minutes later, when court reconvened, Marianne took the witness chair. The lingering scent of gardenia wafted past the prisoner as she rose from the prosecutor's table and walked to the witness stand. Whore, he thought, fighting to hide a sneer tugging at his lips. Y'a ll are whores.

Half-forgotten pictures of the tiny house on the far edge of town where a knot of unpainted, crumbling buildings once stood, rose uncalled before his bleary eyes. Where the bedroom he shared with his skinny, teenaged mother was always covered with layers of cheap, gardenia-scented dusting powder. Where she entertained a string of men while he sat on the steps fighting summer's whining mosquitoes with a bucket of smoking rags, or tightly hunkered down in an old pink blanket, fighting winter's bone-chilling cold.

The faces of those unknown men had long since faded from his memory. Now, what he remembered was hands; hands as big as baseball gloves; hands no bigger than his then childish ones, and patting hands whose touch he tried to dodge as their owners passed him on their way into the house, and that almost always tipped him a quarter on the way out.

Memories of his mother walking for miles to work long hours at a non-union laundry, crowded in.

He sighed, and again glanced back to where she sat beside his wife, her bulk encased in a blue-flowered dress, the one she called her best, her gray hair braided and pulled into a knot at the back of her head. He smiled briefly, then turned back.

Guilt-ridden, Zoe, Loper's wife, watched Marianne take the stand. What happened to that poor girl is all my fault, she thought.

Fourteen

Lisa gripped her pencil and glued her gaze on the unfolding tableau, as Loper's lawyer, his voice filled with guile, approached Marianne. "Mrs. Mavin," he said. "You said Mr. Loper is the man who allegedly raped you. Is that right?"

"Yes."

"You're sure?"

"Yes."

"How long had you known Mister Loper?"

"About two weeks."

"And you're positive this is the man who raped you?"

"Yes."

Anderson's voice sounded mild, almost sympathetic. "How can you be so sure? Wasn't it dark when the attack occurred?"

"Yes."

Anderson stroked his chin as if in deep thought and began striding back and forth before the witness chair. "Do you wear glasses, Mrs. Mavin?"

"No."

"Have you had your eyes examined recently?"

"Yes, and I don't need glasses."

He smiled thinly. "How long have you been married?"

Marianne lifted her head and looked toward the corner of the room where Lisa sat. "Five years."

"Were you and Mister Mavin getting along well when this attack occurred?"

"Yes."

Anderson stopped before Marianne. "Then you would say you were as happy as the average couple?"

The hesitation in Marianne's voice was barely discernible. "Yes . . . as much as we could be."

He let her response slide.

"Then we're to assume you weren't looking for sexual fulfillment outside your marriage . . . is that right?"

Marianne gasped.

Lisa watched a wave of crimson climb Marianne's neck.

Isabel Perkins sprang to her feet. "Objection, Your Honor. That has nothing to do with this case. Mrs. Mavin's not on trial here."

"Withdrawn," Anderson said calmly.

"Sustained," Judge Wright said. "Continue, Mr. Anderson."

Lisa's pencil raced across the yellow sheets as Anderson slipped a hand into his coat pocket, casually took a couple of turns before the jury and again stopped before the witness chair.

"Well, since everything was good at home, you had no reason to want to attract Mister Loper? Is that right?"

Marianne shook her head, then nodded. "No. I mean yes, that's right."

Anderson's lips set grimly as he began pacing. "And you knew nothing about Mr. Loper when he started working at La Belle's? Is that right?"

"Yes."

Anderson stared at the floor as he walked. Suddenly, as if inspired, he lifted his head. "Mrs. Mavin, let me ask . . . have you ever been ice skating?"

A look of confusion crossed Marianne's face. She shrugged. "Yes, when I was a child."

"In a rink?"

Marianne shook her head. "On a pond at my aunt's farm in Minnesota."

Anderson smiled and resumed pacing. "Did you ever venture out to the middle of the pond when the ice was thin, where you were told danger lurked?"

Marianne shook her head. "Never."

He paused, then suddenly shoved his face toward Marianne. "Why not? Was it scary? Didn't the thought of playing with danger excite you? Didn't going out back that night give you that same feeling? Make you feel like you were skating on thin ice?"

Marianne fought for control. "No," she cried.

Perkin's chair overturned as she leaped to her feet. "Objection, Your Honor. Objection."

Anderson turned away. "Withdrawn, withdrawn," he coolly drawled.

"Do you ever wear mini-skirts, Mrs. Mavin?" He turned back to Marianne. A smile widened his mouth. "That must take a certain bravado. You do wear them, don't you?"

Isabel Perkins was again on her feet. "Irrelevant, Your Honor," she bawled.

Judge Wright frowned. "Over-ruled, Miss Perkins." He turned his gaze back to Marianne. "Answer the question, Mrs. Mavin."

The knuckles of Marianne's clenched hands gleamed white against the navy-blue of her dress. "No, I don't. My father didn't approve of them." She hesitated. "And neither does my husband."

Anderson sounded incredulous. "Your husband? Do you mean in this age of the emancipated woman, your husband decides what you do and do not wear? You ask permission to wear mini-skirts when every other woman on the street wears them?"

Perkins objected. "Irrelevant, Your Honor. Why is defense harping on what Mrs. Mavin wears? The law says if she had been stark naked, the defendant still had no right to attack her."

Judge Wright folded his hands on the bench and peered at the attorney over the narrow gold rim of his glasses. "I don't need to be reminded of what the law says, Counselor," he growled. He leaned forward and frowned. "Is that understood?"

A sigh rose from Perkins. "Yes sir."

Several members of the jury glared at Anderson.

Others shifted in their seat.

The judge waved a hand. "Sustained," he said. "Now, may we get on with the work at hand?"

Lisa caught the brief smirk that flitted across Anderson's face before he turned back to Marianne. Anger surged through her. *As always, he's trying to make the victim, the culprit, instead of the bastard who raped her. And that damned judge.* Her hand flew across the pages.

"Have you ever fantasized about having sex with --"

"Your Honor," Isabel Perkins interrupted.

Anderson's voice droned on. "anyone other than your husband?"

Marianne's face flamed.

A gasp sounded from the jury.

Perkins voice rose to a shout. "Your Honor. The law--"

"Sorry. Withdrawn." The smirk returned.

"The jury will disregard that last question," Judge Jackson aid, pounding on the podium. He glared at the defense attorney. "Mr. Anderson, I strongly suggest you change your line of questioning." He paused dramatically. "Now, if that's understood, are you ready to try again?"

Anderson's face flushed. He nodded.

"The court reporter doesn't hear you, Mr. Anderson."

"Sorry, Your Honor. Yes, sir." Anderson stood a moment in front of Marianne and stared at the floor, before he again began pacing. "Mrs. Mavin, did you always leave by the back door?"

"No. That was the first time."

Anderson's voice rose. "The first time. Then why did you do so that night?"

Lisa's hand raced.

"Speak up, Mrs. Mavin. Surely you had a reason."

Marianne dabbed at her eyes. "When shipments of underwear came in, I always took the empty boxes to The Haven where I volunteered." She smiled fleetingly. "It was a small thing to do, and they brought so much pleasure to the children. At The Haven, we always gave them crayolas and paper and put their names on the boxes. They were something the children could call their very own." She glanced toward the back of the courtroom.

"Since you did this regularly, what made that day different?"

Marianne heaved a sigh. "That day, Mr. Loper had hauled the boxes out to the trash before I realized what he was doing, so before Bertha left for --"

"By Bertha, you mean Mrs. Candell, your employer?"

"Yes. She had forgotten to tell me about her appointment until she was ready to walk out. I asked her to give me time to pull my car around to the back and load the boxes, but --"

Anderson broke in. "But?"

"She said she'd wait until I moved my car, but couldn't wait any longer. That she was already running late for an appointment. So I said okay, I'd do that and get the boxes after I closed up. It wouldn't have taken more than two minutes. "

"Hummm. Two minutes. Do you do any other charitable deeds, Mrs. Mavin?"

"No."

"And I understand you only worked part-time at La Belle's. How many days? One? Two?"

"Three. Mondays, Tuesdays, and Fridays."

Anderson smiled, jammed his hands in his coat pockets and took a turn before the jury. "Please continue, Mrs. Mavin. You say in two minutes you would've been gone. Are you implying that my client was lying in wait for you?"

"No, I'm not implying that he was. He said he was." Marianne said slowly. "I thought he was already gone, but even if I'd known he was there, I wouldn't have been afraid. If anything, I'd have felt safer." Red stained her face. "I never would've expected him to --"

Anderson broke in. "Was that the first time Mrs. Candell had left you alone to close up?"

Marianne shook her head. Her reply was a whisper. "No."

"Speak up, Mrs. Mavin," Judge Jackson said.

Marianne cleared her throat. "No," she said, her voice loud.

"What did you do on the other occasions?" Anderson asked. "Park in the front? Your husband pick you up? A friend? Did you call a cab? What?"

Perkins objected.

"Over-ruled," Judge Wright said. "Please answer the question, Mrs. Mavin."

Marianne shook her head. A blank look covered her face. "I, I," she stammered. "I parked in the front."

"With constant reminders on television and in newspapers slanted towards women's safety, I would think that by now, most of them would have learned to stay away from alleys at all costs." A sneer flitted across his face. "Even one of doing a good deed."

Perkins leaped to her feet. "Your Honor," she stormed. "What's defense trying to do? Make Mrs. Mavin out an idiot?"

"What made you think you'd be safe?" Anderson continued.

"Your Honor."

Judge Jackson, apparently jarred from an eyes-open nap, spoke calmly. "Take it easy, Mrs. Perkins. I agree." He turned to Anderson, drew his white, sparse brows together and picked up his gavel. "Mister Anderson," he said, "I'm warning you. Any more hammering at this witness and I'll hold you in contempt." He shifted his gaze from one lawyer to the other and rose. "Let me see you both in chambers right now." He rapped on the podium. "Court's adjourned until eight o'clock tomorrow morning."

As the spectators spilled into the aisles, Lisa saw Marianne hesitate briefly beside the D.A., then hurry to a tall, familiar-looking man who had risen and was elbowing his way toward the door. "Were you going to leave me?" Marianne asked, grabbing his arm.

Revulsion rose in Lisa as the plaint reached her ears. Yes, she thought. The bastard has other fish to fry.

Fifteen

8:10 the following morning.

Zoe Loper, staring at the back of her husband's head, quickly shifted her velvety-brown eyes to a window when he turned, scanned the courtroom, then looked towards her and his mother. She sniffed and turned away. You won't get off so easy this time, she thought, as memories flooded her mind. At ten-thirty on the night he was arrested, police cars, sirens going full blast, had torn through the neighborhood, and with a screech of brakes growled to a stop in front of their house. Car doors slammed. Running feet sounded. Face blanched, Robert leaped to his feet. His chair fell noisily to the floor. Shadows raced past the window where Zoe, elbow-deep in dishwater, stood. Robert raced for the back door.

"Why are the police here? What have you done?" Zoe cried, turning toward him.

Ignoring her, he yanked the door open and came face to face with two uniformed policemen, their drawn guns aimed at his chest.

Shocked, her mind suddenly blank, Zoe held her breath and gaped.

One man yanked Robert around, slammed him face-first against the wall and shoved a gun in his ribs.

"You know the game, Loper. Give me your hands," the other ordered, taking handcuffs from his pocket. As he snapped the cuffs on Robert and read him his rights, they were joined by two men in business suits.

"Get him out of here," one newcomer said and looked at Zoe.

The trio started toward the front of the house.

The newcomer held a letter-sized paper toward Zoe and tilted his head in his partner's direction. "Detective Sergeant Charlie Tippin," he said. "He's Detective Ted Haney."

Numbly, Zoe dropped into a chair and held out her hand.

"Search warrant," he said. "Kids asleep?"

Zoe nodded. "Please don't wake them," she said, her alto voice suddenly high-pitched and un-natural. She started to rise.

He put his hand lightly on her shoulder. "Sorry, Ms. Loper, I'll have to ask you to stay put. Where's your laundry room?"

Tears gathered in her eyes. Shakily, she pointed to a door.

Tippin canted his head toward the opening and Haney left the room. Within minutes, Haney returned carrying a clear plastic bag. In it, the clothes Robert had worn that day. Haney looked at Tippin. "Got 'em," he said gruffly.

"Let's go."

"We got him dead-away this time," she had heard one officer say as the front door closed behind them.

Zoe returned her gaze to the back of Loper's head and sighed. Guilt surged through her. Maybe it wouldn't have happened if I'd forced myself to put up with . . .

'Quit blaming yourself,' a part of her mind told her. 'A woman can't be expected to put up with a man's nightly fumblings forever.'

But he's the father of my children and –

'Yeah, yeah, I know. But when you settle for less, you get less.'

Fighting a losing battle with the memories pushing in, her thoughts returned to the night before Robert was arrested.

After forty long minutes of pinching, prodding and poking at her, Bob's penis had been as flaccid as before he began, and her patience had reached its limit. "Stop," she had stormed. "That's enough."

Leaping from the bed, he verbally attacked her. "If you was half the woman you outta be, you could make Brother Joe here, set up and take notice," he fumed,

Wearily, she picked up her blue-flowered gown lying on the floor. "Yeah, yeah, I know . . . It's my fault," she said, shoving her arms into the sleeveless garment and dropping it over her head. "It's always my fault." Sighing resignedly, she lay down, turned her back to him and lay her head on her pillow.

Sputtering unintelligibly, he plopped down on the side of the bed.

"Bob," she had pleaded, "please lay down and go to sleep."

His sputtering continued.

"Bob, please."

He ignored her.

If only I hadn't, she thought.

But she had.

In a rare fit of temper, she had drawn back a naked leg, slammed her foot against him and pushed. "Go find somebody to help you get it up," she raged.

Arms flailing, he fell to the floor as she sprang from the tangled covers, rounded the foot of the bed and stood over him.

Legs spread, heavy breasts swinging, she had bent, shoved her fist in his face and extended her little finger. "We'd both be better off without that little wonder-toy of yours," she stormed, curling the digit to a droop. "At least you wouldn't be keeping me awake night after night. Get out. Did you hear me? I said get out." Fighting the need to shout, she lowered her voice. "I'm not putting up with this any longer."

Raw hate gleamed from his eyes as he pushed himself off the floor and resumed his perch. "Bitch," he muttered.

Disgusted, she straightened, wadded a blanket and threw it at him. "I'll show you bitch," she had said between clenched teeth. "I said get out. Go sleep on the couch. I've got to get some sleep."

The heavy pounding of the gavel brought Zoe's attention back to the trial.

"Mr. Anderson, are you ready to present your witnesses?"

"Yes sir. In his own defense, Judge, my first witness is the accused, Mr. Robert Loper."

Spectators craned as the handcuffed perpetrator, accompanied by guards and dragging his shackles approached the chair, turned sideways, raised a bony hip onto it, then using his elbows for leverage, shuffle himself into the seat.

Anderson consulted the papers on his table, then rose and walked to Loper. "Mr. Loper, where were you on the night Mrs. Mavin claims you beat and raped her?"

"I was at home."

"Can your wife verify that you were? Had she held dinner for you?"

A lopsided smile crossed Loper's face. He shrugged. "She can if she will, but she was mad cause I'd already et when I got home."

"You'd already eaten?"

"Yes, but she knows I stop by the res'trunt lots of nights fore I come home.. But you know how women are. They never . . . "

Anderson interrupted. "That's true, but how did you get home . . . and what time?"

"I drove home. When I finished eatin' and was ready to go home, my truck wouldn't start, so I called a friend of mine to see if he would come help me out."

"And did he come help you get your truck started."

Loper nodded. "*Yes.*"

"That's all, Mr. Loper." Anderson turned to Perkins. "Your witness, Mrs. Perkins."

"Mr. Loper," Perkins said as she rose and stood before him. "Do you think this friend you called will come forward as a witness for you?"

"Yes ma'am, I think so."

Judge Jackson rapped on the dias. "Court is in recess until eight tomorrow morning," he said.

Sixteen

Blustery winds whipped around buildings, swept the streets, and flung the gritty debris into unprotected faces, as Lisa, legal pad in hand, descended the steps of the courthouse and headed toward the parking lot. That son of a bitch ought to be put away for life, she thought, but with the punitive system the way it is, it'd take a miracle for him to serve it.

As she crossed the street to the parking lot, a man wearing a rumpled shirt and jeans, and holding a child's hand, approached her, the girl struggling to escape his grip, him dragging her along. Memories, long suppressed, rushed full-fledged into her mind.

From the time she was born, Lisa's father had cuddled and loved her, buying her the best of everything. As the only child of Freedom's leading citizen, nothing she ever wanted went un-bought. Rows of dolls sat on the specially-built shelves in her pink and white bedroom. Books, many she was too young to read or understand, filled bookcases beside windows framed with crisp organza.

One night when she was just past eight, her father had come to her room long after she had fallen asleep. She had waked instantly. "What's wrong, daddy?" she'd asked anxiously. "Is mother sick?"

He lifted the covers and slipped into bed beside her. "No, honey," he said. "I just wanted to be with my little girl for awhile. Give me a kiss, then turn your back and snuggle up."

Confused, and strangely uncomfortable, Lisa pecked him on the cheek and rolled over.

Barely touching her, he ran a hand along her thigh, then slid it over her stomach and under her waist. "There now. That better, isn't it?"

Lisa pressed her head into the pillow. "Yes, sir," she mumbled.

"Then go back to sleep, baby. I'm not staying long."

Minutes later, Lisa woke from an elusive dream with the feel of a hand between her legs.

Terrified, she screamed, sprang off the bed and ran towards the door.

Her father was faster. He leaped to his feet and placed himself between her and the door. "Shhh," he whispered, bending towards her. "Don't wake your mother. You know she isn't well."

Lisa gazed at him in the dim light coming through the window and rubbed her eyes. "Wha, wha, what were you doing?"

He knelt before her. "Just loving you, honey, like any good father does."

Lisa felt confused and uncertain. "You . . . you mean my friends daddies does that to them?"

Her father turned on a lamp and shrugged. "If they love their daughters half as much as I love you, they do." He looked into her eyes. "There's something I need you to help me with. Here, let me show you." He opened the slit in his pajama bottom and freed an enormous bulge.

Fear raced through Lisa. Gasping, she stared at the ugly thing and stepped back.

He caught her trembling hand. "Don't be afraid, honey. I won't hurt you, but it's time you learn something about men and their bodies." He looked down and wrapped his free hand around himself. "See . . . this is a penis. See how big it is?" He thrust his lower body forward. "See what it looks like?" He pulled her hand closer to the big, ugly protrusion. "Here, touch it . . . it won't bite."

Lisa tried to jerk her hand away. "No," she whimpered, fighting to stifle her screams. "No!"

"Yes," he said, his voice ragged.

Sobbing, she tore from his grasp, raced to a window and pried at the latch.

Her father bounded across the room. "I'm sorry, honey," he said, reaching for her. "I didn't mean to scare you. I just wanted --"

"Don't," Lisa cried. Pushing her back to the wall, she thrust her fists between her legs, slid to the floor and dropped her head to her knees. Shame whipped through her.

71

Her father patted her head. "Don't cry, baby. Don't cry. I'm going now."

The door bumped shut behind him.

Trembling, Lisa huddled on the floor and waited for the safety of morning when her mother would be awake.

As the following nights came and went, Lisa, afraid she'd make her father again come to her room if she slept in her bed, curled herself into a knot under it, or slept in the closet jerking and moaning in her sleep.

As the sunny days stretched into weeks and her father did not return, Lisa relaxed. The dark smudges beneath her eyes faded and she returned to her bed.

Autumn had painted the tallow tree outside Lisa's windows fiery-red when her father had again entered her room. Throwing back the covers, he pulled her quickly to a sitting position, grasped her hand, wrapped it around his penis and began manipulating it.

"No," Lisa cried, instantly awake. "Don't. Don't." Tears choked her.

He held on tightly. "Wait. Wait honey," he said, his voice sounding strangely choked. "You love daddy, don't you? You're the only one who can do this for me." He half-closed his eyes. "Oh, that's wonderful . . . wonderful. That feels so good, so . . ." His breathing came harder, faster.

Hysterical, she tried to pull away.

He tightened his grip. "No, no, I'll tell you when to stop, " Frenziedly, he worked her hand, groaned and ejaculated. Barely breathing, he spoke. "See. You're the only one who can help daddy get rid of that stuff."

Within a year, he had raped her, and his weekly visits became nightly ones.

Though she felt shamed and dirty, it wasn't until she reached eleven when a lady from the police department visited the school and talked with the sixth-grade girls about sex, that she learned for certain how wrong it was.

Her self-respect plummeted.

Retreating into herself, her life became lonely as she turned her back on former friends and made no new ones.

Seventeen

Homer and Joe, each with his ever- present brown bag, chatted a moment with Les, then hurried down the aisle to their favorite seats. "I guess it'll all be over but the shouting, today," Joe said as he dropped his pillow on the hard pew and sat down.

"Yeah, we can count on it. Those who've been here throughout the trial will likely be here today for the final outcome. Probably even more. According to the Chronicle, everybody's interested in this case, and they want to see whether or not Loper will be found guilty, and if he is, see what kind of punishment he'll draw. Personally, I think he ought to get the chair, or at the very least, be put away for life, but until the state legislature decides whether or not the killing of an unborn child is a crime, the court's hands are tied. And the power of the jury is reduced to recommending time in prison, despite what they think the bastard should get." His voice faded as he watched Marianne, eyes red, face swollen, enter the courtroom and drop to a chair beside her attorney. Poor woman, he thought. Losing her baby and left childless for the rest of her life must be a terrible burden. Thoughts of his daughters rose to his mind. Cristy, who five years earlier, had married an Englishman who hosted an up and coming television show in London, and where they had immediately moved after the wedding. How happy Sally had been that occasionally Margie, after earning a masters in journalism and had worked her way up through the ranks, was now head of the Make New York, New York, Your Home magazine, came home twice a year, plus Christmas, leaving the hustle and bustle of far-off New York behind her. The two of them had visited her once, but after two weeks in the hurry, hurry atmosphere of the city, they decided that their quiet, restful home near the heart of Houston gave them all the city busyness they wanted. Here, they could move as their wants demanded, not be caught up in a constant round of theater, movies and dinners, and the girls could visit them.

"You gonna be here next week for that murder trial?" Joe asked. "Outta be another good one."

Homer, after another sleepless night, lost in a world of memories, didn't respond.

Joe bumped his arm. "Hey, wake up. I said, you gonna be here?"

Jolted back to the present, Homer answered. "No. No, I'll be in New York to spend a day or two with Margie, then I'll be off to London to see Cristy and my first grandchild." He smiled. "Imagine, a grandson. And me a grandpa."

Minutes later, sounds of people pushing and shoving to get in and obtain a seat they considered best, the gallery began to fill. Impatiently, they whispered among themselves as they waited for court to be called to order.

Judge Jackson climbed to his seat, rapped on the dias, called "Quiet," and brought the attention of the onlookers to the fore. After looking around the room to be sure his orders were being respected, he looked at Perkins. "Rumor tells me that you have a rebuttal witness, Mrs. Perkins. Is that correct?"

"It is, Your Honor."

"Then let's bring him in. See what he has to say."

"Mr. David Haverson."

Loper turned a sickly green as he watched a stocky, medium-weight man follow the bailiff into the courtroom, take an oath to tell the truth and settled into the witness chair.

Perkins stood before him. "Mr. Haverson, will you please tell us something about yourself, where you work, and the hours you work."

"I work for the Ease and Comfort bus company and have for the last ten years. And I always work at night."

"What's so special about the Ease and Comfort bus company?"

Haverson smiled. "I guess what's so special about it to me is that it gives me a chance to do a little good for some really nice folks I couldn't otherwise help. I guess that's why I enjoy my work so. You see, I'm a mechanic." He smiled. "A grease monkey, some folks say. When the Ease and Comfort bus company started up about eight years ago, I was lucky enough to be hired and I've been with them ever since. The Ease and Comfort operates solely for seniors. That's their only business. If they want to go to a Casino in Louisiana and gamble a little, or up to the hill country to see the fields of bluebonnets and other beautiful wild flowers that Ladybird Johnson made Texas noted for, we take them. So me and my helper keep the two buses we have in good running order. The buses have roomy, comfortable seats that run the length of the bus, a restroom, and aisles wide enough for the folks that are on walkers or crutches to get through." He paused a moment and shrugged. "I love my work."

"That's wonderful," Perkins paused a moment. "Mr. Haverson, do you know the person sitting at the defense table with his lawyer?"

Haverton looked at Loper. "Yes ma'am, I know him."

"Will you tell us his name and why he's here?"

"Yes ma'am. His name is Robert Loper and he's on trial for rape."

"It's been over a year since Mrs. Mavin was beaten and raped, but do you remember that happening on the 22nd of October of 1997?"

"I do. Vividly."

"Then, let's move on. Have you had occasion to talk to Mr. Loper since that night?"

"Not until two days ago when he sent me word that he needed to talk to me, and to please come visit him in jail. I couldn't imagine what was so important that he wanted me to come to the jailhouse. We've never been that close, but . . ."

"And did you go?" Perkins interrupted.

"Yes ma'am, I did."

"Will you relate to the court the conversation that took place between you two?"

"I can't really recall it word by word, but he asked me to lie for him. To tell the court that I worked on his old truck, or maybe took him home on the night of the rape."

"So, he asked you to perjure yourself?"

"Yes ma'am," Haverson said.

"And what did you do?"

" I refused."

"You refused to lie for him. Is that right?" Perkins asked.

"Yes ma'am."

"Thank you, Mr. Haverton."

Judge Jackson turned his attention from the witness to Anderson. "Questions, Mr. Anderson?"

Anderson shook his head. "None, sir."

Eighteen

Four days later, Lisa, caught up in the unfolding drama, pushed through the crowd of waiting spectators, and when the doors swung open, hurried to a center seat on the front row.

A resounding whap of a gavel brought her to attention, and the day's proceedings to order.

The judge turned to the prosecutor and raised his shaggy brows. "Any re-direct, Mrs.Perkins?" he asked.

Quickly, she rose. "Yes, Your Honor. I'd like to recall Marianne Mavin."

The judge looked at Marianne and nodded. "Please take the stand, Mrs. Mavin."

As Marianne walked to the chair and sat down, Perkins smiled and slowly approached her. "I'll be as brief as possible," she said, her voice soft. "We covered this area the first day of the trial, but I feel it bears repeating." She paused, looked down a moment, then raised her eyes to Marianne's.

"How old are you, Mrs. Mavin?"

"Twenty-five."

"Was there anything unusual about your physical condition on the night you were attacked?" she softly asked.

Marianne nodded. "I was pregnant," she said, her voice suddenly watery.

Anderson leaped to his feet. "Objection, Your Honor," he bawled. "That's been adequately covered. Summation, your Honor. Summation"

"Overruled."

Anderson scowled and dropped to his chair.

Perkins smiled gently at Marianne. "Were you childless for five years because you didn't want children?"

Marianne shook her head. "I couldn't get pregnant."

"Then, pregnancy came as a surprise."

Marianne glanced toward the rear of the room and shook her head. "Not really," she said. "It was planned."

"By planned, you mean?"

"We went to a fertil--"

"Objection, Your Honor. That has nothing to do with the charges against Mr. Loper," Anderson stormed. "He can't be prosecuted for that."

"Overruled, Mr. Anderson. Sit down."

Chagrined, Anderson plopped into his seat.

Leaning forward, Judge Jackson spoke directly to Marianne. "Please continue, Mrs. Mavin," he said gently.

Marianne turned and looked into his eyes. "I . . . we wanted a baby so badly, but for years Len wouldn't consent to being tested, then he did and I became pregnant." She raised her hands, spread them, and dropped them to her lap.

Pain tightened the knot in Marianne's chest that night, as she lay sleepless. Tears slipped from the corners of her eyes. Hate raced through her as pictures of Robert Loper rose before her mind's eye. If only I hadn't lost our baby, she thought.

Tears, like liquid fire, had poured from her eyes as the ambulance rushed through the night to Ben Taub. Though the paramedics had given her a pain-killing shot and encased her arm in what looked like part of a spaceman's suit, they could do nothing for the intolerable pain wrenching her heart.

Susan White, a female interrogating officer, met them at the door, introduced herself and followed them into the emergency room where Marianne was quickly shifted to a cold, steel examination table and draped with a sheet. "I know this is embarrassing, Mrs. Mavin," she said, pulling a tablet from a hip pocket. "But the faster we get the information we need, the faster we can catch the guy who raped you."

"Len," Marianne said, fighting the pain wrenching her.

"Is that the culprit?"

Marianne shook her head. "My husband," she whispered, spreading her legs while the woman peering under the sheet combed her pubic hair. "The man who did it is Robert Loper."

The officer wrote furiously. "Robert Loper?"

"Yes. Please get my husband."

"We've tried your home, and he wasn't there. Where else can we find him?" the officer asked.

"Richard's Friendly Icehouse."

"You sure?"

"He said they always go there."

White tore the pages from the pad, hurried to the door, and after a brief verbal exchange, handed them to someone outside. "Now," she said, returning to Marianne's side, pad open, pencil poised. "Did you know the man who raped you?"

"Not really. He just started working at La Belle's a week or so earlier."

"We'll be in touch," White said, then turned and left the room.

"Relax, Mrs. Mavin," the woman under the sheet said. "I'm going to take a few swabs, now. It won't take long."

Lifting Marianne's foot into a stirrup, the voice from the end of the table said, "Now, the other one, and . . ." She pushed on Marianne's knees. "That's right, open wide."

Pain ricocheted through Marianne's abused birth canal as cold steel was inserted.

"My god," the woman at Marianne's feet bellowed. "Get this woman to surgery. Who's your doctor, honey?"

As the steel was removed and her vagina collapsed, Marianne's cramping worsened and the bleeding became more profuse.

Between sobs, she answered the questions.

"Yes, she was three months pregnant".

"No. Please. Just call Doctor Shaw. He'll know what to do."

Swiftly, she was whisked to an operating room and shifted to another steel table just as Doctor Shaw, his faded red hair standing on end, came puffing in. Yanking his coat and tie off, he hurried over to where she lay silently weeping. Gently, he lifted her hand and bent over her. "Mrs. Mavin?" he whispered. "Marianne?"

"My baby --"

"Ssshhh," he murmured. "Everything's going to be all right, dear. Soon as I wash up, we'll take a look and see what's going on."

"They . . . they took scrapings downstairs," she said.

"I know, dear. I know."

"Is Len here?"

The doctor looked at someone she sensed was standing at her head and slightly nodded.

An hour later, Marianne woke. Where am I, she wondered, looking at a shadowy figure sitting beside the heavily-draped windows. "Where am I?" she whispered.

The person rose and approached her bed. "You're at Ben Taub Hospital, Mrs. Mavin."

"Who are you?"

"Officer Josephine Dickens, Ma'am."

Marianne's memory came flooding back. "Len?"

"We checked Richard's Ice House, but the barkeep said he and his friends hadn't been in all night."

Tears gathered in Marianne's eyes. "He said they always go there."

The officer shrugged. "Maybe they tried a new place." She looked into her eyes. "We'll try your home again in a few minutes."

The memory faded, and her thoughts returned to the trial. Tomorrow, she thought, the jury will make their decision..

Nineteen

Marianne knotted her hands as the jury filed into the courtroom and took their seats.

"Ms, Perkins, are you ready to give your closing statement?" Judge Jackson asked.

"I am, sir."

"Mr. Anderson?"

"Ready, sir."

"Very well. Ms. Perkins."

Perkins rose, paused a moment, then turned her attention to the jury. "Over the past weeks, we have produced and examined a wide assortment of knowledgeable, responsible, trustworthy witnesses and undeniable material facts that proves that Mr. Loper is, without any reasonable doubt, guilty as charged."

"Mr. Anderson?"

Anderson rose and walked to stand before the jury. "From Mr. Loper's testimony, we have adequately covered the facts pertaining to the whereabouts of Mr. Loper on the night of Oct. 22nd of 1997 from the time he left work on the day Ms. Mavin claims she was raped, until he was arrested in his home later that night." He drew in a long breath, then returned to his seat. The judge looked at the bailiff. "If you'll show the jury to their room, we'll await their verdict."

An hour later, the bailiff led the jury back to the courtroom where they assumed their seats. "Have you reached a verdict, Mr. foreman?" Judge Jackson asked

The foreman rose. "We have, Your Honor."

The bailiff's heels clicked loudly in the expectant quiet as he took the folded paper from the foreman and carried it to the bench. The judge's face was a mask as he read the decision, re-folded it, then handed it back.

When the officer returned the paper to the juryman, the judge looked toward the defendant's table. "The defendant will rise," he said.

Holding the queasiness in the pit of her stomach at bay, Marianne sat unmoving, as chairs scraped back and Loper and his lawyer rose. Scarcely breathing, daring not to hope, she waited.

Judge Jackson turned toward the jury. "Mr. foreman," he said, his voice void of emotion, "how do you find the defendant?"

"We find the defendant guilty as charged," the foreman said.

A clamor burst from the women jamming the courtroom.

Hands clapped.

Feet stomped.

A hat sailed into the air.

"Hallelujah. Son of a bitch got what was coming to him."

"Yippee. Put the bastard under the jail. Castrate him."

"Castrate him, hell. Kill the bastard."

Judge Jackson, eyes bulging, jumped to his feet and pounded on the podium. "Quiet," he shouted. "Quiet."

Dazed, Marianne listened as the voices faded to a few whispers and coughs.

The judged rapped again. "Any more outbursts and I'll throw the whole damned bunch of you out. Now, sit down and shut up," he fumed.

The voices silenced, leaving only the shuffle of feet and the sound of seats unfolding.

Jackson, his hair standing in unruly wisps around his reddened face, turned to the juryman. "Did you arrive at a recommendation for punishment?"

The audience held its breath.

"Yes, sir. We recommend that the defendant serve no less than 50 years without chance of parole."

Pandemonium again broke out.

Cheers and shouts bounced off the walls.

The gavel pounded. "Thank you," Jackson said. " Sentencing in ten days."

Now, I can put that emotion-killing Prozac aside and grieve, Marianne thought, tears rushing to her eyes.

She rose on shaky legs and turned to Isabel Perkins, who hugged her tightly, then grasped her arms and held her away. "I'm sorry we couldn't bring murder charges against Loper, but . . . as I told you, a woman has to be four months or more into a pregnancy before a rapist can be sentenced to life. I'm so sorry, Marianne. I wish we could have done more, but until the legislature comes to an agreement on protecting younger unborn babies in cases such as this, our hands are tied," She paused and looked toward the prisoner who was being led out, then turned back to Marianne. "However, since Judge Jackson usually follows the jury's recommendation, you can bet that piece of scum is going to Huntsville for the rest of his life." She turned her attention back to Marianne, looked deep into her eyes. "Are you ready to go back to work? I'm sure that would help you get over all this."

Marianne shrugged. "I don't know," she said. "Dr. Rubin thinks I should, but with all that's happened, I don't know if I ever want to see that place again." She lifted a hand to the faded scar and cringed. "We . . . I wanted a baby for so many years."

Perkins' eyes moistened. "Maybe Mr. Mavin will consider adoption."

Sucking in a quivery breath, Marianne glanced at the chattering spectators crowding into the aisles. You don't know him, she thought. "I'd better go," she said. "He doesn't like to be kept waiting."

The judge turned to the jury. "I thank you folks for serving," he said. "You've been an attentive, thoughtful jury. You're dismissed."

For the first time since the trial began, Carmine relaxed and breathed a sigh of relief.

Thank God the trial wasn't longer, she thought. I don't know how much more I could have taken. Tears rose to her eyes as she made her way to the cloak room to retrieve her purse and other belongings.

Twenty

Lisa tossed the yellow pad into the car, got in and ground the motor to life just as Marianne and Leonard Mavin passed. Mavin, scowling and surly, Marianne, tearful and almost at a run, clinging to his arm.

Bastard's giving her hell, she thought, her eyes following the couple. Blaming her for everything that happened. Making her feel lower than a snake's belly. She glared at Mavin's back, gunned the motor, and tore out of the lot.

As she drove homeward, her thoughts centered on Marianne. Is it possible that she's from Freedom? she wondered. She's the right age. Has the same blond hair, the same blue-gray eyes .

The thought brought a sting of tears to her eyes as childhood memories stirred.

One day after school, Marianne had knocked softly on her door, and Lisa, knowing the maid had already gone for the day, reluctantly opened it. Another dumb present from daddy, she thought.

Glowering, she swung the door open, expecting to see a delivery man. Surprise, and joy she quickly squelched, washed through her when she saw Marianne.

Marianne smiled. "Lisa, can you come out and play?" she asked, twisting a strand of hair around a finger.

Lisa clutched the doorknob and frowned. "No," she blurted. "I told you, yesterday, I don't want to play with you anymore."

"Why?" Marianne said, her voice verging on tears. "Are you mad at me? Don't you like me anymore?"

"No, I don't," Lisa said. "And I don't want to play with you. Just go home and leave me alone."

Tears spilled down Marianne's cheeks. "But . . . but, I like you," she blubbered. The rope of hair grew tighter under her busy fingers. "You can have Bo Peep," she wheedled, her voice strangled.

Lisa laughed scornfully. "I don't want your stupid old doll," she said. "Doll's are for babies." She shoved on the door. "Go home and leave me alone. I don't ever want to play with you again." She slammed the door shut, and through the window had watched Marianne, head down, walk slowly across the adjoining spacious lawn wiping her face with the tail of her dress. She watched until her best friend entered her house, then with tears pouring from her own eyes, rushed to her room.

Twenty-One

Marianne scowled and stirred water into the rich brown gravy for the fourth time, then lifted the lid from a small enameled pot and glanced at the over-cooked vegetables inside. Another dinner ruined, she thought, turning off the burner. She blinked back tears and looked at the clock. Resentment filled her. "It's getting worse and worse," she muttered. "While Leonard and the boys stop-off at the Icehouse, I prepare our meal, then sit and wait. Well, no more."

She sighed and opened the oven door, spooned a dab of potatoes onto a plate and topped it with a scrap of country-fried steak and a bit of the now-watery gravy. Entering the living room, she fell into her recliner.

"Marianne, you know how it is," Len had said, when she first raised objections to his lateness, "If I'm gonna ride with 'em, I gotta go where they go." His voice had slurred. "Anyway, I ain't doin' nothing lots of other men don't do."

"That doesn't justify what you're doing, Len. They're not you. The money you think you're saving on gasoline, you're spending on alcohol." She gagged and turned away. "To say nothing of the way you smell. If I were blind and deaf, the stench alone would announce your arrival."

"The money I'm wasting? What about you? Hell, you spend it."

A trace of anger sped through her. "Please stop cursing. You know I only buy what we need."

He smirked drunkenly and wagged his head. "Yea, yea, me too. I just buy what I need."

"What about all those bar-flies you treat? You need them?"

His face contorted. "Bar-flies?" he bellowed. "They're my friends never the . . . never the . . . jus' the same."

"Please, Len, " she said, her anger fleeing. "Quit the car-pool." Her eyes stung with unshed tears. "All it's doing is causing us trouble and using money we'll need to renew our lease. You know it comes up in two months."

He grabbed her by her arms, shoved his face in hers and shook her. "An' you crazy, Miss High and Mighty. Whassa matter? Ain't I s'ported you so far?"

She jerked away, stepped behind a chair and blinked back tears. "Len, stop. You're hurting me," she cried. "I work too, you know, and the little money my parents left is almost gone, then what will we do when the next payment is due on our home?" She rubbed her aching arms. "I don't know you, anymore," she whispered.

A sly smile slipped over his face. "Too bad, too sad," he had muttered, staggering to the bedroom.

A talk she'd had with her father sprang to mind. One afternoon, eyes closed, her feet rhythmically pushing the ground, she had been sitting in the broad, white swing behind the house waiting for Len when a voice pulled her from her reverie.

A sliver of fear skittered through her. "Oh, she said, opening her eyes and seeing her father, "You startled me." She giggled.

Her father smiled. "Sorry," he said, dropping heavily into the seat beside her. As they pushed the swing into motion, Amber, Marianne's big tabby, leapt into her lap.

Her father turned to her and smiled. "You're looking mighty pretty," he said. "Going out?"

Marianne smiled. "Yes, sir," she said, glancing at the new watch circling her wrist.

His smile broadened. "The new school teacher's son? He's quite a handsome lad."

Shaking her head vigorously, Marianne pushed the cat off her lap and brushed the front of her pink, silky dress. "No, sir. Len."

"Oh . . . I see you don't have your camera. You losing interest in photography?"

Instantly on guard, Marianne, remembering the accolades she had received when she won a national school-magazine's award for best picture of the year. She shifted uncomfortably. In the excitement it had stirred, she had even considered making a career of it, but . . . She shrugged and dismissed the dream.

"No, sir. It's just that Len said he sees enough of the woods without taking me out there to make pictures." She smiled.

Silently, her father leaned forward, propped his elbows on his knees and watched Amber, tail haughtily aloft, stalk off.

A pair of scolding mockingbirds squawked past.

At last, he spoke. "Honey," he said, slowly dropping each word into the vacuum, "you know your mother and I haven't objected to your seeing Len through the summer, but . . ." He pushed himself erect and turned back to Marianne. "We feel his coming around so often is not the best thing for you right now."

Marianne's discomfort heightened. Sudden tears stung her eyes. "Why not?" Lifting a hand to her hair, she began twisting a strand around a finger. "He's-"

Her father held a palm toward her. "Wait . . . wait . . . hear me out." He drew in a deep breath, dropped his hands to his lap, and looked toward the lush, green hills in the distance. "He seems to be a nice enough young man. I'm not saying he isn't, but . . ."He turned his gaze back to her. "The boy doesn't seem to have any ambition."

Marianne flicked the tears from her eyes with a finger. Her mind reeled. "That's not fair," she flared. "He's only been out of school a year, and--"

"And he's still working at Don's garage."

Marianne felt blood rush to her face. "Just because he gets dirty and greasy and likes to . . ."She paused. "He's as good as anyone else," she said defensively, yanking the lock of hair tighter.

"No need getting all riled up," he soothed. "We're just talking."

Marianne tightened her jaw. "He likes working with his hands."

Her father nodded slowly. "There's nothing wrong with that, if that's what he wants, but what about his future?"

Realization that she and Len had never discussed what she romantically thought of as their future sped through Marianne. She stared at her father and blinked back tears. "I don't know. We haven't discussed it."

Her father again looked toward the peaceful hills. "Then, what about your future? Your mother and I hope you're not thinking of pushing your education aside."

Relief sped through Marianne. "Oh, no, Father, I'd never do that," she said brightly. "I'm looking forward to college."

He nodded. "Have you given any thought to Len's . . . background?"

"Daddy. You sound like-"

"Like a father?" He shrugged. "Marianne, what you do is of vital interest to us." He sighed heavily. "Look, your mother and I are only asking that you look at the facts intelligently before you get any deeper into this relationship. Then, if you decide that's what you want . . ." He spread his hands and pulled in another deep breath. "You know, this time next year, you'll be leaving for college." He sighed and stood up. "Just think about it, honey. That's all we ask." He turned to leave, hesitated and turned back. "You know, in Austin you'll be meeting young men from all over the country . . . all over the world, in fact. And from all walks of life. Rich men, poor men, men in between, and besides their maleness, they'll have one other thing in common. They'll all be pushing for an education."

Marianne squirmed. Unchecked tears splashed down her cheeks.

He leaned down and patted her shoulder. "Sorry, baby. I didn't mean to make you cry. I just want you to think." He tipped her face up and kissed her forehead. "Why don't we pray about it?"

Pulling her thoughts back to the present, she rose, returned her partially-emptied plate to the kitchen, poured tea into a glass and stared blankly at the clock. What's happening to us? she wondered, setting the untouched tea in the sink and returning to the living room. And where is it leading us?

She reached for the remote-control. Too tired to follow a story line, she tuned in a small local station whose survival depended on large fees paid by theaters, clubs and ice-houses, in and around Houston, to present and promote them in nightly thirty-minute segments. A theater in The Woodlands, where some singing great was presently appearing, filled the screen.

She lay her head against the chair-back and closed her eyes.

"Now, to our next hot-spot," the jovial, tuxedo-clad host said. "Take it away, Lawrence."

As the KHIP cameras began scanning the interior of Monterey's Icehouse, Marianne's lips parted slightly. Her soft snores broke the professional chatter.

Thirty minutes later, Marianne pulled up her legs, curled into a knot, and looked about. Her mind raced. Wh . . . wh . . . where am I?

She lifted a hand to the scar tracing up from her eye.

Reality swept through her.

Her breathing slowed. Another nightmare, she thought. Will they never end?

She hunched her shoulders and glanced toward the bedroom where the table-lamp still glowed.

Hopelessness nudged her. Breathing heavily, she levered the chair and sat up.

At the rape-crisis center she had regularly attended, talking about the rape had kept the nightmares at bay, but now . . .

She rose and shuffled to the window, raised the blinds and glanced at the parking lot, then dropped, exhausted, into the nearby overstuffed chair.

Memories tumbled through her mind.

For two years after entering high school, she, like most of her friends, had adored Freedom's quarterback from afar. Then, shortly after Christmas of her junior year, the dark-headed, rugged-looking senior had bent from his heroic position and sought her out. Her, a preacher's daughter.

She thought she would faint the day he had caught her arm and stopped her in the hall between classes.

"Hi, Marianne," he said, his lean, tall body making her five-feet-six feel almost petite. "You got time for a coke after school?"

Her legs went rubbery beneath her. She struggled for composure. "Well... ," she said, hesitantly meeting his eyes with hers. "I, I guess so." She smiled weakly.

"The Dog House okay?"

Marianne shrugged. "Sure," she said, past the sudden knot in her throat. Bravely, she brought up another smile and glanced toward her best friend, Doris Snyder, who was waiting a few feet away. "Sorry, I've got to go." Heart pounding, she turned away.

"Four-ten okay?" he called after her.

"Okay," she tossed over her shoulder.

Doris, eyes wide and brimming with excitement, smiled as Marianne joined her. "Four-ten?" Doris' eyes grew wider. "You have a date with . . . "

Marianne nodded and sucked in a long, shuddering breath. "He wants me to . . . to meet him at the Dog House," she mumbled.

"Ohhhh," Doris rhapsodized, "The biggest man on campus invited you to have a coke with him? How lucky can you get?"

Marianne shrugged. By the time she reached her locker, her legs felt as if they would no longer support her. "He probably wants some help with trig," she said, clumsily turning the dial and yanking the door open, not daring to hope for more. That's all it is. He just wants some tutoring. After all, he and Susie Pope have been a pair since grammar school. Her heart plunged. She drew a quivering breath. "I'm sure that's all it is," she added, swallowing her self-imposed disappointment.

But a second date had followed. And a third. Delirious with joy and blind to his need for constant adulation, Marianne had felt privileged.

Now the future looked bleak.

Twenty-Two

Lisa pushed through the back door of The Red Wine Inn, hurried to her car and flopped into the seat. Another day without enough rest, she thought, but Sunday is only twenty-four hours away and like the movie I never work on Sunday.

Pulling into the near-deserted street, she reached in her bra for the night's earnings and counted it as she drove. One hundred from Edmond Snyder, one sixty from Charlie Pikes, a new, unknown customer and two hundred from Cadance Tinsley, a NASA big-wig lawyer, whose wife, he claimed, was killing him with boredom. He makes me feel better about myself than anyone, she thought. Driving automatically, she recalled the night's scene with him and smiled.

Momentarily pausing in the arched entrance of the dining room-bar, he had caught her eye, and frowning, sauntered to her table. "Damn, I hate you sitting out here like a common whore," he said, pulling out a chair and plunking down in it.

Lisa took a sip of soda water and shrugged nonchalantly. "Then, don't look," she said. Instantly, she regretted her words. "Look, Cade," she continued, softening her voice, "what would you have me do? Pretend I'm someone I'm not? At night, I sell sex. That's what I do."

He covered one of her slender hands with his. "Dammit, I admire your honesty, but I'm tired of playing games with you." He paused. "*The usual,*" he said to the waitress who walked up. As Dixie turned away, he called after her, "*make it a double . . . and another soda for my friend here.*" He looked at Lisa and motioned with his head. "*See what you're doing? You're making a drunk out of me. If you'd just let me set you up somewhere . . . You know, there're some beautiful condos over on Harvey."*

"*I know,*" Lisa said, tired of being pressured. "*I've seen them.*"

"*Well?*"

Lisa frowned. "*Cade, you know the answer . . . you can't afford me.*"

"*The hell I can't.*"

"*You'd make payments on the condo and give me a couple of credit cards, but what I need is cash. Cold, hard cash! Besides, look what you'd be taking from your wife and daughter.*"

"*They get everything they need. Look, dammit, I'm in love with you. Besides, Coleman's schooling's not near the finish line.*"

Lisa looked into his steel-gray eyes. "*The truth is Cade, that you're in lust with me and lust always ends.*"

His face reddened. "*That's a lie and you know it,*" he muttered. "*Dammit, I'm not some love-struck adolescent mooning over his first girlfriend. I love you.*" He ducked his head a moment, then snapped it back up. "*What've you made tonight?*"

Lisa lifted a hand to the low-scooped neckline of the fitted red dress she was wearing. "*Not enough,*" she said. But from all indications, there's another two hundred waiting, she thought, glancing at a man seated at the bar. "*Why?*"

The red in Cadance's face deepened. He picked up a shot of bourbon and tossed it down, lowered his hand, and popped the glass to the table. "*Damn you, Lisa. It's never enough. You sit here making eyes at men as if I were blind, deaf and dumb.*" He turned and glared toward the bar. "*One of them your next john?*"

A queasiness shot through her. Softly, she stroked his hand. "*Cadance, please don't be mad,*" she said, gazing into his eyes. "*You don't know what it's like to beg for food, to wear other people's castoffs, to hunt for a place to sleep so you won't be molested or killed. Well, I do. I've lived through all that, and I don't want to ever do it again. For once, I'd like to live on your side of the street.*" Her voice hardened. "*And I will,*" she said, determination filling her. "I will!"

He turned his hand, gripped hers and squeezed. "*I know,*" he said, his anger dissipating. He leaned back and smiled. "*Look, I got two hundred in my pocket that's just begging to be spent.*"

Quickly, she glanced toward the bar, then back at Cadance. A known source is always the safest, she thought. "*I know where you can spend it,*" she had teased. "*Want me to show you?*"

Twenty-Three

Zoe Loper pulled her dark hair into a silky French twist, pinned it in place, then lifted the brightly-flowered dress lying on the bed and dropped it over her head. Gazing at herself, she stood before the mirror, smoothed the soft fabric over her hips and smiled. Now, for a bit more color, she thought.

Bending close to her reflection, she picked up a cylinder from the dressing table, swivelled its contents to the top and ran the bright red tip over her full lips. Her tongue flicked out and moistened the paint. She turned, checked her appearance then smiled and turned again. I feel like a new woman, she thought, picking up a vial of perfume.

As frustration had dropped from her life with Robert's imprisonment, twenty pounds had dropped from her frame. At first, she had merely belted the dresses in, then tiring of that, had tried sewing tucks in their waists, but when repeated alterations no longer hid the too-full sleeves and excess fabric drooping about her body she had given up. Now, paycheck by paycheck, she was building a wardrobe from fashions she carefully selected from Walmart and Marshall stores.

Angus Jerguson's admiring glances ran through her mind. Her self-esteem heightened.

Holding her breath, she thought of the previous morning when she had boldly slipped her wedding band off. When, after spreading her hand and gazing at the white strip of flesh circling her finger, she had brazenly opened a drawer and shoved the ring beneath a stack of neatly-folded panties. Just for today, she had told herself.

Her conscience had battered her mercilessly when Jerguson's obvious admiration had first expressed itself with glances that held a moment too long and smiles that suggested more than professional interest. Then yesterday, when he had bent closer to her teller's window and asked her to lunch she had frozen. *"We're not allowed to mix socially with bank patrons,"* she said.

He made a joke of it. *"Oh, that's no problem. I'll simply shift my accounts elsewhere. Will that help?"*

Zoe felt heat rise to her face. She shook her head. *"I, I can't, Mister Jerguson. I'm married."*

He glanced at her ring finger and smiled crookedly as she pushed his bank book toward him. *"Hey, I don't see a wedding band."*

Zoe felt her blush deepen. *"I . . . took it off to clean it,"* she lied, lowering her eyes and blinking away the sting of tears.

He looked into her reddened eyes. His voice lost its teasing tone. *"Sorry, Zoe. I didn't mean to be pushy."*

She lifted her head and smiled. *"See you tomorrow, Mister Jerguson."*

He tipped his hat and smiled ruefully. *"Maybe I'll have better luck next time,"* he said, his joviality returned.

Zoe had smiled and nodded.

Luck had been with her the day she'd lost her job at Mulo's Credit office because of Randy Mulo's busy hands. He had laughed when she mentioned sexual harassment then at the end of the day he had handed her a check for the previous weeks work and said he would mail the additional three day's pay to her. Stunned, she had gathered her purse and dignity, and face burning, had left. As she entered First State Bank to exchange the paper for cash, she remembered they had lost a teller to marriage only a week earlier and had heard they were interviewing applicants for the job. Zoe asked to speak to the manager.

"Ordinarily, Ms. Loper, we only hire through an agency," the manager said. *"But since you're here, tell me about yourself."*

Zoe told him that she had been with Mulo for eight years, and that she had been dismissed because she wouldn't go along with his recent pawing.

"You shouldn't have to," he said.

"I'm no saint, Mister Quinn, but I have lived a straight life."

He frowned. *"Loper? Loper? Why does that name sound familiar?"*

Zoe wanted to cry. Instead, she swallowed her pride and lifted her head. Braving herself, she looked directly into his hazel eyes. *"Probably because two weeks ago my husband was sentenced to Huntsville for rape,"* she said, her voice firm. *"However, I don't believe my children should pay for his mistakes anymore than they've already paid."* She took a deep breath. *"And they will if I don't soon find suitable work."*

The following Monday she stood behind a teller's window.

Drawn back to the present, she avoided the mirrored reflection of her eyes as she dabbed a drop of Emeraude behind each ear. *"Angus is not just any man off the street,"* she said. *"He's somebody."*

'What if this somebody lawyer makes a move on you again?' her conscience cautioned. 'Will you accept it? Will you date him? What will the children think? More importantly, what will they do, since he's not their father'.

She tilted her head thoughtfully. They will adjust. Besides, in another six or eight years Jim and Jolanda will be grown and gone, she thought, and where will I be? Alone and forty, that's where I'll be. Gathering courage, she stared at herself in the mirror. *"Yes,"* she whispered. *"I'll date him. Robert never was much of a husband when he was here."* she whispered. *"And I'm tired of life without a man."*

'What if Robert's released early? You know it's possible. They're paroling them every day.'

She glanced resentfully at the un-opened letter she'd received from Loper the day before. I'll deal with that when it comes up, she thought, but right now, I want to feel pretty, young, and desirable. I can't wait for him to get out of prison. I have two children to raise.

Twenty-Four

Robert Loper cowered alongside the fence, his back pressed to the wire, his eyes in constant motion. He glanced at the lowering sun and begged it to stand still. Just before the red ball would disappear below the horizon, prisoners would be herded from the yard into the gray-walled dining room, given a meal of beans and rice, then . . .He shook with fear.

During times of outdoor recreation, instead of walking or running or joining the murderous group playing volleyball, he sought solitude. Curling himself into a knot, he tried to make himself invisible, as he had done today.

As dread of the coming night filled his mind, he felt as if a giant hand had grabbed his middle, squeezed his belly to his backbone then slammed him hard against a brick wall. He breathed in shuddering gasps.

He knew well the hell awaiting him under the blazing lights anchored in the cell-block's high ceiling. From the time he entered Huntsville one month earlier, he had nightly been gang-raped and tonight would be no exception. Panic threatened to choke him.

Feeling as helpless as a rat with his hind-part caught in a trap, the more he had struggled, the worse his situation had become.

After dinner two weeks earlier, Loper's misery had increased when Big Richard, a burly lifer who could choke a man to death with one hand, walked up behind Loper, pinned him to his massive chest, and laughing uproariously, yanked his head back and forced his lips apart. "*Might's well quit fightin'*," Richard said, leaning against a wall and capturing Loper's writhing body with a leg. "*It's for your own good.*"

Looking down, Loper saw Garner, a chunk of metal in his hand, step forward.

"*Ain't gonna hold 'im forever,*" Richard growled. "*Get it done.*"

In horror, Loper had watched the metal arc toward his mouth and crack against his teeth. Pain, like none he'd ever known, assaulted his senses. Now, an increase in oral sex had become an added part of his nightly torture.

Bile filled his throat.

Always, after Big Richard and his cronies were through with him, he fell, bleeding and retching, into his bed.

The raucous peal of the dinnertime-bell knifed into Loper's mind. Sucking in a shaky breath, he pushed himself to his feet and stumbled forward. Eyes downcast, he followed the crush of men. Smells of the nightly diet poured through the door as he entered the building. He gagged.

After a surly prisoner filled his tray, he found a seat, mashed and stirred the dinner into a puree, then sipped at the meal.

The bell clanged. He sighed, picked up the metal dish and placed it atop the stack at the end of the table.

His feet slowed as he shuffled from the dining room.

A guard rapped him on the shoulder with a billy. "*Get going, bastard,*" he gibed. "*Ain't got all night.*"

Loper nodded meekly and imperceptibly quickened his step.

The guard glared and stuck him again. Harder. "*I said move, scum. Move.*"

Loper's thoughts trailed through his head as slowly as his feet inched along the corridor. Marianne's blue-gray eyes and slender body rose in his mind. Hate consumed him, as momentarily he roused from his stupor.

"If I ever get out of this hell-hole, I'll get even with you if it's the last thing I ever do," he swore.

She stared at him accusingly.

He sneered. Bitch. Whore. Slut. You don't know the meaning of rape. He took another unsteady step. All I give you was what all you bitches beg for anyway with all your smiling and flirting. You otta been happy. He felt himself getting hard. He grinned. I'm ready, he thought. Takin' it always makes me hard, even if Zoe couldn't.

The bright lights of the cell-block loomed before him. Swallowing, he slouched toward his cubicle.

Lights out, when the individual doors would clang shut for the night, was hours away. Until then . . .

Big Richard lifted a hand to his face and gave an effeminate, mocking wave as Loper trudged past his cell. *"Hi, lover-boy,"* he said.

Loper's supper jiggled to his throat as he turned his head toward the bully and wrested a smile to his lips.

Twenty-Five

Marianne sighed, picked up the novel she had dropped to her lap, and again forced herself to read words that for her held no meaning, before putting the book aside and allowing her thoughts to return to Len.

He tried to make himself invisible. she realized. Even in school she had contributed to Len's macho attitude, had felt loved and protected by it.

Maybe there is another woman, she thought, remembering the night of the attack, when hour after slow hour had passed before the police had finally found him. She shrank from her thoughts as falling tears freckled the front of her dress. *"Mama,"* she mumbled, *"if only I could talk to you."*

She'd always been able to discuss anything with her parents until three months before her wedding when their lives were cut short by a drunk who broad-sided their car.

At first, immersed in pain and loneliness, she'd refused to discuss the wedding with Len. Then one night when he kept pushing for marriage, she had returned the tiny diamond to him.

In time, the fog inhibiting her thinking had lifted and she realized that wherever her parents were, their wish for her happiness continued. When Len again approached her with the ring and talk of marriage, she had agreed and they had moved ahead with wedding plans. Though the church had not pushed her to move, she knew they needed the parsonage for the new minister they had hired.

In a private ceremony, with their closest friends, his family, and her only aunt present, she and Len had quietly married.

She smiled faintly. Then, convinced that distance would ease her pain, she and Len had left the mid-Texas town for Houston and a new life. One week later they had rented the duplex. The first two nights they slept on the floor, but by noon of the following day, they had a mattress from Mattress Mac's, and with the treasured furniture she'd brought from her former home, they had set up housekeeping.

Shaking off the memory, she rose, walked to the window, and looked down at the cars lining the parking lot. Why do I torture myself, she thought, gazing at the empty space next to hers. He's not there and it's probably better that he's not. If he were home, all we'd do is fight anyway.

Again she scrutinized the lot. I guess I was alone from the start and just didn't know it.

Bitterly she turned away and dropped into the overstuffed chair beside her.

Twenty-Six

As Channel Four sprang to life, the news-anchor looked out at Marianne. *"This afternoon,"* he said, *"a child was found wandering around and crying outside Pasadena Mall. Between sobs, the six-year-old told investigating officers that on her way to school this morning, a man had lured her into his car with candy and took her to a wooded area where he molested her. Then, after riding around a while, he went to Popeye's, bought her some chicken wings, then drove to Pasadena Square and put her out."*

"An unnamed woman leaving the mall noticed the child, alone and crying, and called the police. Officials are asking that anyone who knows anything pertaining to this case, to immediately notify the authorities."

Sickened, Marianne punched the TV off. Pain, like a river, gushed through her. *"I'd kill him with my bare hands, if he'd touched one of mine,"* she muttered through clenched teeth. Conjured pictures of her rape-aborted child flashing before her eyes, fueled her anger. If I had one, she thought.

Dissolving in tears, sobbing inconsolably, she slid to the floor and wept as sleep slowly overtook her. Long after midnight, she woke, her eyes hurting and swollen, her inner pain lessened. Drained, she rose. Fighting to still the wild ideas running rampant through her mind, she trudged to the bedroom, where she eased onto the vanity bench, picked up her hair brush and automatically began stroking her hair.

Momentarily pausing, she leaned forward and gazed at herself. A child's face, innocent and pleading, rose unbidden before her. She caught her breath. Poor little thing, she thought. How many more will have to suffer before these animals are stopped?

103

Dragging in a deep breath, she stared into the mirrored image of her blue-gray, red-rimmed eyes. A feeling of helplessness seeped through her. She sighed. Except for the police, what can anyone do?

She sighed, crawled into bed, and picked up the novel from where she'd tossed it. Already half-way through the text, she read a few pages more, then unable to concentrate, put a marker in place and closed the book.

Twenty-Seven

Leonard Mavin stopped on the threshold and squinted at Marianne asleep in the recliner. She's a goner for sure, he thought. Pursing his full lips, he hauled in a deep breath then clamped his mouth. 'fi can get outta here without her waking up, I'll be hunky-dory. Easing the door shut, he shook his head and tried to blink away the fogginess obliterating his vision.

Drawing himself up to his fullest height, he hunched his shoulders as if preparing to tackle an opponent, bent forward, then lurched toward the bedroom. His foot struck a table leg. Glass shattered.

"*Damn*," he muttered.

Marianne bolted upright. Her eyes sprang open. "*You're home. You're finally home*," she cried, vaulting out of the chair. "*Where have you been? I've been worried sick about you. I called the plant and they said you'd checked out two days ago. Where have you been?*" She glanced at his feet. Tears filled her eyes. Accusation filled her voice. "*You've broken Mother's dancing girl.*"

"*Big deal*," Len mumbled, staggering forward. "*Damned thing wooden there, it wooden get broke.*"

Marianne hurried after him. "*And you're drunk.*" she said. "*Is that why you didn't come home? Where have you been?*"

He bent and yanked a suitcase from under the bed. "*Wooden you like to know?*" he mocked. Jerking a dresser-drawer open, he flung its contents into the case then opened the closet door.

Hysterical, she clutched his arm. "*Len, stop. Stop. What are you doing?*" she cried.

He turned and grabbed her shoulders. *"You stupid, or what? What's it look like I'm doin'?"* He glared and gave her a shove.

As her foot snagged on a dropped tee-shirt, she hit the floor with a thud.

Shame singed his numbed brain as he watched her struggle to her feet and rub her hip.

"Why? Why are you doing this?" she asked.

Her face swam before him. *"Jus' can't deal with all this shit anymore."*

"Doesn't our marriage mean anything to you?"

Anger replaced the shame. He sneered. *"'parently didn't mean nothing to you or you'da left that jailbird alone."*

"You know I didn't do anything."

Ignoring sleeves, socks and pant legs dribbling from the edges of the suitcase, he slammed it shut, latched it and tucked it under an arm. *"See ya, Toots,"* he said and walked out the door.

Numbly, Marianne stood by the big double-window and watched Len stumble to his pick-up and rumble out the driveway.

Memories of her parents surfaced. In Freedom, folks had always held them up as an ideal couple, she remembered, as had the local newspaper when they did a weekly series on church leaders. They had the kind of marriage I thought we'd have, she thought.

Smiling softly, she could almost hear her mother sing as she prepared and packed food for some sick or needy family; could see her father studying, preaching, visiting the sick, managing the church's ball team.

And on spiritual issues, she thought, they found no difference between God and His image. The way they saw it, each was so tightly wrapped in the other, that regardless of color, social status, finances or sins, the two could never be separated.

And that belief ruled their lives, Marianne thought. Their essence. Not that I ever felt left out. I'd was part of it. I always knew my happiness was of paramount importance to them. She smiled through tears as scenes from her childhood rose before her.

Dressed in whites or pastels with matching hats and gloves, she'd sit beside her mother in the second pew of the big, mid-town church, her legs primly pressed together, a wad of forbidden bubble-gum hidden in her jaw and wait for her father's eyes to pause on her as he scanned the congregation.

She adored her parents. They were always there, she thought, and now, in the mess I've tangled my life into, I know if they could speak, they would urge me to work my way through the difficulty Len and I are having.

"Unfortunately, though, Len is a factor I can't control," she murmured.

The trance-like state Marianne had, for months, lived in, suddenly vanished. For the first time she saw the stark reality of her situation as she watched the vermillion ball on the horizon pale and dive into inkiness. She sighed, drew the blinds and settled into the recliner.

Twenty-Eight

Lisa opened her eyes, glanced at the clock and jumped out of bed. Frenziedly, she ran a brush through her hair and threw on some clothes.

Grabbing her books, she yanked the door open and came face to face with her landlady, who stood, hand raised, ready to knock. "*Oh, Letty,*" she gasped, staring into the hard dark eyes. "*Can we talk when I get--*"

"*Ain't nothing to talk about,*" Letty broke in, holding out her hand.

Lisa scratched around in the bottom of her bag, her mind working frantically. Damn, I forgot to keep rent money out. Surely the old bitch won't put me out.

On her way home from The Red Wine Inn that morning, she had mailed a check to the Greater Gulf Coast Academy where Coleman was enrolled, then whipped by Bank One and deposited all the night's earnings but ten dollars into the night deposit box.

Coleman comes before you, or me, or anyone else, she thought, a picture of her son rising before her. Her jaw tightened as her fingers found the loose bill. She thrust it towards Letty. Gas money, she thought. But what the hell? I'll withdraw a little. "*I'm running late, Letty,*" she said. "*I'll give you the rest of it when I get home.*"

Letty glanced at the money and shook her head. "*I want it now. All of it.*" A sneer distorted her thin lips. "*What'sa matter? Didn't you work last night?*"

"*Please, Letty,*" Lisa said, ignoring the jab. "*I'm running late.*"

"*That's your problem.*"

Fighting to quell her rising anger, Lisa laid the money on the hall table. Her voice took on an edge. "*Letty, please. You know I'm good for it,*" she said, hating herself for begging. "*I've never tried to skip out on you.*" Seething, she hurried to the entrance, grasped the knob and yanked the door open.

Without waiting for a reply, she slammed the door and ran to her car. "*Bitch,*" she muttered, throwing a towel over the bare springs of the seat. "*You'd think I'd tried to cheat her.*" She scrambled into the car, coaxed the motor to life and careened away from the curb.

As she cooled off, a picture of Coleman rose before her. She smiled.

Paralyzing fear had swept through Lisa the day Coleman turned six.

They were on the way to Levert's Day Care when he turned his clear, blue gaze toward her. "*Mommy,*" he said, "*why can't me and you, uh, I mean, you and I, stay home at night? I don't like to stay with Miss Ross. She talks all the time.*"

Sucking in a shaky breath, Lisa reached and patted his leg. "*You know why, honey. I've told you. I work at night.*"

He squirmed and looked out the car window, then turned back to her. "*But why don't you work in the daytime?*"

"*This pays more, honey,*" she said. "*And I need to make all the money I can.*"

"*Is it hard to mop all them . . . them . . . those offices?*" he asked, again correcting himself.

Lisa swallowed the guilt in her throat at his innocence. "*Sometimes,*" she said, the lie bitter on her tongue. She forced a smile. "*Maybe some day I'll be able to stop, but not right now.*" She eased her breath out. I can't put it off any longer, she thought, her heart skipping a beat. I must do something. She had blinked back tears. "*What say we talk about something else?* "

That summer, they had taken their usual jaunt to Mississippi to play in the waters along the man-made beaches. She could hear him now, howling happily as the out-going tide pulled sand from beneath his feet or the in-coming one splashed his chest while he stood ankle-deep in the water.

While there that year, she made inquiries about entering him in the military academy, where, she'd been told, a few years of training transformed boys into young men. Though aghast at the cost, she had returned to Houston determined that someday he would attend. Meanwhile, she would buy a home there. Somewhere, back off the beach, she was convinced, a place she could afford awaited her.

And events had proved her right. Only two years later, he was enrolled in the Academy, and after weeks of searching, she had found the perfect place for them. Located just north of the Louisville and Nashville Railroad where houses were cheaper, she had immediately contacted a realtor. Though cutting deeply into her savings, she had made a large down payment on the tiny house, and later, deciding the place could pay for itself, she rented it to an elderly couple, which had proven to be a smart move. The old man liked to putter, and with her approval and paying for any needed material, he kept the place in excellent repair.

Remembering, she smiled as she sped along Bissonette. The University of Houston suddenly loomed before her.

Pushing the memories aside, she left the car and scurried into a building. Excitement raced through her. That's where we belong, she thought, entering a classroom. We'll have a good life there.

Twenty-Nine

Marianne, back turned to the building, glanced quickly about the parking lot. Except for a few cars sitting before the restaurant, and hers and Bertha's parked some twenty feet away, the area was deserted. A paper bag, caught by a light June breeze, skittered past. What am I doing in this eerie place, anyway, she asked herself. My first loyalty is to myself, and after Loper . . . She shuddered. She turned her head and saw Bertha hurrying to La Belles' front door. Thank God, she's ready, she thought, shifting her attention back to the wind-swept tarmac.

Bertha closed the door and locked it, then straightened, jammed the key into her pocket and smiled. "*Well, another day, another dollar,*" she said. "*You ready?*"

Marianne nodded and hurried to her car. "*Goodnight,*" she called over her shoulder.

Bertha waved. "*See you in the morning.*"

Since Marianne's rape and her return to work three weeks earlier, the two women, by tacit agreement, always left the store together and followed one another out of the parking lot to the traffic light on the corner where they parted. Marianne watched the tail lights of her employer's car disappear in the heavy stream of traffic, then glanced in her rearview mirror just as a ragged sedan, tires squealing, barreled away from an all-night store, bullied into the lane behind her, and smacked into her bumper.

As the impact threw her into the steering wheel, somewhere outside she heard glass shatter.

Her head slammed into the windshield, then back against the headrest. Horns blared. Cars crowded past. Dazed, she lifted a hand to her bleeding forehead and looked into the rearview mirror.

The driver yelled, jumped out of his car, and ran towards her. A chill ran down her spine.

She reached for the can of mace and poised a finger over the release valve. Don't be afraid, she told herself. And above all, don't get out.

The incensed motorist, gesturing wildly, bent and shoved his dirt-streaked, bearded face close to the window. *"What's the matter with you, lady? "* he snarled. *"Didn't you see that light turn green?"*

She lowered her window a bare inch and pointed toward the convenience store. *"We can call the police from there."*

He stared at her, then flapped his hand and turned away. *"Police, hell. You better learn how to drive."*

The following morning, Marianne groggily rolled to her side and punched the snooze button on the clock. Groaning, she swung her feet from the bed and pushed herself upright. Events of the previous night raced through her head. Where are all the Lancelots and Galahads of yesteryear, she wondered. Or did they ever exist except in the minds of writers? If they're alive today, where are they? Why do I keep finding cowards instead of real men? Even Len . . . She forced thoughts of him from her mind.

Carefully, she straightened, raised a trembling hand, and massaged her neck.

As the throbbing in her head mushroomed, the ticking of the clock atop the bedside table grew louder. Irritably, she snatched it up and hurled it against the opposite wall. *"Damn you, shut up,"* she cried. Startled, she slapped a hand over her mouth. Gasps poured from her. Tears filled her eyes. She stared at the shattered timepiece.*"What's happened to me?"* she asked, *"Cursing. Throwing things. I don't even know myself anymore."*

'You'll feel better when you get the venom out,' a voice within whispered.

Quickly she took inventory. *"I guess I do at that,"* she muttered. *"Maybe anger's not that bad, after all. At least, some of the pain in my head has let up.*" A picture of her father suddenly rose before her inner eye. 'Even Jesus had a temper,' he seemed to say.

As she shuffled to the kitchen, the raging face of the man who had confronted her the previous night, rose before her. She shuddered. What if he had broken the window and attacked me? Would anyone have stopped? Better not count on it, she thought.

Loosened tears suddenly streamed down her face. "*It, it . . . I've had enough these past months to drive any woman crazy,*" she railed. "*Rape. Losing my baby. A pending divorce.*" Sudden determination surged through her. "*But no damn more. I'm tired of being a victim.*"

Two days later, a full-page ad in the Houston Chronicle jumped out at her.

Women, it read. Take charge of your life. Our justice system, as always, is skewered toward men. Women are raped. Wives beaten. Children are molested. And those responsible, after serving an average of a year to a year and a-half behind bars, are being freed. If you have been used, abused, or are confused, and are ready to take charge of your life, call 719-552-8753.

Marianne quickly read the rest of the advertisement where case examples of abuse were spelled out, then lowered the paper and stared blindly out the kitchen window. She trembled with excitement. This may be the answer for me, she thought. As she ran a finger down the scar falling from her hairline, she re-read the ad and reached for the phone.

"*Bertha,*" she said after the initial greeting. "*Can't we take inventory Sunday instead of Monday or Tuesday?*"

Bertha stalled. "*Why would you want to do that? Have you forgotten I have a dinner engagement Sunday?*"

Marianne's spirits dropped. "*I guess I did, but –*"

"*I'm sorry, but Sunday's out of the question. Why do you want off? You were okay yesterday.*"

Marianne cleared her throat and drew in a deep breath. "*I know yesterday was only my third day back, but after leaving you last night, I was involved in a little accident. But that's not the reason I want off.*" She hesitated a moment. "*There's a seminar I want to attend that's really important to me.*"

"*And of course, it's on Monday and Tuesday.*" Bertha's impatience zinged through the wires. "*What's so important about this seminar that you can't wait and catch it the next time around?*"

Marianne felt heat rise to her face. I'm not begging, she thought. And I am going. "*It's a course on self-defense.*"

"*What do you mean, a course on self-defense?*" Bertha's voice was cold.

"*It's for women who have been abused, and after all that's happened to me, I don't merely want to take it. I need it.*" Even if it means my job, she thought. The wire hummed in her ear. "*Bertha, are you there?*"

"*Yes. Yes, I'm here.*" After her earlier coldness, Bertha suddenly sounded almost apologetic. "*Look, I didn't tell you earlier because . . . well . . .*"

Marianne waited.

"*Well, I had to hire someone to fill in while you were out. I hope you understand.*"

"*Of course I understand. Why shouldn't you?*"

"*Well, because of that, things have changed.*"

"*What are you trying to say?*"

Bertha seemed to struggle for words. "*I've asked Maggie to continue working on your days, beginning Monday,*" she said. "*There's not, not . . .*"

Marianne's thoughts whirled. There's not enough work for three people. "*You're saying it's nothing I've done. It's just that I've had to be off work too much. Is that it?*"

"*Well, it did create a problem.*"

"*Sounds like we're down to an either/or situation.*" Marianne's heart suddenly lightened. "*No problem. No problem at all. If you'll just mail my check.*"

Thirty

A hum of voices spilled through an open door into the noisy hall where Marianne tensely waited in line to pay the seventy-five dollar course fee. She prayed no one would recognize her. Before entering the building, she had turned up her coat collar and scrunched her shoulders. So far, so good, she thought. Now if I can get through the line and into a seat . . .

She glanced at the women ahead of her and mentally pushed them forward. The line moved, and moved again. Finally, she stood before a well-endowed redhead seated at a table.

The woman looked up and smiled. *"Hi,"* she said, holding a pencil poised over an open register. She lowered her head. *"Name and address please."*

Marianne felt heat rise to her face as her mind flashed back to the publicity the court case had aroused. She reached for a name.

The woman's eyes softened. She relaxed her hand and looked up. *"If you don't want to give your name it's okay, but we will need an address of some kind to send the mail-outs to."*

Marianne felt the blush deepen. Tears stung her eyes.

The red-head tapped the book with a finger. *"Only a handful of women ever see this,"* she said.

Shakily, Marianne sucked in a breath and bent forward. *"My name is . . ."* she whispered, then shook her head and straightened. *"Just send them to Post Office Box 1897, Houston, 37981. I'll get it."*

The pencil scratched. *"You'll find our mail-outs very helpful,"* the woman said as Marianne turned away. *"Almost as informative as what you'll learn here today."*

Small groups of women clustered about the auditorium chattered among themselves. Others, surrounded by empty seats, their arms folded tightly across their chests, stared straight ahead and spoke to no one.

Looks like they don't want to be seen, either, Marianne thought. Relief filled her as she scurried down the aisle to the front. Except for a few seats, the entire length of the row was empty. I can see and hear everything from here, she thought, and no one can turn around and look at me, and I can be the last one out. Breathing easier, she dropped into a seat near the center of the stage and relaxed.

Minutes later, a tall, slender woman ascended the steps, walked to the center of the stage and tapped on a microphone set up on a podium. A hush fell over the crowd.

"*Ladies,*" she said into the quiet, "*my name is Julia Best, and believe me when I say I know how you feel because I've been there.*" She lifted the microphone from the stand and began to pace. "*Seven years ago, and I haven't forgotten one moment of it, I was severely beaten, raped, and left for dead. Only by the grace of God and my sturdy constitution, did I live to see the bastard who took away my self-respect behind bars.*" Her voice gained force. "*Look around you, ladies. Every woman present is here because she has suffered at some man's hand and now has determined to do whatever is necessary to defend herself and her children. As we all know, pedophiles are as rampant in today's society as the rapists and woman-beaters who abused you.*"

Marianne sat riveted as the speaker paused, paced the length of the stage and again turned to the audience. "*Before you leave here today, you'll learn that locking your doors and windows is never enough. Never enough, because it doesn't keep a rapist out. Why?*" The lecturer dramatically bent forward. "*Because most rapes, beatings, and killings, are committed by those you greet with a smile and an open door.*"

A murmur of agreement swept through the room.

The lecturer straightened, looked toward the back of the room and nodded. "*In the papers being handed out, you will find all the techniques we'll be speaking on today. Tomorrow, you'll learn how to use them.*" She laughed. "*Don't look so horror-stricken. You won't actually gouge one another's eyes out, or crack any Adam's apples but you will learn the quickest and most effective way to stop an assailant using whatever is available, including your hand."*

As the woman's voice faded in her ears, Marianne removed a stapled sheaf of papers from the stack passed to her and handed the remaining ones over her shoulder to a woman seated directly behind her. Slowly, she began turning the pages. Shock and nausea surged through her. I can't do this, she thought. Pictures of Loper ran before her inner eye; Loper, in a fit of rage, beating her, raping her; Loper, his eyes filled with scorn, watching her each time she took the witness stand; Loper, handcuffed and flanked by two armed policemen, turning a last hate-filled look toward her as he was led from the courtroom.

She lifted a hand to the scar on her forehead and shuddered. Determination filled her. Oh yes I can, she thought, steeling herself. I'd gut him if I had to.

After hurrying down the hall to a restroom when the group was dismissed for lunch, Marianne returned to her seat, pulled a sandwich and thermos from her bag, ate, then rested her head on the chair-back and closed her eyes.

Forty minutes later, the crackling of the microphone roused her.

As the afternoon wore on, a series of lecturers mounted the stage and by the time three o'clock arrived, she was tired, her brain crammed with advice, and she was happy the day's seminar was over. Kicking shins, grinding heels into an assailant's foot, biting, butting his nose with one's head, grabbing his testicles and hanging on with all one's might if the assault reached that point, were all taught. Gouging eyes with keys, if keys were available. If not, with fingers, stiffened for the attack, all bled into one gigantic tactic.

"See you at nine in the morning," the last speaker said.

Marianne rose and joined the crowd-filled aisles. A feeling of sisterhood swept over her. As she cleared the door, she lifted her head and pushed her hair back from her face. So what if I'm recognized, she thought. I've done nothing to be ashamed of.

Thirty-One

As Lisa, drooping from exhaustion, rose and picked up her books, Cadance Tinsly popped into her mind. Why don't you leave me alone? she thought. I'm not ready to tie myself down to you or any other man. Probably never will be. Besides, when my degree is in my hand, I'm leaving Houston and you wouldn't like that.

Her rational mind came into play. 'He could make life a lot easier for you,' it whispered. 'No more all night stands. No chance of getting AIDS . . .you know he's clean. Besides, the man's in love with you.'

Bitterness streamed through her. Love. Of course, love. And just how long will this love last? Her mind fled back to the dark-eyed boy she'd fallen for at sixteen, the only love she'd ever known . . . the one who ran when the burden of a family had grown too heavy for his young shoulders.

She sniffed as Cadance returned to her mind. You're no different from any other man. About the time I'd get used to having you around, you'd decide it's all over. As it is . . . She choked back her thoughts. Besides, I'll soon be putting all that behind me.

Caught-up in the noisy stream of youth laughing and bouncing along the hall, Lisa pushed thoughts of Cadance aside and turned her attention to the rest of the day. One more class then home for a few hours sleep, she thought, weaving through the on-coming crowd.

As she drew near the auditorium, a vaguely familiar face seemed to float out of the crowd towards her. Marianne Mavin, she thought. I wonder what she's doing here?

Suddenly, she remembered briefly glancing at a notice on the bulletin board about a two-day seminar. Of course, she's attending the course on self-defense.

The following day, Lisa skipped her last class and waited at the building's entrance for Marianne who stood talking with two other women. Why am I doing this? she questioned herself. Why do I care how she's doing?

A picture of Marianne in court slipped through her mind. *"Because she reminds me of myself,"* she whispered, *"before . . . "* Desperately, she fought the memories welling up. Tears stung her eyes. What are you doing, Lisa? she silently asked herself. Getting maudlin in your old age?' A faint smile tugged itself onto her face. Yeah. You are pushing twenty-eight, you know.

She glanced at Marianne, then abruptly turned her back to the building and flicked away the tears with a finger. Maybe . . . just maybe I can help her. At least I can listen if she needs to talk. She clamped her jaw. And that son of a bitch she's married to . . . Disgust filled her. I've wondered how long it took that bastard who called himself your husband to learn that you'd been raped that night, because he was at Monterey's till way past midnight.

At first, it seemed he had refused to join his friends in their fun until Trixie came along and got her claws in him.

From her nearby table Lisa had seen Trixie watch the rowdiness for awhile, then toss a bill on the bar, pull her neckline lower and, hips rolling, saunter to the table. She looked at Len, smiled invitingly and in her high-pitched, little-girl voice, said, *"Hi, good looking. You here for a good time, ain'tcha?"*

Len's friends, and the women crowded around them, laughed.

Lifting one of his arms from the table, Trixie wrapped it about her waist and held it, then pushing a heavy breast close to his mouth, snuggled against him.

Len blushed.

One of his companions guffawed as he reached for a girl and pulled her to his lap. *"Aw, come on Len,"* he said. *"Loosen up. Have a little fun."*

"*Yeah,*" another broke in. "*We know you ain't got much, but go on, give her what little you do got.*"

The raucous laughter burgeoned as Trixie dropped a hand below the table.

Len squirmed.

"*Hell, loosen up Len. Enjoy yourself. Your old lady ain't gonna know nothing 'bout it.*"

"*Yeah, quit acting like a saint. Hell, screwing's what a man's born for.*"

Within minutes, Len, grinning foolishly, had followed Trixie out the door.

Bitterness swept through Lisa. She snorted. Men's brains are always in their pants, she thought.

Dismissing the memory, she turned and watched the women bend closer to Marianne as she turned her face slightly and brushed her hair back.

Absently, Lisa raised a hand and rubbed a smooth white line that stretched from just below her ear almost to her chin.

Only once, when the cut was still fresh and livid had Coleman asked her about it. He was eight at the time and she had gone to the Mississippi coast where he was enrolled in the Academy, to be with him over the Easter holidays.

He frowned and gently touched the ugly red streak. "*What happened, Mom?*" he asked, staring hard at the scar.

Heart-heavy, she looked into the honest depths of his deep-blue eyes. "*Oh,*" she lied, "*I just slipped in the bathtub.*"

He flung his arms around her and buried his head in her neck. "*Please be careful Mom,*" he whispered, his voice strangled. "*Don't let anything happen to you.*"

Tears clouded her eyes as she hugged him tight. "*I won't, darling. I promise I'll be more careful.*"

His arms tightened.

She felt the warmth of his tears slide toward her collar.

"*You're the best mom in all the world,*" he mumbled.

Tenderly, she held him. "*You know what?*" she said at last. "*I think Miss Vonay has found a house for us.*"

Coleman laughed and pulled away. *"Can we see it today?"*

"How about Monday?"

The scene faded.

Suddenly aware of rubbing the scar, Lisa dropped her hand and glanced toward the spot where Marianne had stood. She was gone. Spinning about, Lisa saw her less than ten feet away, walking, head bent, toward the parking lot.

Keep your mind on your business, dummy, she scolded herself. Pictures of Coleman excitedly looking through the house in Mississippi slipped quickly through her mind. Her heart lightened. Another few months and school will be out. Then, it's off to the coast for the summer.

Pushing the thoughts aside, she hurried behind Marianne. *"Hi,"* she said, catching up.

Marianne jumped. *"Oh,"* she said, glancing at the books in Lisa's arms. *"You startled me. Are you an instructor?"*

Lisa shook her head. *"Student,"* she said, meeting Marianne's blue-gray gaze. *"Sorry I startled you."* She stuck out a hand. *"I'm Lisa West. You got time for a coke?"*

"Of course," Marianne said shaking Lisa's hand.

After placing their order and settling into a corner booth at The Round About, Lisa removed her coat and looked at Marianne. *"How was the seminar?"* she asked.

Marianne glanced down at her hands which lay folded on the table-top and shrugged. *"All right, I guess,"* she said. A rueful smile played briefly over her lips. *"I just hope I'm never forced to use any of their teachings."*

Lisa narrowed her eyes and studied Marianne through a fringe of false eyelashes. *"After what Loper did to you, I'd think--"*

"I only hope I never again face such a situation."

Desperately, Lisa wracked her brain, looking for something to say. *"You'll probably think I'm nuts, but . . ."* she finally blurted, *"did you ever live in Freedom?"*

Marianne nodded and lifted a questioning gaze to Lisa's. *"I was born there,"* she said, surprise lining her voice. She lifted her brows. *"Why?"*

That really was crazy, Lisa thought, asking her something like that. What if she is Marianne Rowe? What'll she do when she learns I'm a whore? Get up and walk out? After all, she is a preacher's daughter.

Dragging in a shaky breath, Lisa pulled her gaze from Marianne's and stared blindly out the window. Don't be so neurotic, she told herself. Who's gonna tell her? You? Anyway, what difference does it make what she thinks? You'll probably never see her again. Forget needing someone to talk to. When you and she were kids, you shared all your secrets. Well, most of them, she thought, remembering her father's visits to her room. Except for that, of course, they weren't so big. Now . . . Besides, chances are she's probably not the Marianne you knew.

Sighing, Lisa pulled her thoughts back to the moment, looked at Marianne and shrugged. *"Just being nosy, I guess,"* she mumbled, doubt racing through her. *"I lived there as a child."*

Marianne, her face bright with anticipation, leaned forward and stared at Lisa. *"You did? Where?"*

"Sunshine Lane. Next door to a preacher and his--"

Marianne's eyes widened. *"Next door to me? You're Lisa Bailey?"* She giggled.

Lisa nodded. *"Crazy, huh?"* she mumbled, blinking back tears, recurring shame shooting through her.

"I can't believe after all these years, we . . ." Breaking off, Marianne grasped Lisa's hands. *"Why did you leave without saying goodbye? The day after you told me you hated me, I knocked on your door."* Marianne laughed. *"You know me. I never knew when to give up. Anyway, your father answered the door and said you'd gone to live with an aunt in Virginia. I thought that was funny since your own mother was so sick . . . but who was I to question your actions? After all, I was a child."*

Marianne's eyes reddened. Tears dampened her lashes. *"I thought I'd done something terrible, but I didn't know what it was. All I knew was that you were gone and that it was all my fault. It was years before I stopped blaming myself."*

Tears of guilt stung Lisa's eyes. As open and honest as ever, she thought. *"I'm sorry,"* she said. *"I never meant to hurt you. I just had to--"*

Marianne, apparently lost in memories, smiled crookedly. *"I remember getting down an atlas that day and asking mama to help me find the town where--"*

Lisa pulled in a deep breath. *"I didn't go to Virginia,"* she said bluntly. *"I came here."*

Puzzlement filled Marianne's face. *"You came here? Why?"*

Shaking her head, Lisa frantically sought to change the direction their conversation was taking. *"How are your mom and dad?"*

A look of sadness quickly settled over Marianne's features. *"They were killed in an automobile accident almost two years ago,"* she said. *"And yours?"*

"Dead too," Lisa said. I hope, she thought. *"Mother had--"*

"I remember. Terminal cancer. I didn't know what that meant at the time, but . . ."

Marianne freed Lisa's hand, dug in her bag for tissues and blotted her tears. *"What a beautiful ring,"* she said, looking at the gold, gem-encrusted band circling Lisa's finger.

Lisa lifted her hand and jiggled the ring with her thumb. *"A trinket John gave me,"* she said off-handedly.

"John?" Marianne said as if savoring the word. *"Any children?"*

"A boy."

Marianne grew pensive. *"Ohhhh, how lucky you are,"* she murmured. Tears glistened in her eyes. *"I'll never have children."*

Hours later, with phone numbers exchanged and many questions still hanging unanswered, Lisa smiled self-consciously and reached for her coat. *"I could talk all night,"* she said, glancing quickly out at the dark, *"but I'd better go."* Time for work, she thought.

Outside the restaurant, each turned toward her car. "Call me," Marianne called as she drove away.

Painfully undecided, Lisa watched Marianne turn onto Bissonnette and disappear in a river of red tail-lights. Her eyes filled with tears as memories of the night she left Freedom crowded in.

By the time she had reached twelve, her father was having nightly intercourse with her, and she knew that until she could get away, there was nothing she could do but live in the trap called love that had caught her.

And in the church-going, mid-Texas town of Freedom, she knew that no one would ever have believed their sainted mayor could commit such a dastardly sin, even if she'd had someone to turn to.

For months, she thought about leaving, but too scared to go, and too scared to stay, she chose what she considered the lesser of the two evils and stayed. There, she figured she at least had a certain amount of safety.

Her self-respect plummeted.

Her life became lonely as she turned her back on former friends and made no new ones.

Then one night soon after her twelfth birthday, after her father had made two trips to her bed, Lisa made her decision. She had to leave home or kill him. Either, she knew, would hurt her mother, but, she reasoned, killing him would hurt her worse.

She saved her allowance. Then one night just past two, as soon as her father left her room and pulled the door shut, Lisa dressed, crawled out the window and made her way to the highway.

Constantly glancing over her shoulder, she had run until she thought her lungs would burst, then panting, had slowed to a walk. By following a pattern of running and walking, when the eastern sky lightened, she was far to the south.

As the sun slipped over the horizon, she heard an automobile approaching. Fearfully, she crouched behind a roadside bush. It can't be the police, she thought. The siren's not on. Besides, daddy'll tell everybody I've gone to Aunt Emma's for the summer cause he don't want anybody to know what he's been doing. He's always after me not to tell.

Her heart beat faster as she held her breath and watched an old car slowly materialize over the hill behind her. In the brittle light of a Texas summer morning, she saw an elderly black couple inside.

Frantic, she ran to the edge of the road and waved her arms. What am I gonna tell them, she worried, as the car wheezed to a stop. Quickly, she ran to it.

"*Wha'choo doing out here in these woods by yourself, child?*" the woman asked.

A lie sprang easily to Lisa's lips. *"I went camping with my big sister and her friends, and I guess everybody in her car thought I was in the other one when they started home. Anyway, I got left. Will you please give me a ride?"*

The woman looked at the tall skinny man under the wheel. *"Wha'choo think, Henry?"*

"Huump," the man said. *"Likely story's all I gotta say."*

"You know we can't leave this child out here by herself. Someum happen to her, an-"

"An you'll be blaming me for the rest of my life."

"Please, please," Lisa cried, tears rising to her eyes.

The old man squinted his black eyes and looked hard at Lisa. *"You sure you not running away from home?"*

Lisa shook her head. *"Y,y, n,yes sir."* she said.

He snorted and jerked his thumb over his shoulder. *"Get in,"* he mumbled, then turned to the woman beside him. *"If I get in trouble with the law . . ."*

"Thank you, thank you," Lisa cried, scrambling into the back seat. *"If I can just get to a town where I can call my mother, she'll come get me. When my sister gets home and I'm not there, she'll go crazy."*

In Norris, the car stopped at an H.E.B. grocery. A pay phone hung from the store's front.

The woman smiled at Lisa and patted her hand. *"Here's a quarter, baby. You can call your mama collect from over there."*

Rubbing sleep from her eyes, Lisa thanked them for the ride, told them goodbye and walked to the phone. Picking up the receiver, she pretended to dial and silently mouthed words until they left the parking lot and rumbled away. She had noticed a Greyhound Bus sign two blocks back. She'd be in Houston by nightfall.

Once a month after that, she called home. If her father answered, she hung up. If her mother answered, she cried at her mother's confusion.

If I could only have seen her before she died, Lisa thought. But that's how things are. You accept the bad with the bad.

But, now, things were looking up. Another few months and she'd be a bona-fide, college-degreed journalist. I haven't done too bad, she thought, excitement trailing through her.

Thirty-Two

Happiness trilled like a symphony through Marianne as she slowly drove home, mentally repeating every word she and Lisa had exchanged, seeing every nuance of emotion that had flitted across Lisa's face. *"Thank you, Father, for sending her back into my life,"* she whispered. *"If ever I needed a friend, it's now."*

Questions, yet unanswered, filled her mind. Other than seeking a degree in journalism, Lisa hadn't said anything more about herself. Not really. After a brief answer about the eye-catching ring she wore, and saying she had a son, Lisa had changed the subject.

Is John her husband, Marianne wondered, and she simply refuses to wear a wedding band? Nothing unusual about that. It seemed that many women, some with children and a man who was obviously their father, no longer hung onto the tradition of stating their status with a gold band.

Women were freer here than in Freedom, or they seemed to be.

She sighed and twisted the circle on her own hand. It's time I put this thing aside and forget about Len, she thought. He'll never change and thank God I no longer need him. The accuracy of the thought excited her. Self-confidence, like a bubbling spring, rushed through her. Even if he tried to come back, I wouldn't have him, she thought. I've grown used to living alone and like it. I like it. She laughed as the truth of the thought spun through her. I don't need him now or ever. She touched the packet of papers lying on the car seat beside her. And with all I learned at the seminar, I'll probably find it laughable that I ever thought I did.

Her self-esteem soared. I can take care of myself, and as for sex . . . . Loper's face loomed between her and Westheimer Street. Clutching the wheel, she shook off the vision. *"You took care of that."*

As she rolled into the parking pad in front of the apartment building, a familiar restlessness that had gripped her recently again took hold. She turned the motor off, then sat and looked at the hedges fencing the barren, wind-scrubbed cement lot, the mildewed brown tiles covering the sides of the building. Sadness momentarily slipped over her. This place is a constant reminder of the past, she thought. If I were smart, I'd move now that I can afford to. But, her prudent up-bringing argued, the lease doesn't run out for another three years. Moving would be foolish. There's no point in deliberately wasting money.

She shrugged. I know. I'll wait.

One month after her divorce from Len was finalized, Marianne had celebrated her twenty-sixth birthday.

A week later, she received a letter from Leon Shaler, the lawyer in Freedom who had handled her parents business. He wrote that a lump sum of ninety-five thousand, five hundred dollars her father had accumulated through CD's and careful investments, was now hers, that the small fortune would be transferred to her bank as soon as she informed him of her wishes.

Joy and sorrow battled within her. She had always known that should she be living when her parents died, she would inherit whatever money they'd managed to save, but she'd expected nothing beyond the modest amount she had gotten at their death. Certainly not wealth.

Now, no longer pressed to work, she could spend more time discovering who she was and what she wanted to do with the rest of her life.

Thoughtfully, she slipped the straps of her purse over her shoulder and gathered the stack of hand-outs she'd received. Picking up the can of mace she had bought at the seminar, she got out of the car and mashed a button on her key-case. The lock whooped in response.

Gripping the can in one hand, the handouts in the other, she hurried across the deserted lot and entered the tiny lobby.

At her door, she picked up the Houston Chronicle, grappled with her key, entered the apartment and threw the unopened paper on a table.

The following morning when she picked up the newspaper and opened it, her eyes were drawn to a story near the bottom of the page.

Late last night, it began, an exclusive apartment complex near the Galleria became the scene of the assault and rape of a twenty-year-old.

Marianne cringed as the horror of her own experience again rushed through her.

Thirty-Three

Mike Donovan's shoulders sagged as he plopped down on one of the sleek white couches, fished a writing pad and pen from an inner pocket of his jacket and lifted his bloodshot eyes to Jackie McSwain's. I'm getting too damned old for this crap, he thought. He faked a smile. *"Now, if you'll just tell me exactly what happened, Miss . . ."* He let the sentence hang as he opened the pad and placed it on his knee.

The woman knotted on the couch opposite Donovan looked at him through swollen slits. *"I, I don't know how he got in,"* she stammered, barely moving her ruptured lips. *"I locked the door when Da . . . "* She stumbled over the name, then added, *"When my friend left."*

Donovan dropped his eyes and scratched ovals on the tablet. These bastards and their power-plays, he thought. Raping a woman, then beating her to within an inch of her life. *"What time was that?"* he asked.

"A little after one."

Mack Herman, who had been on the force for two years, entered the room from the back of the apartment with Joe, a rookie, following him. *"No sign of forced entry,"* he said.

Donovan snorted softly. Damned upstart. Putting on a show for the new man.

He had never cared for Mack. Too much of a know-it-all, but a damned good cop to have at the scene of a crime. Never missed anything. Donovan's voice grated. *"You sure you checked everything? Had to get in someway."*

129

Mack's face reddened. His lips thinned. "*Windows are bolted. Patio door's locked.*" He pulled in a breath and repeated himself. "*No sign of forced entry anywhere.*"

Someone knocked on the door.

Donovan glanced up at Joe and tilted his head toward the door. "*Lab men, I guess,*" he said. "*Let 'em in.*" He closed his eyes and pinched the bridge of his nose. Damn, what I wouldn't give for a good night's sleep, he thought, then dropped his hand and looked across at the woman. "*You ever see your assailant before tonight?*"

Jackie sat mouse-still. "*I don't know. He had a stocking over his head.*"

Donovan leaned forward to hear the whisper. "*Sounds like he thought you might recognize him.*"

Jackie remained silent.

Donovan propped an elbow on his knee and turned to Mack. "*Y'all go round up anyone who's still standing around out there and see if any of 'em saw or heard anything. You can come back tomorrow and get the rest of 'em.*"

As the two patrolmen left the apartment, Donovan straightened and turned back to Jackie. 'How in hell can a man expect a woman to go anywhere looking like that?' he asked himself. "*Sorry,*" he said, "*but I gotta take you over to Ben Taub and let 'em look you over.*"

The knot that was Jackie curled tighter. Her voice gained volume. "*All they gonna find is I been with a man.*"

"*And that man raped you. Right?*"

She ducked her head. "*Yeah, but . . .*"

Easy, Donovan thought. "*DNA testing can identify him once he's caught,*" he said softly.

Tears trembled in Jackie's voice. "*I,*" she stammered, "*he . . .*"

Donovan leaned forward. My God, she's just a kid, he thought. "*Yeah?*" he urged. "*He what?*"

"*My friend . . .*"

Donovan cleared his throat. "*You trying to say you and your friend went to bed before this guy got in?*"

Jackie stared at her shaking hands and nodded. "*I had just let him out and was running my bath when I looked up and there was this guy.*"

I don't know where he came from, but I don't see how DNA testing can help."

"*Does your friend have a key to the apartment?*"

"*Yea, but--*"

"*But you think he wouldn't've have come back?* " His eyes narrowed. "*He the only one got a key?*"

Jackie nodded.

Donovan sighed, slipped the pad and pen into his pocket, then rose and walked tiredly toward the door. "*I'll wait while you get your coat.*"

Shrugging with resignation, Jackie pushed herself off the couch and shuffled to the entrance closet.

Son of a bitch's probably been wanting to play rough all along, Donovan thought. She just wasn't prepared.

Thirty-Four

The following morning, Lisa punched the TV off, swiped a brush over her hair, shoved long legs into green slacks and snatched a shirt from the closet with a force that left the clothes racks clattering. Buttoning the blouse as she went, she grabbed her keys, locked her apartment door behind her and flew to her car.

A touch, and the Lexus purred to life. Carooming from the parking lot, she wheeled into the early-morning traffic of Richmond Avenue and pointed her car east. Eyes wide, she darted and bullied her way to River Oaks Boulevard, turned again and zoomed toward a district housing some of Houston's wealthiest.

Here, residents who lived off money made decades earlier from oil fields and cattle dwelt besides the nouveau riche whose livelihood was derived from computer companies, stock-market trading and slick deals made with banks and savings-and-loan companies.

Near enough to be called exclusive, yet not within the bounds of these territories, building contractors had erected multiple apartment complexes. Neat, clean, designed for singles or couples without children, they appealed to the foot-loose and fancy-free among both retirees and working folks.

Minutes later, Lisa saw these showy buildings with their precise landscaping and frescoed exteriors shouldering through the Houston smog. She careened around a corner and braked into a parking slot. "*Oh, God,*" she muttered, locking the car, "*Am I responsible for this?*" She hurried to the front of one-eleven, jabbed the doorbell, then breathing jerkily, worried the welcome mat with a foot as she waited. A moment later, she pressed her ear to the door and again pushed the bell.

A chain rattled, a key turned, and a tiny space appeared between the door and its facing. An eye peeked out.

"Oh, Lisa," a strangled voice said, flinging the door wide. *"I'm so glad to see you."*

Silently, her mind spinning, Lisa embraced the slumped figure that fell into her arms until Jackie sniffed, pulled away and turned toward the kitchen.

"Want some coffee?" Jackie asked. The gurgle of liquid pouring into a vessel sounded. *"Seems like that's all I want now."*

"No, thanks. None for me." As Jackie turned away, Lisa had studied the swollen, blackened face, the ugly bruise encircling her neck clearly made by merciless hands. She stumbled to a couch and dropped onto it. It's been years since I've seen anyone beaten this badly, she thought.

Coffee sloshed to the floor as Jackie slouched in and set the steaming cup on the long, marble-topped coffee table. She plucked a Kleenex from its box and blew her nose. As she sat down opposite Lisa, her housecoat fell open exposing bruised flesh that reached from her knees to her crotch.

Lisa's throat constricted as she leaned forward. *"I heard what happened on the morning news and recognized the front of the building. I hoped it wasn't you."* She paused and let her throat relax. *"You're sure you didn't know the man . . . that it wasn't David?"*

Jackie nodded slightly. *"David wouldn't've done this. He loves me,"* she mumbled.

Lisa had her doubts. She had known too many men who took out their hates and frustrations with their fists. Her voice softened. *"Has he ever wanted to play rough?"*

"Well yes, but--"

"But you think he's too nice a guy to slap you around." Lisa leaned back, crossed her legs and began tapping the air with her dangling foot. *"Right?"*

"You . . . don't understand. Me and David are in love."

Lisa pulled in a deep breath and fought to quell her growing irritation. Humphhh, she thought. Teen-agers fall in love. And men who're tired of their wives. She looked out a window and focused her attention on a woman walking past as she waited for her anger to subside. When she again turned to Jackie, Jackie was silently weeping.

Lisa drew in a series of short breaths, then spoke. *"Why are you so dead set on defending David?"* she asked. *"Just because he's keeping you doesn't give him the right to beat you or force unwanted sex on you. You're the same as married. It just isn't legal."*

"I know." Jackie said, lifting her head and meeting Lisa's eyes. A spark of fire shone from them.

"Look, when I encouraged you to get off the street and let him put you up, my God, it wasn't so he could use you for a punching bag."

"Why do you keep harping on David?" Jackie flared. *"I told you it wasn't him. Don't you think I'd know? He's good to me. Just yesterday, he . . ."* The brief tirade changed to a dull whine.

With AIDS spreading like wildfire, I'm glad Cade finally convinced me to leave the streets, Lisa thought, twisting the diamond and sapphire ring he had given her. She smiled faintly.

Our wedding ring, he had called it two months earlier when she had succumbed to his continued pressure and moved into the sumptuous apartment. But I have no desire to make our arrangement permanent, she thought wryly. I have other plans for my future.

A picture of Coleman's laughing blue eyes rose before her. Soon, you and I will be together, she thought, her heart like putty. At least, until you graduate and begin following your own path in life. Sadness enveloped her, then slid away as she sighed and brought her attention back to Jackie's monologue.

"won't give him a divorce. Everything seems so hopeless," Jackie moaned. *"You know what I mean?"*

Lisa leaned back against the cushions, re-crossed her legs and again patted the air. *"I know,"* she murmured, *"but . . ."* Guilt filled her. *"Look, I'm probably being a fool, but in a way I feel responsible for what happened! After all, I did talk you into--"*

Jackie's voice strengthened. *"Nobody talked me into anything,"* she said. *"You just helped me straighten out my thinking. Remember? You said, If David wants you, you're a fool to stay on the streets and risk getting AIDS. Be his full-time mistress, you said."* Jackie cleared her throat.

"Them words are stuck in my mind like honey in a jam pot." Her eyes met Lisa's. *"Like I say, what I done wasn't nobody's fault but mine."*

Relief spread through Lisa. A moment later, she stood up. *"Is there anything I can do for you? Shopping? Anything?"*

Jackie shook her head. *"I got plenty of food, and like I said, all I want's coffee, anyway."*

Lisa walked to the door. *"Then, I'll be going,"* she said, watching Jackie rise and stumble to the door. *"You're sure there's nothing I can do?"*

Jackie nodded. *"I'm sure. Time's all I need now."* The corners of her swollen lips turned up in a caricature of a smile. *"Thank you for coming,"* she said, opening her arms. *"You're a good friend."*

Lisa hugged her close and massaged her shoulder. *"I hope they catch the son of a bitch who did this to you."* Releasing Jackie, she stepped back and pulled the door open. *"Let me know how you're doing."*

Jackie's eyes reddened. She nodded. *"I will,"* she whispered.

Deep in thought, Lisa slowly drove home. What's happening to our world? she wondered, and why isn't something done to stop it? Last week that poor little four-year-old was raped and left for dead near the dome, then that eighty year old woman some son of a bitch raped and beat to a pulp. Nothing seems to stop them.

Anger sped over her. The bastards are multiplying faster than the cops can jail them. And with the penal system turning them loose on the public time after time, what can we expect but more of the same?

She pulled into her parking slot, locked the car, and entered her condo. Thoughtfully, she crossed the spacious living room to the bedroom and sank into a paisley-covered chair before the dressing table. Her imaginings brought a picture of Jackie's bruised and swollen face before her. *"No matter what she says, I still feel responsible for her,"* she muttered.

Blinking away the image, she stared into the mirror into her own green eyes, then slicked her hair back from her face.

Centering her thoughts on herself, she bent closer to her reflection. *"You're beginning to look a little seedy, dear,"* she murmured. *"It's time for a change, and with Cade out of town . . ."* The thought of spending a day at Conray's Beauty Salon brought a rush of well-being. The perfect pick-me-up, she thought, and reached for the phone.

Thirty-Five

Three days later, Lisa lifted the shrilling phone to her ear. *"Hello,"* she said, then from years of habit, added, *"This is Lisa."*

"Lisa," Marianne's voice sang over the line, *"I'm glad I caught you. This is Marianne. I hope you haven't seen the latest Harrison Ford movie,"* she continued. *"I don't remember the name of it, but I want to see it and I don't want to go alone. Interested?"*

"Hey, thanks for asking," Lisa replied, happiness welling in her. *"I'd love to go. From the reviews, it must be great. Say, you sound mighty chipper this morning."* She smiled as she tried out the newest expression she had picked up from her favorite professor.

"Well," Marianne drawled, *"I don't know about that, but who knows? After making a few trips to Almeda, and coming away unharmed except for my wallet, I think I've finally shucked my shell. Anyway, the movie's playing at Leow's over on Forty-Five. I thought maybe we could have dinner, then go . . . if that's all right with you."*

"Sounds perfect. Where do you want to eat? The Olive Garden? Chili's? Luby's? They're all over that way."

Marianne laughed. *"What I'd really like to do, is go to The Red Wine Inn. I know a lot of hookers hang out there, or so I've heard, but I've also heard that their seafood is out of this world, and I'm hungry for some. That sound good to you?"*

Gnawing fear momentarily blotted out Lisa's thoughts. Her heart skidded to a halt, then banged against her ribs. Frantically, she considered her options. Marianne would drop her like a hot potato, she feared, if she ever learned the truth about her, and the friendship was far too important in Lisa's climb to respectability to risk losing.

On renewing the friendship, she found that the love she'd once held for Marianne had merely been hibernating, ready to again incarnate, given the chance. Now, fear of losing that love reared its head.

Tonight, I'll tell her the truth about myself, she thought.

Don't be foolish, an inner voice answered. What's to be gained by it?

Nervously Lisa sucked in a deep breath. You're right, she thought, eagerly grasping the advice. I'll tell her later. Breathing easier, she turned her attention back to Marianne.

Her mind raced furiously. Damn, what a choice. Of all the places Houston has to offer, for Marianne to choose the Inn. Now, what can I do?

"Lisa, are you all right?" Marianne asked, her voice puzzled. "*Lisa? Lisa, can you hear me?*"

Lisa pursed her lips and quietly released her breath. "Sorry," she said. "*I was just thinking. The Red Wine Inn could be quite an experience.*" A novel idea filled her mind. Wear a disguise. Would Marianne think she was crazy? The answer came back quickly. Not if you make a game of it.

"*Tell you what,*" she said. "*Why don't we turn the evening into real fun and go in disguise?*"

Marianne laughed. "*Go in disguise? You mean . . .?*" She paused, then giggled. "*That really does sound like fun, but . . . have you ever?*"

"*Once,*" Lisa laughed. "*It's surprising the things you learn when people don't know who you are.*"

"*Okay. Let's do it.*" Marianne giggled again. "*Shall I pick you up?*"

"*It'll be more interesting if we simply meet there.*"

"*What time?*"

"*Anytime between now and say . . . seven-thirty? That sound okay?*"

Marianne laughed uncertainly. "*Well . . . sure, but how will we recognize one another? Pin a flower in our hair? Wear a scarf? What?*"

Lisa laughed. "*That'd take the fun out of it. Why don't we pretend we're guests at a murder-mystery dinner and we're looking for the killer? See how long it takes to cut through one another's disguise?*"

Marianne laughed gaily. "*Okay . . . see you there.*"

Lisa bent close to the mirror and studied her reflection. Except for the whitened scar tracing along her jaw and under her chin, her creamy skin had remained flawless. Not bad for my age, she thought. Good genes, I guess.

Meticulously, she applied makeup then pulled her emerald green eyes wide and inserted brown contacts. Finished, she looked at her reflection and smiled. Still look like Lisa, she thought, but not for long.

Slipping into a "fat" body suit, she cupped her full breasts, lifted them into the built-in bra and laughed. Now, no one will recognize me any more than Cade's wife did when I went to their house to get a look at her, she told herself, pulling on a curly blond wig.

Thirty-Six

"Hey, whatsyaname, how about another shot of ol' Jack?" a voice called from the other end of the bar.

Andy Polk tightened his jaw and tossed the towel over his shoulder. He gritted his teeth. *"After three months, you ought to remember my name,"* he muttered as he carefully added the glass to the nearby stack. A regular sitting close by, spoke up. *"You're not the first barman he's irritated,"* he said. *"They all know him. He goes all over town giving 'em hell."* He chuckled. *"I don't know. Maybe prodding people's his way of having fun."*

A feeling of resignation filled Andy. *"Of all the damn things that've happened the last year or so, I never thought I'd ever end up tending bar here."* A feeling of resignation filled him. His shoulders drooped. As he rounded the lacquered mahogany corner and sauntered toward the offending customer who was checking his image in the polished mirror behind the bar and smoothing his sparse combed-over gray hair with spit as he shifted his gaze from one scantily clad artist's conception of a beautiful woman to another, Andy's spirits drooped.

Avoiding the man's bleary eyes, Andy lifted the fifth of Jack Daniels from under the counter and filled the glass the drunk pushed towards him. *"Six-fifty,"* he said, holding out his hand.

The man fumbled in his pocket. *"Don't look like I got it right now,"* he whined. *"Put it on a tab."*

"We don't run tabs."

"Damn you, anyway. Old Jimmy did."

"Old Jimmy's dead," Andy said roughly. *"You gotta deal with me, now, and I don't run tabs."* He narrowed his steel-gray eyes, stared at

the man and shoved his hand closer. *"You know the game plan. Pay up or get out."*

The old man straightened up and importantly puffed out his chest. *"You know who I am?"*

The intoxicated voice garbled the words.

"Yeah, I know." Andy, tired of the nightly ritual, caught the eye of a burly black standing, arms folded, alone by the door that led to the street and motioned with his head. As the bouncer walked up, Andy jerked his thumb toward the offender. *"Jake, Mr. Gardner, here, says he's ready to leave. You want to help him out?"*

Jake scowled. *"Come on, Sam, let's go,"* he said. Ignoring the drunks threats, he gripped the man's arm with a massive hand, hauled him off the bar stool and quickly shunted him out the door.

Andy sighed, filled an order for a waitress, returned to the unpolished glasses and gazed around the huge, L-shaped room. Moments later his hands stilled as he focused on a blue-swathed figure paused just inside the door to the lobby. Quickly he took in the high cheekbones, the full red lips, the sable-dark hair hanging in bangs over her forehead and plank-straight down her back.

Automatically, he set a glass in place, and to keep from staring, turned away.

From the corner of his eye, he watched her stand for a minute as if uncertain, then look around the room and walk toward him. She's either a tourist or a conventioneer, he guessed. There's no way I'd forget something that gorgeous.

"Hi," he said as she reached the bar, and head turned, lean against a stool. *"Can I get you something?"*

"Yes," she said. *"I'd like a Shirley Temple."* She nodded slightly toward a darkened corner of the room. *"And if it's all right, I'd like to sit at that table in the corner."* She turned and smiled at him.

He looked into her blue-gray eyes. Dixie's holding it for her regular, he thought, but hell . . . He turned and took a quick glance at the clock hanging behind the bar, then turned back to her and cleared his throat. *"Dixie,"* he called, wagging his hand. *"Over here a minute."*

Dixie, order pad in hand, was headed for the kitchen. Frowning, she turned to him. *"What you want, Andy? Can't you see I'm busy? I've gotta-"*

"I know. I know. This young lady wants that table over there," he said, pointing. *"Can you help her out?"*

Dixie pursed her lips. *"It's reserved,"* she said. She looked around the crowded room, then looked at the stranger. *"You sure another one won't do you just as well?"*

"Well," the stranger said, *"I'd really rather -"*

"No, another won't do," Andy broke in, anger edging his voice.

Dixie turned and glared at him, then motioned for the girl to follow her. Jaw set, she flounced off.

"I'll bring your drink right over," Andy called. After carefully surveying the room and seeing no one she thought might be Lisa, Marianne, who considered her friend far more adept than herself at seeing beneath people's façade, smiled. Arriving first had given her the advantage she had wished for in this disguise game she and Lisa were playing. From the corner of her eye, she studied the women around her. Though some were dressed more expensively than others and their hair-dos were salon-done confections, their differences seemed to end there. Their carriage and voices, ranging from nasally shrill to sexy contraltos, were much like those one would encounter anywhere.

She shrugged and shifted her chair so both the archway leading to the lobby and the door that opened onto an outside wooden gallery were clearly in view, then unsnapped the floral-bedecked cover of the bracelet-watch dangling from her wrist. Only ten minutes left of the meeting time she and Lisa had set. Her smile broadened.

"Hello," a voice beside her said.

Startled, Marianne jerked her head around to see a stranger bending over her.

"Care to dance?" he asked, the smell of liquor strong on his breath.

"No," she snapped, her lips curling in distaste. He probably took me for a hooker, she thought, watching him stalk away. Within moments, a second man, then a third approached her as if they were taking turns. What are these jerks doing? Seeing who'll score first?

She laughed at her thoughts and again looked toward the archway where a woman, boldly surveying the crowd, stood talking to a host. Marianne narrowed her eyes and stared.

Could that be Lisa? As she watched, the woman entered and began slowly circling the room. No, Marianne decided. She's too skinny. Lisa carries more weight than that. Besides, she's a redhead.

Marianne lifted a hand to the wig covering her own blond hair. You're one to talk, she thought, smothering a giggle. But all's fair in love and mystery. As Marianne watched, the woman laughed loudly and sat down at a table in the back of the room.

Again, Marianne glanced at her watch. Only ten minutes remained of the promised meeting time.

Mike Donovan entered, removed his hat then stepped to a familiar darkened spot just inside the door. As his eyes adjusted to the murky light, he quickly scanned the crowd.

At the far end of the bar, Charlie Kuran, his attention apparently focused on the glass of amber in his hand, perched alongside three small-time hoods. Al Green, a slick lawyer who had gotten Burl Jackson acquitted of bank-embezzling, was sitting at a table laughing it up with a couple of whores. Jake Stern, an acquitted rapist, sat alone at another table.

He stared at the woman seated at Lisa's table.

"*Good evening, Mister Donovan,*" Roger said, interrupting Donovan's chain of thought. He motioned with his head. "*The only thing we have left is over there, if that'll suit you.*"

Donovan, never shifting his gaze, shook his head. "*I'm not staying,*" he said. As Roger walked away, Donovan leaned forward and squinted at the woman. Has Lisa changed her hair color again? He snorted. One damn sure way to find out, he thought. Automatically hitching up his pants, he ran a hand over the hand-carved, turquoise-buckled-belt that had set him back several hundred dollars weeks earlier, smoothed his salt and pepper hair, circled the spot where several couples were dancing and stopped before Marianne.

Tense with anticipation, Marianne frowned and shook her head. "*No.*" she said, looking beyond Donovan to a heavy-set blond standing in the entrance.

142

Wearily, Donovan pulled out a chair and plunked down in it. *"I haven't asked you anything yet,"* he said.

"How dare you," Marianne railed. *"You can't just --"*

Donovan sighed and shoved his badge towards her. *"Don't get your dander up, Mrs. Mavin,"* he said. *"I'm harmless. Really I am."* He leaned back, dug a quarter from his pocket and laid it on the table beside the badge. *"You can call the precinct for verification."*

She stared at him. Her face burned as she recognized him. Tears stung her eyes. *"Oh, Mr. Donovan,"* she said in embarrassment. *"I'm sorry. I, I didn't recognize you. Please forgive me, I didn't . . . I thought you were another one of these jerks trying to hit on me. I'm sorry."*

Donovan smiled. *"Forget it,"* he said. *"I'll have to say, though, I can't blame them for trying. You make a lovely brunette."*

Marianne smiled. A feeling of gratitude slipped over her. They won't bother me, now, she thought. *"Thanks,"* she said, glancing, in turn, toward each of the entrances to the room.

"You expecting someone?" he asked.

Marianne nodded and stared at an obese woman fast approaching her table. Surely that isn't . . .

"Hi, " Lisa's familiar voice said. *"Sorry I'm late. You been here long?"*

Marianne shook her head. *"I thought I had you fooled,"* she said, staring at Lisa in astonishment. *"How did you recognize me?"*

Lisa grinned, shrugged and pulled out a chair.

Donovan, looking puzzled, swept his gaze over Lisa, then narrowed his eyes and stared hard at Marianne.

"Gotta be good at something," Lisa said, then turned to Donovan. *"What're you doing here, stranger?"*

Donovan laughed. *"Stranger? You're one to talk. Looks like you're puttin' on a little weight there."*

Lisa laughed, pushed her chin high and looked down her nose at him. *"Putting on weight. You know me better than that."*

He laughed. *"Indeed, I do. You still in school?"*

"Yeah," Lisa said, dismissing the subject with a wave of her hand. *"Looks like you need some rest. You look bushed."*

"*Hell, I am tired. But you know* . . . " Donovan's voice bled out as his pager beeped. After a quick glance, he rose. "*Gotta go,*" he said, heading toward the front door where a bank of phones lined a small section of the wall.

"*I would never have made it, without him,*" Lisa said, following him with eyes filled with love. "*He's watched out me for years.*" Like a father would, she thought.

Thirty-Seven

As Cadance Tinsley's key sounded in the lock, Lisa sighed, dried her hands on a kitchen towel and gave a last-minute glance at the dining table. Everything was done the way he liked it. Silver polished to a sheen. Crystal reflecting candlelight. Dishes turned so the delicate, painted roses climbed along the left-hand side of the china. Fresh, hot-pink roses cascaded from a cut-glass vase.

The musky scent of the flowers suddenly sickened her. Smothering a sigh, she hurried forward and smiled as Cadance swung the door wide. Kicking the door shut, he gathered her close, thoroughly kissed her, then releasing her, slid a hand down the length of her body and cupped a buttock while the other pulled her closer.

Hungrily, he kissed a path up a cheek and across her eyelids, then down to the pulsing hollow in her throat, before returning to her mouth. "*I adore you*," he whispered against her lips, teasingly brushing his mouth back and forth over hers. Slowly, painstakingly, he removed her blouse and unhooked her lacy bra, then stepping back slightly, gazed at the creamy, blue-veined mounds jutting toward him. Swallowing hard, he bent, and moving from breast to breast, tongued their pink tips to hardness.

Breathing heavily, he straightened and glanced toward the dining table. "*Let's skip dinner*," he mumbled. "*You're what I'm hungry for.*"

Lisa nodded.

While his lips clung to hers, he tore off his tie and shirt and dropped them to the floor, then scooping her into his arms, hurried to the bedroom.

Later, Cadance relaxed in a recliner and watched Lisa clear the table. *"Dinner was great, honey, even if we were late getting it,"* he said.

Lisa looked up from where she was clearing the table and smiled. *"Thank you,"* she said. How formal you've gotten, she scolded herself. *"Chicken paprika always holds over well."*

"Did you have fun while I was gone?" he asked.

She shrugged. *"Uhhh, the usual. Bought a new dress. Some cosmetics. A new bracelet."* She drew in a breath. *"A wig,"* she said softly.

The recliner thumped to the floor as Cadance frowned and leaned forward. *"A wig? Why on earth did you buy a wig? I thought you were going to Rush Whachamacallim's for a new hair-do."*

Careful girl, Lisa told herself. *Stay in character.* She smiled mysteriously, reached up and patted her hair. *"I did. You like it?"* She turned her head from side to side.

Cadance relaxed, pushed on the chair-back and picked up The Chronicle from the table beside him. He grinned. *"It's beautiful, honey. Sorry I didn't notice when I came in, but all I could see was you."* His grin widened. *"With a sexy girl like you around, all I could think about was hauling you off to bed."*

The sheer negligee Lisa wore parted as she wagged her hips at him and laughed. *"It's good to know I still have enough pizzazz to drive a man crazy,"* she said.

"Witch," he muttered, unfolding the paper.

"Hummm, I see there's been another rape," he said, watching Lisa walk to the couch facing him.

"There's never an end to it," Lisa said. *"And there won't be until women takes things into their own hands. "*

"Our country can't afford for people to go taking the law into their own hands. You know that."

Lisa's temper flared. *"That's dumb reasoning. What if that woman had been your wife? Would you still feel so self-righteous?"*

Cadance threw the paper aside and gripped the chair arms. His eyes suddenly blazed. *"Regardless of how heinous the crime, who commits it, or who it's committed upon, everyone must be given his chance before the bar."* His voice rose. *"Even rapists."*

Lisa flung herself off the couch and glared at him. *"No need to get mad."* she said. *"We're just talking."* She walked to a window, yanked the drapes closed and turned back to him. *"But at the risk of raising your blood pressure even more, I repeat my question. What if that had been your wife? Or you daughter? Or even me, for that matter? Would you still defend the bastard who did it?"*

His face blanched. *"My daughter? Daisy? Hell, I'd kill the bastard, if I had to kill him in his cell.*

Thirty-Eight

Two weeks after making her decision, Zoe again removed her wedding band and dropped it into the change purse in her handbag. Despite her initial conclusion, it took that long to bring herself to act. Sleeplessness hounded her as she fought her battle. Rationalization worked only long enough for her to take the ring off, look guiltily at the lighter flesh encircling her finger and shove it back on.

One week later, she realized she needed help to make a decision she could live with. I can't go on day after day, constantly torn by right or wrong, she thought. That night she determined that come morning, as soon as the children were out the door and on their way to their bus stop, she would immediately dress for work, go to the nearby Saint Matthew's Catholic Church and hopefu lly be able to talk to Father McAheeney. Surely he would help her solve her dilemma. Prayer alone hadn't helped.

The following morning, heart pounding, she climbed the steps, chose a seat, and began to pray. When at last she realized she was too close to the problem to rely on herself to receive an answer, she went to Madam Ophilia for a card reading. Nothing would be lost in her rendition of the truth. With a few shrewd questions, the rotund woman had ascertained Zoe's needs, then told her what she wanted to hear.

That night, the ring came off.

The following day, when Angus Jerguson stepped up to her window and glanced at Zoe's hands, he raised his eyebrows. *"Am I reading too much into your lack of a ring, or . . . "* Lifting his eyes heavenward, he leaned forward, patted his chest and whispered in a low falsetto. *"Be still my aching heart, while I feast my eyes on yon beauty."* He looked at her from beneath lowered lids and smiled.

Zoe felt a rush of blood to her face, but held her head high. "*I haven't felt married for years Mister Jerguson. I only tolerated the union because of the children."* She felt her blush deepen. "*I've decided to quit living a farce."*

The teasing tone left his voice. His face smoothed. "*Let me take you to dinner tonight, Zoe. We can talk about it."*

Zoe dropped her gaze. Excitement skittered through her. She hadn't seriously entertained the idea of actually dating him. Until now, her thoughts had been more fantasy than reality. Her stomach fluttered. Her knees shook. *Dare I?* she wondered. *What will I do? How will I act? What have I got myself into?*

Except for Jerguson's daily flirting which had made her feel desirable, and the sheer sexual attraction of the man, she would have backed off, scared, as she had done so many times before. Even now, she considered doing just that.

"*I get off at five."* Shocked, she heard the words leave her mouth. "*I, I mean--"*

"*I'll be waiting out front."* He quickly pivoted and left the bank.

As the clock on the far wall spun closer to five, Zoe felt she was a zombie working in a vacuum. Twice during the previous hours, she had made errors.

Rodney Brown's sparkling green eyes had peered at her from a bed of deeply-entrenched wrinkles. "*I don't believe this is right,"* he said, laying the small pile of bills on the counter. "*You feeling all right, today, Missy?"*

Zoe smiled at the shrunken old man. "*Yes sir,"* she said, re-counting the money. "*Just a little foggy, I guess."*

He smiled in his lop-sided way. "*Better leave that for over-the-hill-folks like me,"* he said. "*You're too young and pretty to act senile."*

Zoe quickly counted the cash into his hand. "*Sorry, Mister Brown."*

"*I'm just glad I caught it before I left. You know, living on a pension . . ."* His voice faded as he tipped his old fedora and turned away.

The other customer, Delwood Bryan, wasn't so nice. He counted his money, handed it back to her and snapped, *"Better keep your mind on business, Toots. You shorted me ten bucks."*

Dorothy, at the next window, looked at her and smiled patronizingly.

As the day wore on, both relief and fear rushed through Zoe when the minute hand swung to four-thirty and the bank guard locked the door and lowered the blinds. Her hands were clumsy clunks of ice as she lifted her tray free of the drawer and set it on the counter before her. Steeling herself, she counted and assembled the money in neat, hundred-dollar stacks and laid the checks beside them. The silver she would do last. As she tallied and bound the bills, her mind roamed to the night before her. She kept yanking it back. The adding machine whispered under her rapidly-moving fingers. At last, the job was done. She balanced.

Giving way to relief, she carried her tray to the head cashier, gathered her purse and jacket and turned toward the door. Pausing just inside, she drew in a deep breath and nodded to the guard. *"Goodnight, Mister Goode."*

He tipped his hat. *"Have a nice night, Mrs. Loper,"* he said.

A tremor of guilt zipped through Zoe. *Does he know? How can he?* She glanced back at him. He was holding the door for Peggy Wade and saying the same thing. Relief whooshed through her.

"Zoe," a voice called. *"Over here, Zoe."*

The constriction in her throat threatened to choke her. She gulped and looked toward the curb. There, holding the door of a Porsche open, stood Jerguson. Unsteadily, she walked toward him. *What does the night hold?* she wondered.

Tense and doubt-torn, Zoe surreptitiously studied her companion's profile from the corner of her eye as he skillfully entered the southbound traffic of Highway Forty-Five. Handsome almost to the point of being pretty, his clean profile and dark head rose majestically above a snowy shirt whose two top buttons stood free. Chest hair gleamed through the triangle against sun-bronzed skin. His coat and tie rested on the console between them.

He glanced at her and smiled. *"So, Zoe, how was your day?"*

In a strained voice that sounded completely foreign to her, she related the episodes concerning the errors she'd made that afternoon. *"Other than that, the day progressed according to plan."* She pressed her legs together and chuckled hoarsely. *"Just dull, dry, bank work."*

He frowned and glanced quickly at her. His voice dropped. *"Hey, Zoe . . . relax. We're only going to dinner."* He reached out and patted her tightly-clenched hands.

Drawing in a jerky breath, she stared out the window. *"I know,"* she whispered. *"It's just that--"*

"That you've never done this before."

She blinked back tears and nodded.

For a time they rode in silence. As he clover-leafed onto NASA One Road, he again glanced at her. *"You been to the zoo since the renovation?"* he asked.

She shook her head. *"Not yet, but I plan to take the children as soon as the weather permits."* She felt warm relaxation seep slowly through her.

"Yes, wait 'till summer and it's too hot and muggy." Briefly, he looked at her and smiled, then turned his eyes back to the road. *"But then, that's Houston. By the way, I wish you'd call me Gus. Everyone does."*

Zoe toyed silently with the name and found herself relaxing more and more as he drew her out. Excitement spread through her. *This is fun and God knows I need a little of that in my life.*

Her thoughts turned toward home. Minutes after accepting Jerguson's invitation, she had called and talked to Jolanda. After telling her and Jim to spend the night with their grandmother, she added a lie. *"I'm going out with the girls,"* she had added. *"I'll be late getting home."*

Guilt-filled, she stared out the window. Heat suffused her face. *What nerve, sending them to Rosa's while I'm out with another man. God, what kind of a person am I turning into?* She heaved a sigh.

"Zoe?" Jerguson said. *"Are you all right?"*

On edge again, Zoe turned her head to face him. He was bending toward her, his face filled with concern.

She forced a smile. *"Sorry. Just thinking."*

He grinned. *"Thinking's out of bounds for tonight. Fun's the word. Hope you like seafood."*

She pushed tighter into the bucket seat and smiled dimly. *"If it swims in the gulf, I love it."*

Jerguson smiled.

At Highway One-Forty Six, he turned south into the little city of Kemah, zipped over the high-rise bridge, made another turn, and within minutes pulled to a stop before Landry's Seafood Restaurant.

A hostess greeted them just inside the door. *"Good evening, Mister Jerguson.,"* she said, smiling.

"Good evening," Jerguson said, then smiled and looked down at Zoe. *"Going up."*

Zoe trembled. Her mind raced. Oh God, what am I doing here? Robert would kill me. Her hands turned cold at the thought. Her legs shook. She took a deep breath and, with Jerguson gripping her elbow, entered an elevator for the third floor where they were shown to a table looking out over the water.

"Here we are, Zoe," Jerguson said, handing her into a chair. *"Some of the best seafood in town."*

Her mind in turmoil, unable to study the menu lying before her, she glanced at Jerguson. *"It all sounds good, Mister . . . "* She felt the blush return. *"I, I mean Gus."* The name felt strange on her lips. *"Please order for me."*

He smiled. *"Whatever you say."*

His voice hummed in her suddenly sound-stricken ears as he gave the uniformed waiter their order, then reached across the table.

Quickly, she dropped her hands to her lap and watched boats hurrying to berth before the dusk that hovered over Galveston Bay blackened the waters.

Two hours later, her hunger satiated, her head spinning from wine and unaccustomed attention, Jerguson confidently led her from the restaurant.

Six weeks later the soothing strains of The Blue Danube flowed over, around, and through Zoe, as she, held tight in Gus' arms, followed his smooth steps. Momentarily indulging herself in day-dreams, she lay her head on his shoulder and closed her eyes.

I could go on like this forever, she thought.

'Stop thinking that way,' a chorus of voices seemed to say, as they gathered like storm clouds on the edge of her conscience. *'Don't keep tempting yourself with thoughts of love! Forget those romantic dreams!'*

Swallowing hard, she lifted her head and pulled slightly away from Gus.

Puzzled, he looked down at her then stopped dead still. *"Something wrong, Zoe?"* he asked, his eyes not quite meeting her up-lifted ones. *"I thought you said you loved to waltz."* Dropping her hand, he walked over, muted the CD, then turned back to her. *"What's going on, Zoe?"*

Numbly, she shook her head and shrugged. *"Nothing . . . nothing,"* she mumbled, hating herself for her weakness. *"It's just . . . "*

Patiently, he slipped his arms around her and, pulling her close, stroked her hair. *"That conscience of yours beating you to death, again?"*

Desire surged through her. Teary-eyed, she nodded. Placing her hands on his chest, she pushed away from the burning heat of his erection. *"I can't go on this way,"* she said. *"I just can't. Please . . . take me home."*

For weeks, now, she had battled against giving in to her own sexual urges. *"No,"* she had always argued when their love-making became too hot. *"I'm married. I, I can't. My children—"*

Now . . .

"Can't, Zoe, or won't?" he interrupted. *"I've grown to love you. You know that. Besides, who'd ever know?"* He paused and tipped her face to his. *"You know I'd marry you in a minute if--"*

Zoe lifted her hand and blocked his words with her fingers. *"Don't,"* she whispered, her thoughts a jumbled confusion.

Sucking in a deep breath, Gus suddenly bent, covered her lips with his, picked her up and turned toward his bedroom.

Oh, God, she thought, her fragile hold on denial weakening. *Who am I fooling? He's right.* At last surrendering to love, she flung her arms around his neck. *"I love you, too,"* she whispered.

Holding her captive with his lips, he stood her on her feet and began to slowly undress her, then loosened his trousers and dropped them to the floor.

Thirty-Nine

Tuesday, April 7th.

As Lisa's mind wandered, she dropped her pen, pushed the notebook aside, then propping her elbows on the table, gazed moodily out the window. Images of news reporters scrambling for the juiciest stories, the best views, the most attention-getting words, rose in a foggy curtain between her and the thundering rain that had washed in.

'*Do you really want to join their ranks?*' an inner voice asked.

What difference does it make? she argued. *Want to or not, it's what I'll do . . . it's what I've been working for.* She turned, looked at Coleman's picture resting on top the TV and smiled. *It's where our future lies.*

Her thoughts skipped to the academy, where the sturdy eleven-year-old was too quickly leaving childhood. "*Time is passing so fast, I can't keep up,*" she murmured. Sadness seeped through her. "*I'm losing too much of him.*" Tears flooded her eyes. "*Anyway, what else can I do besides . . .*"

She glanced around the condo, then turned back to the window and wiped the salty streaks from her face. Absently, she again ran a finger down the notebooks stacked before her, picked up the pen and began to write. Startled, she paused as Marianne's face wavered between her and the pages. Thoughts of the day they had met and the hours they had spent over burgers and cokes pell-melled through her mind. *Why am I remembering all that?* she questioned herself.

'*You're back into the story of the rape and trial, aren't you?*' an inner voice asked.

Thought-filled, she again laid her pen down and ran a finger down the spines of the notebooks. *"Yes,* she muttered, *"But as soon as I write my thesis, it's into the garbage with all this."*

'*What a shame no one but Professor James will read about the horrors and repercussions of the rape she experienced.*'

Anger flashed through Lisa. *"The horrors and repercussions she experienced?"* she muttered. *"Don't be a damn fool! Hell, I could write a million books about rapes and beatings, and, and . . . "*

'*Then do it and quit talking about it!*'

"Do it?"

Startled, she picked up the pen and began doodling, as her thoughts flew back to her childhood, to her teens. A sentence formed in her head.

I was a pawn, she wrote.

Again, she glanced around the apartment. *"And I still am,"* she said.

She set the sentence down below the former one, then fused them.

I was a pawn and I still am. She laughed bitterly.

"A pawn for what? Food? Money? Existence?"

Her mind worried the words. *"Yes! Hell yes! All of the above!"*

'*Love?*'

"Love?" Her laughter swelled. *"Never!"*

As her laughter peaked and fell away, she wiped her tears, bent to the paper, and furiously copied the words she had written until the page was filled then flipped it over and continued.

At last drained, she pushed the material aside, rose heavily and trudged to the bedroom. *Thank God Cade's not here tonight,* she thought. *Maybe I can get some sleep. "Love? How funny!"*

Quickly squelching threatening hysteria, she picked up a book and climbed into bed.

The following morning, she woke with the phrases she had written the night before ringing in her ears and the scent of coffee filling her nostrils. *"I was a pawn, and I still am,"* she whispered to the walls. *"I was a pawn and I still am,"* she repeated to her mirrored image as she brushed her hair.

Making her way to the kitchen, she addressed the coffee pot. *"I was a pawn,"* she muttered, carrying the pot and a cup to the table. *"And I still am!"*

She filled the mug, sat down before the open notebook and stared at the pages filled with the scribbled sentence. *There must be something here for me to learn*, she thought. *Otherwise, why wake up with this on my mind?* Calmly, she studied the words, propped her chin in a palm and looked out on another bleak day.

An unfamiliar sense of shame suddenly seared her. *"I am a pawn in a game that passes for love,"* she admitted.

Heat rose to her face as pictures she had long repressed moved before her inner eye; as she watched the child she had been make her way into the darkness, into the city, and into the streets which were at once a haven and a threat. Sadness engulfed her. *"The streets were my home,"* she whispered in her pain.

'*Write it,*' the voice within commanded.

Through her tears, she wrote.

'*Now, combine the two.*'

"I was a pawn in something that passes—"

'*No, no!*'

"What?"

'*In this thing called love.*'

"All right. All right!"

She scribbled.

I was a pawn in this thing called love.

The streets were my home.

"There. Does that suit you?"

She re-read the lines. *There is a certain rhythm there.* Excitement skittered through her. *This could be the beginning of a poem!*

'*Whoa there. Not so fast. Use present tense.*'

"Okay."

"I am," she began.

'*And contractions, stupid.*'

She whispered the words as she followed instructions.

"I'm a pawn in this thing called love,"

The streets are my home."

Her mind surged with ideas as she laid the pen aside and stared, unseeing, out the window. Smiling, she lifted the cold coffee to her lips, then wide-eyed, turned back and removed a notebook from the stack. *"With a little imagination someone could turn this material into a best-seller."*

The voice returned. *'Someone? Why not you?'*

"Me?" The thought astounded her. Violently, she shook her head. *"You've lost it, Lisa. You've really lost it this time. . . however . . . "*

Excitement stirred. Possibilities she had never considered swam wildly through her mind. She looked at the words she'd written. *First, I'll finish this poem*, she promised herself, *then . . .*

Lisa angrily shifted the load of books in her arms, locked the door behind her then stomped to the dining table and dropped the stack onto its surface. Quickly, she withdrew a manila folder marked completed assignments and rifled through its contents until she reached the paper Professor Brian had handed her an hour earlier.

He had frowned as he paused beside her desk. *"What's going on with you, Lisa?"* he asked. *"Your work's not up to par."*

Lisa shook her head. *"I don't know,"* she said, unaccustomed meekness tinging her voice. She glanced briefly at him, then lowered her eyes to the grade scrawled in red at the top of her paper. A quiver of fear shot through her. *Another damned D*, she thought, as he strolled on past her. *At this rate, I'll never get my degree. Why are my grades falling? I work as hard as ever, but it's like I'm slogging backwards through mud.* She groped for a reason. *Cade*, she thought. Her face grew hot with anger. *He's the reason. Keeping him happy eats up all my time. Days I don't have classes, he's there for lunch, and unless he's out of town, he's there every night.* Resentment had gripped her.

Now, paper in hand, she plopped into a chair, looked around the lushly furnished town-house and laughed harshly. *Here, I've fooled myself into thinking I'm living the good life, when what I've done is shackle myself to my benefactor's timetable. Benefactor, hell! He's my jailer!*

Sudden illumination filled her consciousness. Laughter died. Her heart lightened. *"I've always cherished my freedom,"* she muttered to the empty room, *"but I've foolishly given it away. Instead of studying, I'm cooking. Instead of studying, we're tumbling into bed. Instead of studying, I'm serving him until he goes home. No wonder my grades have suffered."*

She rose, a smile on her face. *Someway,* she thought, *I'll reclaim my freedom.* She again looked around the room. *Material things are not worth my failure or my misery, and especially not the future of my son.* She looked at the latest picture of Coleman smiling at her from atop the television, walked over and picked it up. Her heart grew buttery-soft as she hugged it close. *"You're the only male in my life who counts,"* she whispered.

She replaced the picture and again turned her thoughts to Cade. *I hope he understands, but I'll be surprised if he does. Men don't understand that nothing replaces freedom. Or that sometimes women simply grow tired of them and their demands. They think that option belongs only to them.*

Memories of Billy flooded her mind. After running away from home, she had lived on the streets, doing whatever was necessary to survive. At sixteen, hardened by life, she met him and her heart melted. With hair as dark as a grackle's wing, and eyes as blue as the good-luck marble she carried, Billy promised her a future.

And he'd tried. They'd both tried. He'd found work as a dishwasher in an all-night restaurant and she'd cleaned floors for a janitorial service, which left their days free for one another.

Two months later she was pregnant. Three years later, he was gone.

How hard I fought the truth, she thought. *Until finally I accepted the fact that he wouldn't be back.* One of the many times hope had brightened Coleman's eyes rushed to her mind.

One of Texas' sudden weather changes had swept in and caught her unprepared. Holding Coleman close, Lisa shivered and opened the door to The Salvation Army store.

The scent of laundered age had rushed out. Quickly glancing around, she located the nearest bin of children's clothes. *Girl's clothes,* she thought grumpily. *Why don't they quit changing everything around?*

At three, Coleman was growing so fast it was hard to keep him in clothes. Today, she hoped to find a sweater of some kind that would fit him. And if luck was with her, a coat that would last him through Spring.

After giving him an extra squeeze, she leaned back slightly. *"How about a little kiss before I put you down?"* she asked.

He laughed, threw his arms around her neck and planted a wet kiss on her lips. *"When's daddy coming home?"* he asked, drawing away, his face suddenly still.

Lisa's heart momentarily froze as she stared into the guileless agate-blue eyes. *I must be honest with you*, she thought. *"I don't know, baby,"* she said, the loss she constantly fought, assailing her.

Coleman puckered up his face. *"Coman wants daddy,"* he cried.

She forced a smile. *"I know, baby. So do I, but until he decides to come home, you and I will just have to take care of one another."*

He patted her face as his eyes filled with tears. *"Don't go way, Mommy,"* he said, anxiety coloring his voice.

Lisa brushed away his tears and pulled him closer. *"Never, darling,"* she whispered, laying her cheek on his head. *"Never. Mommy will always be here. Okay?"* Fighting tears, she smiled.

He nodded solemnly.

Playfully, she nuzzled his neck until he giggled then set him on his feet. *"Hold on to me,"* she said, *"so I won't get lost."*

Tears blinded her as she felt his tiny hand grasp her skirt. Billy had been gone now for three weeks, and though hope lifted her heart each time she saw a slender male back topped with smooth, dark hair, she knew in her heart she was wishing in vain. He toughed it out as long as he could, she thought. *He won't be back.*

Six weeks later, fiercely determined to dig out of the poverty that was slowly drowning her, Lisa returned to the streets she had known so well.

Within weeks, she moved a few blocks away to a roomier apartment. And after talking with Betty Nohil's mother who lived across the hall, she had hired the teenager to spend nights in her home with Coleman.

Leaving home each night wearing faded blue coveralls over short skirts and cobwebby stockings, her face barren of makeup, Lisa retained the illusion of working with the janitorial service.

Another month and she bought the old Honda, whose interior was ragged, but whose motor ran well.

And she opened her first bank account with five dollars she had managed to save.

Scorning pimps and pleased with the advances she had made, Lisa moved her "business" from street corners to bars and hotels. With paint and powder covering her face, she could pass for a woman in her late twenties. Besides, her customers didn't look too closely. That wasn't where their interest lay. And no one else mattered.

The first night Lisa worked the Red Wine Inn she had bravely approached the dining-room manager.

"What'll you charge to hold my left-over food in the cooler until I go home every night?"

"Hold your food?" The manager narrowed his eyes and boldly surveyed her. *"A roll in the hay."*

She shook her head vehemently. *"No deal. I only do that for money."*

"Hell, electricity's money."

"Yeah, but . . . Aw, forget it," she said, turning away. *"I was just hoping--"*

"Hey, not so fast. You live alone?"

"Why do you want to know? What difference does that make?"

He shrugged and smiled shrewdly. *"Maybe none. Maybe lots. Do you?"*

"No. I have a three-year-old boy, if it's any of your business."

His eyes took on a far-away look. His face grew still, softened. *"Me, too,"* he muttered and looked away. *"Yeah, we can take care of it,"* he said, his voice suddenly gruff. *"No problem."*

Abruptly, she pushed the memories aside and thought about the men who had passed through her life. She sneered. *Every one, without exception, called the shots, but not this time,* she thought resolutely. *I'm done with that,*

Three days Lisa found an apartment she felt she could afford. Then, the picture of Coleman disappeared from its resting place atop the TV, gradually followed by things she'd clung to through the years; the crystal figurine of a woman swaying in dance, her expression dreamy, her flowing shawl, a delicate sheet of glass lifted from her shapely body by some unseen breeze; a three-legged donkey, one ear oversized, molded by Coleman's tiny hands when he was five; a faded, well-marked copy of Scarlett. Others.

Now, she could breathe easier.

Tomorrow, she thought, she'd make her move.

From behind lacy panels, Lisa watched Cadance wheel his Ferarri into the space beside hers, crawl out and head for the building. Her stomach lurched sickly as she steeled herself and crossed the room. Gripping the doorknob with a sweat-slicked hand, she gulped and swung the door wide when she heard his footsteps.

He grinned and kicked the door shut. *"Does this mean you're ready for fun and games?"* he asked, reaching for her.

She shook her head and quickly stepped back. *"No,"* she said. *"It means . . . "* She pulled in a shaky breath. *"It means I'm leaving."*

He scowled. *"Leaving? Where're you going? You didn't tell me you had a trip planned. Hell, I'll be in town all week."*

Her knees were rubber beneath her. *"I'm leaving for good,"* she mumbled.

His voice rose. *"For good? What in hell's going on here?"*

She spread icy hands and looked past him. *"I've just realized that this simply isn't enough."*

"Enough for what?" He glared and waved his arms. *"Looks pretty good to me."* He bent towards her. *"Hell, what do you want? The Taj Mahal?"*

She closed her eyes and shook her head. *"No, That's not what I mean,"* she said. Frantically, she searched for words, then sucked in a steadying breath. *"I mean I'm tired of catering to a man,"* she blurted. She eased her breath out and stared at him. *"A cab will pick me up in an hour."*

He turned and glared at the suitcases stacked by the door. *"You're moving,"* he sneered. *"Just like that, you're moving?"*

She swallowed the lump of fear lodged in her throat and nodded. *"Just like that."*

"What've I done to deserve this?"

"Nothing." She dropped her hands into her pockets. *"Nothing,"* she repeated, hoping to soothe his rising anger. *"It's me."*

His eyes narrowed. *"Then what in hell're you talking about?"* he bellowed. *"Well? I'm waiting."*

Silently, Lisa turned away.

He grabbed her arm and spun her around. *"Don't turn away when I'm talking to you. You got some explaining to do."*

Her anger flared. *"Stop man-handling me, you bastard,"* she said, her response automatic. She struggled to pull away. *"I don't have to explain anything to you, and I'll turn away whenever I damn well please."*

He gripped her arms, picked her up and brought her nose to nose with him. *"I bought and paid for you, you slut, You owe me,"*

"I owe you nothing," she screeched.

"I've given you--"

Tears of rage blinded her. She poked at her chest with a thumb. A laugh tore from her throat. *"What you've given me? What you've done is rob me of my time, my freedom, my inde-"*

Cadance sneered and threw her to the floor. *"Your freedom?"* He laughed harshly. *"You call sitting in a whore-house waiting for some Super-John to come along, freedom?"*

Ignoring the bolt of pain that shot through her hip, she pushed herself to her bottom. *"You ought to know. It's how I met you,"*

Palm spread, he drew back his arm and stood over her, then apparently changing his mind, turned and stalked to the suitcases. *"What's in here?"*

Lisa pushed herself upright. *"Nothing that belongs to you. Your ring and car keys are on the table."*

He glanced at the table and curled his lip. *"You expect me to believe a whore?"* he jeered. *"Where's the silver?"* He snatched her purse from where it teetered atop her train-case and plunged his hand into it. *"Where in hell's the keys to 'em?"* he bellowed, kicking the luggage. A wicked grin covered his face as he withdrew the switchblade she carried and flicked it open. *"Better get your ass over here and open 'em up,"* he mocked, *"or I'll do it for you,"*

"Here," she cried, jerking the keys from her pocket and tossing them to him.

Cadance snatched them from the air and unlocked a case, held up a flimsy rose-red garment and laughed. *"Ain't nobody else gonna enjoy this*," he muttered, slicing into the gown. Wild-eyed, he dropped it and reached for a white silk dress.

Lisa rose and limped painfully to a couch. Calmly, she watched him shred his way through her clothing. Peace washed through her. *Thank God, the really important things are at the apartment,* she thought.

At last, his anger spent, he dropped the knife, stalked to the door and pushed it open. "*See ya around, slut,*" he muttered.

Forty

Marianne's foot was a blur as she spun around and slammed it at the balding head of her opponent.

Chong Wang ducked. *"You good,"* he said, his sing-song voice serious. *"You protect self, now . . . but must remember . . . other person maybe better."* He smiled and playfully wagged a finger at her. *"Must practice every day."*

Marianne reached for her towel and mopped her face.

"Chinese say, yao te kao, jen ch'ien ts'ao," Chong said.

Bewildered, Marianne stared at him.

He smiled gently. "In America means, when one wish to . . . to . . ."He stopped, looked at the floor, frowned and seemed to struggle for the next word. *"Ex-cel,"* he said, obviously pleased with himself. Speaking slowly, he started over.

"When one wish to ex-cel,
Before ex-pert, prac-tice well."

Marianne smiled and nodded agreement. *"Yes. Practice makes perfect."*

Chong scrunched his wrinkled face. *"How long you come here? One month? Two month?"*

Her eyes met his. *"Soon be six months."*

He raised his sagging brows and shook his head slightly. *"You not quit? You want black belt?"*

Marianne laughed. *"You know I'm not working for a belt. I just want to be able to protect myself."*

He pointed a finger at her and nodded sagely. "*Control self why you do good. You need belt, too. Next week start kick-boxing. Like karate, need control.*"

Marianne lifted the towel to her face. "*Thank you,*" she said, again wiping sweat. "*I'm grateful for all you've taught me.*"

Chong smiled and bowed. "*I grateful you come,*" He raised his brows. "*You come Thursday?*"

She turned toward the showers. "*I'll be here,*" she said.

As water from the shower spilled over Marianne's head, she centered her thoughts on the following day. Two months after Len left, she had, on Doctor Rubin 's advice, resumed her three-days-a-week stint at The Haven, hoping that by working with the children of the abused women, her own grief would lessen.

At first, she refused the extra hours the manager tried to press on her. Constantly on guard, she never allowed the children she worked with to worm their way into her heart. Emotionally exhausted at the end of each day, she would return home, promising herself never to return.

The haunted eyes and frail body of little Illyse Pinyard rose before her tightly clenched eyes. From the moment the youngster had walked into The Haven, Marianne's heart had gone out to her. *Poor baby,* she thought. Distrust shone from Illyse's sidelong glances as her mother, her brother, and herself settled in.

Illyse ignored all attempts at friendliness while her mother sought work during the days that followed. Bowing her head and hunkering her shoulders tight each time a staff member approached, she played alone.

After days of useless coaxing, it was decided to allow the child to come forward if and when she was ready.

Weeks later, as Marianne sat reading to a small group of pre-schoolers, Illyse sidled up. Fear shone from her eyes. An uncertain smile trembled on her lips.

Marianne smiled down at her and spoke softly. "*Would you like to join us?*" she asked.

Without answering, Illyse quickly turned and ran to a corner of the room she had claimed as her own, turned her back and stared at Marianne from over her shoulder.

Then, day by day, hugging a battered doll tight to her chest, Illyse inched closer. Another week and she drew close enough to run a shaky finger down Marianne's arm.

Resisting the urge to lift the child into her arms and kiss away her fears, Marianne forced herself to smile and continue reading.

The following week, as Marianne stood on the sidelines cheering on a relay team, Illyse approached and leaned against her legs.

Hesitant, her stomach in knots, Marianne squatted and casually slipped an arm around the tot's shoulders. Within days, they had become friends.

Sadness filled Marianne as she rinsed the last bit of shampoo from her hair and opened her eyes. Grief over the loss of her own child filled her heart as she reached for a towel.

Forty-One

Stunned by the horde crossing the television screen, Marianne dropped into a chair and avidly studied every face the camera caught.

"*Under Judge Shiler's orders,*" the anchorman said, "*two hundreds inmates were released from Huntsville today to alleviate over-crowding. Officials want to stress, however, that these men were incarcerated for crimes such as auto-theft, etcetera. They are not violent offenders, therefore not a threat to the community.*" The anchor looked at his partner. "*Now, Judy has some refreshing news about the job market. Judy?*"

They didn't show them all, Marianne assured herself, *but thank God they didn't turn the worst ones loose.* She shoved thoughts about her rape aside and smiled. *I can take care of myself, now,* she thought, remembering the statement Chong had made earlier in the day.

"*Next time you come,*" he had said rising from the floor where a well-placed kick had placed him. "*Young man will work with you.*" He grinned and dragged his sleeve across his sweating face. "*You too good for me. You need young man.*

Forty-Two

Zoe's heart raced as Gus kicked the door shut, covered her eager lips with his and pressed her tight against his erection. Her breath fluttered in her throat. Raw desire surged through her.

"*God, you're gorgeous,*" he muttered, at last releasing her mouth, his voice a rough whisper. "*I love you.*" Leaving her lips, he traced a path of kisses past her chin, down her neck, across, then up to her ear and eyes, before again grasping her lips with his.

"*I love you, too,*" she whispered between kisses, hating that words so inadequately expressed her feelings.

Maddeningly slow, he loosened the pins in her hair and sifted its dark sweep through his fingers before letting it fall thick and free around her shoulders and down her back.

Blinded by a sudden rush of tears she quickly blinked back, she fumbled with the buttons of his shirt. Tonight must by perfect, she thought, dropping her hands and loosening his belt.

Cradling her in his arms, he carried her to the bed, sat her on it then knelt before her.

Between a deluge of kisses, he slipped her dress over her head and unhooked her bra, cupped her full breasts in his hands, bent to them and circled their rosy peaks with his tongue.

Her breath shortened. Hungrily, she unzipped his pants and grasped his hardness.

After a sharp intake of breath, he eased her to the pillows, slipped her panties off and began tenderly massaging her clitoris. As her need peaked, his fingers drove deep into the innermost chambers of her womanhood.

Wild with desire, she pushed his hand aside. *"No,"* she whispered, tugging on him, urging him to top her, her fingers hardly meeting around his long, velvety shaft. *"I want you. You,"*

Quickly hoisting himself beside her, he entered her and moving in a rhythm as old as eternity, stroke by stroke timed himself to her rapidly-mounting hunger. Tense and sleek with sweat, she groaned as the blaze in her belly neared its zenith. Cupping his buttocks with her hands, she held him tight as he drove deeper and deeper into her. *"Now . . ."* she moaned, peaking, *"now . . ."*

Contentedly, she sighed, opened her eyes and met his gaze. Pushing himself to his hands, he pressed his pelvis hard against hers and slowly, gently, rocked. *"You're perfect,"* she whispered, the recurring waves of passion fading, the hardness of his penis melting away. *"You're absolutely perfect."*

Again kissing her, he rolled to his side and pulled her head to his shoulder. *"I love you so much, Zoe,"* he said, *"But what are we gonna do about it? I can't go on like this . . . I want you with me every minute of every day, every night, every . . . you know after he's been in prison for seven years, you can get a divorce. Until then, we can--"*

Dread flooded Zoe's mind. *"I know,"* she said, pulling away. *"Seven years are a long way off. But is it right to desert a man because he made a mistake? And what about the children? They must be considered. Is it right to make them suffer?"*

"They're suffering now, aren't they? Can it get any worse?"

Thoughts of the humiliation and shame that kids at school, mimicking those in the neighborhood, had heaped on Jim and Jolanda ran through Zoe's mind. Breathing jerkily, she pulled away from Gus, rose on suddenly shaky legs and slipped on her robe, then stilling her fear, turned and looked at him. *"This is our last date,"* she said. *"I won't see you anymore after tonight."*

Eyes wide, Angus leaped from the bed. *"Our last date? What are you talking about our last date? What's wrong with you?"*

Zoe walked to a window and cracked the blinds. *"The children's grandmother is no fool,"* she said, looking out. *"She knows I'm seeing someone. She just doesn't know who and she said that after tonight, she'd no longer keep the children."*

"*Hell, that's no problem. Hire someone . . . I'll pay them.*"

She shook her head. "*It's not that simple. They love Rosa. I wouldn't feel right entrusting them to anyone else, and with me gone all the time, they need someone they love and can rely on.*" She glanced back at him.

Stark naked, Gus stood stiffly erect, clinching and unclenching his fists. He glared at her. "*So this is it? We're through?*"

Zoe bowed her head and blinked back tears. Not trusting herself to speak, she nodded.

"*Damn it, Zoe,*" he said, slamming a fist into the wall. "*Why didn't you tell me sooner? Why'd you let me fall deeper and deeper in love with you?*"

Zoe turned to the window and closed her eyes. Tears coursed down her cheeks.

Crossing the room, he turned her to face him. "*Don't shut me out, Zoe. Look at me, Why didn't you tell me this months ago? And tonight . . . why did you wait until after--*"

Zoe lifted her wet face to him. "*Because I'm weak,*" she whispered, her knees like water. Spreading her hands in appeal, she looked into his eyes then dropped her gaze. "*I'm in love, too, and I've hungered for love for so long that--*"

His grip on her arms tightened. "*Doesn't that count for anything?*"

"*It counts for everything. Everything but my children's welfare. They come first.*" She struggled for breath. "*Please . . . please understand. If I'd told you earlier, we'd have spent the night fighting and I couldn't risk that . . . I wanted . . . no, I needed one last, perfect evening to remember.*"

Gus stared hard at her, then turned on his heel and headed for the bathroom. "*Get dressed,*" he muttered. "*I'm taking you home.*"

Forty-Three

When Marianne entered The Haven, her co-workers looked up, mumbled a greeting and somberly turned away. She shrugged and glanced out a window at wind-whipped, low-hanging clouds. This weather's affecting everyone, she thought. As she walked toward a playroom where colorful child-made drawings covered the walls, Ruby Lofton emerged from her office and crooked a finger at her.

Avoiding Marianne's gaze, Ruby dropped into the worn leather chair behind her desk, drummed her fingers on the scarred desktop, sighed and met Marianne's questioning gaze. *"Have you seen the morning paper?"* she asked.

Marianne shook her head.

Ruby opened a deep bottom drawer, reached into it and lifted out the Houston Chronicle. She drew in a deep breath, cleared her throat and held the daily toward Marianne. *"Maybe you'd better sit down,"* she said, motioning to a chair across from her.

Their eyes locked.

Slowly, Marianne lowered herself to the chair, took the paper and unfolded it across her lap. Pulling her gaze from Ruby's, she looked down.

The headline jumped out at her. Meningitis raging among children in several local schools. She frowned. *What does this have to do with me?* she wondered.

Quickly, she scanned the article, then raised questioning eyes to Ruby's. *"What's this about?"*

Ruby averted her eyes and sucked in a deep breath. *"It seems that Illyse has contracted the disease and is very sick . . . is actually in the hospital."* she murmured.

Alarm clutched Marianne. *"How could that be? She's not in school."*

"But Jason is, remember? Apparently, he brought the germ home."

Lowering her head, Marianne voraciously read the devastating news. *"How did you learn about Illyse?"* she asked. *"Did Mrs. Pinyard call?"*

Ruby stared into Marianne's eyes. *"Yes. About twenty minutes ago."*

Marianne sucked in a shaky breath. *"What can we . . . I do?"* she whispered, feeling totally helpless.

"Other than relieving Mrs. Pinyard at Illyse's bedside, nothing that I can see."

Ruby paused as if waiting for Marianne to speak, then rose, circled the desk and laid an arm across Marianne's shoulders. *"Why don't you take a day or two off, dear?"* she asked gently. *"I know how close you've grown to the child. Maybe by Monday . . . "* She left the sentence hanging. *"Joan Masters will fill in until you get back."* Bending, she pecked Marianne's cheek then turned, moved to a window and looked out.

Numb, Marianne rose and stumbled toward the door.

A car door slammed.

Ruby's voice followed Marianne out the door. *"There's Joan, now,"* she said. Her voice lightened. *"Take care, dear. See you next week."*

Marianne, her mind glutted with grief, stared at the movie through a curtain of tears. Around her, the world continued undisturbed. Patrons whispered, crunched popcorn and slurped sodas.

After an interminable time, the film ground to a halt.

Unaware of the crowd pushing and shoving toward the exit, Marianne sat immobile.

A voice penetrated her silence. *"Miss, Miss,"* it said. *"The movie's over."*

Dazed, she removed a ticket from her pocket. *"I'm going to see it again,"* she said.

172

Forty-Four

The notice appeared in the social pages of The Houston Chronicle.

The 1982 class of Robert High School, it read, will hold its fifteenth class reunion at the Holiday Inn in the French Quarters in New Orleans, La. on Saturday, June 5th. Anyone knowing the where-abouts of any of the following members of that class, please write Kathy Godchau at 5182 Old Indian Trail, New Orleans, La 86741.

Cynthia Thomas
Romana Wilkins
Zoe Fahularo
Gayle Perkins
Josephine Dawes
Edgar Dawkins
Roger Landler
Emmett Argeron

Zoe threw a cursory glance at the page, saw her name and did a double-take. Memories of the worry-free days of school, immediately followed by the image of Gilberto Guriano ran through her mind.

She had seen him only once after she married and had found his dark good looks and obvious admiration of her as exciting as ever.

It had happened outside Gil and Louie's Restaurant just off Saint Charles.

Eyes aglow, Gil grasped both her arms and searched her upturned face. *"Zoe,"* he said. *"At first, I thought these old peepers were deceiving* me, *but it is you. You got time for lunch?*" He released her and motioned with his head. "*They still got the best gumbo in town.*"

Zoe nervously lifted a hand to her hair and wished she were anywhere but there in her out-dated, too-short dress and frumpy, flat-heeled oxfords. In a welter of confusion, she shook her head. "*No. No, I can't,*" she stammered. "*I don't have . . . I'm in a hurry.*"

"*At least a cup of coffee,*" he said.

As if he hadn't heard her, he quickly took her elbow, guided her through the door past a line of people waiting to be seated and waved at the man behind the cash register. "*Hey, Louie,*" he called, motioning with his head. "*The lady and I are going to the office. Send a waiter.*"

Louie looked up from making change and nodded.

Gil smiled, then grasping Zoe's hand, led her through the dining room, past the kitchen and into a spacious office. Quickly, he closed the door and flipped on the lights. A massive desk, its polished surface stacked with papers, stood in one corner of the room near mural-covered windows through which sunbeams shone. Along that same glass wall, three unlit candles waited in silver holders atop a linen-covered table.

Zoe tensed. "*All set up for a tete-a-tete.*" she whispered.

"*Not exactly,*" Gil said, guiding her past giant pots of greenery. "*But it is a touch of luxury we enjoy.*" He waved toward the desk. "*Back here, away from the noise out front, I can get a tremendous amount of work done in half the normal time.*"

Questions shone from Zoe's eyes.

"*Oh,*" he explained. "*I'm part owner.*"

After seating her, he walked to a clothes-tree and removed his coat.

As trim as he was back then, Zoe thought as she watched Gil unbutton his collar and loosen his tie. "*Gee, I'm impressed,*" she said, smoothing the snowy linen.

He dismissed the subject with a shrug, sat down opposite her and motioned to the candles. "*All right if I light these? They're never used.*" He grinned. At her nod, he picked up a book of matches from the table and struck one to the cylinders. "*Now, tell me. What's going on in your life?*" He gazed into her eyes. His face settled into sobriety. "*You know,*

I tried to get in touch with you after graduation, but . . . " He drew a deep breath. *"Your mother told me you had married and moved away."* He leaned toward her. *"Why, Zoe? Why didn't you let me know?"*

Memories, trapped in Zoe's mind for years, swept the past forward. *"I couldn't,"* she mumbled. *"I just couldn't. You know my parents were dead-set against my seeing you."*

"You mean against the mafia and my Italian background."

She shrugged. *"The two were the same to them. After Daddy heard that your Dad was connected to the mafia, he was scared to death for me, and . . ."* Pausing, she studied her hands. *"There was no changing their minds, even after the truth came out. They simply couldn't see beyond their suspicions."*

"I loved you, Zoe. I think I still do."

Zoe raised her eyes to his and nodded. *"I loved you, too."*

Sucking in a deep breath, he covered her hands with his and for a moment they sat silently gazing into each other's eyes. At last he broke the spell. *"Ancient history,"* he said, his voice barely audible. The volume rose as he loosened her hands, smiled gently and leaned back. *"Tell me what's been happening in your life all these years."*

Zoe, eager to retreat from the dangerous grounds they were treading, swallowed the knot in her throat and looked away. *"Bob works with an oil refinery,"* she said, trying for nonchalance. *"We move around a lot, but what can I say? It's a living. A good living and he likes what he's doing."* God will never forgive me for all these lies, she told herself.

"That's good." His face again sobered. *"Please . . . I've often wondered if . . . Is he good to you?"* Again reaching, he covered the hand that was nervously fingering a candle-holder. His eyes sought hers. *"I wish we could've made it, Zoe,"* he said softly. *"I think of you often. Sometimes, I think, too often."* He rose, leaned across the table and lightly kissed her lips.

Heat flooded her face. Regret rushed like quick-silver through her. She freed her hand and dropped her gaze. *"Don't."* She shook her head and pulled away. *"We were just kids,"* she whispered, her voice shaky. *"And I was afraid to marry anyone without my parent's consent."* She rose. *"I'd better go."*

Gilbert quickly rounded the table-corner and stood before her. *"Please stay. I didn't mean to get out of line."* Eyes pleading, he smiled gently. *"We haven't even ordered."*

Shaking her head, she turned toward the door. *"I shouldn't even be here,"* she had said. *"I need to go."*

As the memory faded, she looked out the screen door to the yard where Jolanda and Jim were playing and laughed softly. If I'd gone along with your plans, I wouldn't have them, she thought. And I'd never have met Gus.

Gus, she thought, her heart sinking. *Another relationship gone awry.*

Forty-Five

Tears of laughter that only moments before had blinded Lisa, dried as she drove deeper into the darkness. The musky smell of marshes filled her nostrils. As her car sputtered and died, she frantically pumped the accelerator and coasted to a stop. Fear skittered through her. The last sign of habitation she remembered seeing now lay a mile or so to her back, where a clutter of unlighted shacks stood like gray ghosts along this twisted, untamed coastline. Homes to the fishermen hereabout, she had thought when she sped past them.

Her jaw hung slack as she stared in disbelief at the gas gauge. What happened? she asked herself. I should've made it back to I-10 easily. Now, what do I do? My God, anyone could be out here . . . I could wind up being food for the fish and no one would ever know. Coleman would never know. The thought of him, alone and battling the world as she had, sobered her. *"Be damned if that's so,"* she muttered. *"That'll never happen,"*

Sucking in a tremulous breath of courage, she switched off the car lights and strained to see through the engulfing blackness.

From somewhere across the great expanse of water, the lonely, sonorous moan of a freighter's horn drifted shoreward. Mosquitoes whined and nipped at her when she lowered the windows.

Quickly, she cranked them shut and slapped at the insects.

A rap sounded on the window.

Sweat, gathered on her face and body and worming along her scalp, turned icy. Gasping, she jerked her head toward the noise. A circle of light pressed against the glass blinded her.

"*Kin I hep, Ma'am?*" a male voice asked. "*Ma'am? Ma'am? You awright? Kin you hear me?*"

Numbly, she shook her head. Where did he come from? she wondered. I didn't pass anyone.

"*I live jus' cross the street over there,*" he said. "*You sure I cain't hep?*"

She nodded.

"*Didn't mean to scare you, Ma'am. Just thought you needed some hep.*"

Headlights, beam on high, rounded the bend behind her. Lisa froze as the vehicle drew near, forfeited its whine and stopped. Violent trembling shook her.

A voice called out. "'*Zat you, Louie? Whatsa matter? You got trouble wid your car again?*"

The light shifted from Lisa.

"*Yeah. Damn old flivver up and quit on me again.*"

"*Who'zat in the car?*"

Louie lifted his shoulders and spread his free hand. "*Doan know, man. Some lady won't say nuttin'.*"

Lisa held her breath as the man threw a leg over the door of the stripped-down pickup, stepped to the ground and joined Louie.

For the first time in years, Lisa thought of prayer. *Lord? Lord? Look, I'm out of practice, here, but get me out of this and I promise -*

Louie turned the flashlight back on Lisa. "*Ma'am, if you just crack your window a little so you kin hear me . . .*" He hesitated a moment, then bent to the glass. In the faint reflected light, dark gaps showed in Louie's yellow-toothed smile. "*Ain't meaning you no harm, Ma'am, but you outta gas?*"

"*You checked the tires?*" the newcomer asked.

"*Yeah. They okay.*"

Lisa, braved by her attempt at prayer, lowered the window a bare inch. "*I . . . I think I'm out of gas.*" Her voice squeaking through her suddenly-narrowed throat, sounded like that of a stranger.

Both men chuckled.

"*Women,*" the newcomer said.

"*We can fix that easy,*" Louie said. "*Plenty of gas up at the dock.*"

Do they expect me to go with them? Lisa wondered, visualizing herself sandwiched between the two sinewy men. "*The dock?*" she asked. Her voice trembled.

"*Yessum. Don't worry none. We be back in a few minutes.*" They turned and climbed into the truck. "*Just sit tight,*" Louie called. "*We be right back.*"

Lisa drew in a quivering breath and sighed it out as the truck rattled into the darkness, then reached up, removed the curly, black wig and tossed it into the back seat. As many times as I've made this trip, how in hell did I take I-10 instead of 12, she wondered.

'*Tired,*' came the answer.

The ka-plunk, ka-plunk of a motor roused Lisa from the half-sleep she had drifted into. Swiveling her head toward the noise, she saw the men had returned, and Louie, flashlight in hand, had dropped to the ground. *Thank God, they're back*, she thought, watching him turn, lift a huge gas-can from the bed of the truck and walk towards the back of her car. Moments later, fumes of raw gasoline filled the air.

"*Try 'er now, Miss,*" Louie said, pressing the light to her window. "*See it she'll crank up.*"

Apprehensively, Lisa pumped the accelerator, then reached for the key and turned it. Except for the grinding of the starter, nothing happened.

Pushing the pedal to the floor, she again tried. Again, the motor didn't catch. Now what? she thought, silently cursing the salesman who had sold her the car.

"*Got another fifty thousand miles in her, easy,*" he had said, handing her the ninety-day warranty that two days earlier had expired.

Damn him, anyway, she thought.

Louie tapped on the window. "*Hold on a minute, Miss,*" he said. "*Pop ya hood . . . lemme take a look at the carbrater.*"

The strong smell of gasoline again filled the air.

"*Now try'er,*" Louie called.

Holding her breath, Lisa again twisted the key. Relief washed through her as the motor sprang to life.

Slamming the hood shut, Louie rounded the front of the car, and grinning, walked up to her window.

" '*few gettin' the mileage you oughtta be gettin' outta this little thang, you got enough gas there to take you a long way,*" he said.

Lisa dug a twenty-dollar bill form her purse and lowered her window. "*I can't tell you how thankful I am for your help,*" she said, holding the money toward him.

Vigorously he shook his head and backed away. "*Oh, nome, nome,*" he said. "*You don' owe me nothin'. Jus' glad to hep out a little. Don't get much chance of that out here in the boonies.*"

"*But --*"

Still shaking his head, he turned, climbed into the waiting truck, then turned back toward her and waved. "*Good luck, Ma'am,*" he said. "*You be careful, now.*"

Some forty miles beyond the Louisiana-Mississippi State Line, Lisa exited I-10 and worked her way to the coast. Turning east, she followed Beach Boulevard past flamboyant gambling casinos to the fenced-in sprawling grounds of what Elsie Vonay had told her was once the veteran's hospital, turned north a few blocks, crossed the railroad and stopped before a darkened cottage. She smiled as her car lights flashed over the freshly painted sides of the house. Deeply-buried feelings of peace washed through her.

Each time she came here, she silently blessed the day she had bought the house she and Coleman would soon call home. And the elderly couple who had rented it. As agreed, they had made up for the little rent she charged and by her buying the needed material, kept the place in first-class condition until two months earlier, when the wife was stricken by sudden illness and they had moved to Biloxi to live with their only daughter. Even now, they came by once a week to check on the place until Lisa could claim it for good.

And that's not too far away, she thought, her smile widening. She turned off the motor and stepped out of the car. Standing a moment in the silence, she closed her eyes and gratefully sucked in the salty air and the sweet aroma of flowers bedded beside the house and along the fence. Then, peacefully sighing, she climbed the steps and fitted the key in the lock. Lucky, lucky me, she thought.

And tomorrow I'll see Coleman.

It seemed that each time she had visited him over the last year, he had grown inches as he made his trek toward manhood. New shoes and uniforms were a constant expense. But what more could I want for him than to be an officer in his country's service, she would ask herself. If he chooses to go that route. And if he doesn't, when he graduates he'll still be fitted to do whatever he wants. She smiled and shrugged. It's his choice, she thought.

Minutes after a quick shower, she was in bed and asleep with the phone close at hand.

Three hours later its ringing woke her. She stared at the clock and lifted the receiver.

"*Mom,*" Coleman said, "*are you awake?*"

She laughed. "*If I wasn't, I would be now. Are you ready for me to pick you up?*"

He hesitated. "*Well . . . not exactly.*"

Lisa's heart leaped. "*Not exactly? What do you mean by that? Are you sick?*"

"*No . . . no m'am,*" he stuttered.

She swung her feet off the bed and bolted upright. "*Then, what's wrong?*"

For a moment, silence greeted her. Her voice grew sharp. "*Coleman? Coleman, answer me, What's wrong?*"

"*I . . . I guess I kind of got in a fight.*"

"*A fight, I can't believe that, You've never . . . who were you fighting? What were you fighting about?*"

"*Uh, uh, about a girl.*"

She could almost see him cringe, see his ears turn red. Oh God, don't say that, she thought. You're only a baby. You shouldn't be interested in girls yet. "*Keep talking,*" she said. "*No . . .wait, I'll be right there. Meet me at the office.*"

Quickly, she dashed water over her face, dabbed on lipstick, ran a brush through her hair, dressed and was out the door seven minutes later. Gravel spun from beneath her wheels as she backed out of the driveway and raced toward Beach Boulevard.

Her mind churned furiously.

The tall gates to the academy she had once admired as elegant, she now saw as barricades. Frantically, she dug in her purse, withdrew her ID card, and shoved it at the lanky, wrinkled guard slouching sleepily towards her. *"I'm in a hurry,"* she said, her nerves stretched to breaking. *"My son --"*

"Take it easy, Ma'am. I'll have to call." He shook his head. *"It's mighty early for visitors."*

Lisa bit back a retort as he turned and sauntered to the guard shack. *Bastard*, she thought. *I don't care what time it is, Coleman needs me,*

Through the glass enclosure, she watched him lift a phone and speak into it. Grinning, he replaced the instrument, slowly turned and pushed the controls. The gate swung open.

Bastard, You could've done that to start with, Lisa thought, as she tossed her head and sailed past.

The facade of the administration building seemed to glower at her as she parked in front and entered. In the glass-fronted office immediately to her right, she saw Coleman, head bent, waiting. Her heart lurched. Sucking in a deep breath, she yanked the door open.

Smiling sickly, Coleman looked up and rose. *"I'm sorry, Mom,"* he said, his voice muted. Tears slipped to his cheeks.

As Coleman started towards her, a door in the rear of the room opened and a uniformed man stepped out. Coleman stopped short, turned and saluted.

The stranger returned the gesture. *"At ease, West,"* he said, then turned to Lisa, his smile quick, but friendly. He extended his hand. *"Ms. West, I'm Colonel Batting."*

Gripping his hand, she stared into his dark, flinty eyes.

He released her hand and turned to a man at the room's only desk. *"Hold my calls, Monroe,"* he said, leading the way into the spacious office he had emerged from and waving them to a seat.

Anxious to hear the details of Coleman's trouble, Lisa perched on the edge of a square, cushioned chair drawn up before the desk. *Okay, I'm here*, she thought. *Let's get it over with.*

Batting cleared his throat. *"I'm sorry we couldn't allow Coleman to leave the grounds until you and I could talk, but to maintain discipline in an establishment like this, the full co-operation of parents is needed. I'm sure you understand."* He gave a cursory glance at a sheaf of papers spread before him, then looked up and smiled. *"Coleman has a fine record with us,"* he said. *"This is his first time before me,"* Turning his head, he gave Coleman his full attention. *"Why don't you tell your mother your side of the story, Mister West?"*

Lisa's insides quivered as she stared at her son.

Pushing himself as far back in his chair as the seat permitted, Coleman began to twist the cap he was holding. His face flushed. *"Well,"* he mumbled, *"it started--"*

"Speak up," Batting commanded.

Coleman gulped noisily. *"Yes, sir. Yesterday when some of us went to the movies in Biloxi, Joe Fernay heard me tell Mike I thought a girl I saw was cute, and he laughed and said that I was stupid or I'd know she was a, a . . . "* His face turned fiery as the words rushed out. His eyes pleaded with her. *"A whore, Mom, A whore, So I hit him."*

Lisa forced her voice past the knot gathered in her throat. She turned to Batting. *"What does this Joe Fernay have to say, Colonel?"*

Batting sat forward and motioned toward the front room. *"West, you can wait in there now."*

As the door closed behind Coleman, Batting smiled. *"Looks like you've reared quite a little Galahad there."* His eyes searched Lisa's face. *"Please don't look so distraught . . . we're only trying to extend the teachings you began."* He chuckled. *"Regardless of the actions of certain military men these past years, our aim is to turn out officers and gentlemen, though the term, gentlemen, seems to be old-fashioned to some."*

"And Joe Fernay?"

"Joe admitted he knew nothing whatsoever about the girl. It seems he and Coleman are always vying for top position in everything, and he just wanted to rile Coleman." Rising, Batting smiled and held out a hand. *"I hope that clears things up and that you two enjoy your time here. Good day, Ma'am."*

Lisa's heart beat a tattoo against her ribs as she drove Coleman to his barracks and waited while he packed a bag. My god, she thought, he fought over a girl he hasn't even met? She sighed nervously. If that wouldn't scare a woman into going straight, nothing would.

Tears stung her eyes. Thank God, as soon as I can get my degree, I can put that life behind me and at last be free. *"If only that opening on The Mirror will come through,"* she whispered.

Forty-Six

The headache Zoe had waked with persisted throughout the day, unaltered except for brief periods by over-the-counter pills she had periodically taken. Now, the agony hung just behind her eyes, stretched up to her hairline, then wrapped around to the back of her skull.

"Did, too," Jimmy cried from the living room, his voice wavering on the edge of tears.

"Didn't either," Jolanda said. *"You're nothing but a cry-baby, always wanting your way,"*

Zoe sighed heavily and walked to the living room where the two children stood before the VCR, Jimmy clutching a Power Rangers video with one hand and frantically blocking Jolanda's efforts to shove a Pocahuntas tape into the machine with the other. *"Stop it,"* Zoe cried. *"Now, who–?"*

Jimmy's tears spilled over. *"Shuh, shuh, she won't let me watch--"*

Jolanda propped her hands on her childish hips and glared at her younger brother. *"We watched that yesterday, Jimmy, It's my turn to choose,"*

"Didn't either," Jimmy yelled.

Zoe held out a hand to Jolanda. *"Give me the tape,"* she said.

Jolanda screwed her face into tight lines of accusation and glowered at Jimmy. *"See what you did,"* she fumed, handing the film to her mother.

Jimmy sniffed, gripped the Ranger closer to his chest and watched wide-eyed as Zoe tucked Jolanda's tape beneath her arm and reached a hand to him.

"Now yours," she said.

Tears, hanging in the cups of his eyelids, loosened their hold on his lashes and rolled down his face. *"But . . . but--"*

"I don't want to hear it," Zoe snapped. Plucking the video from his hands, she removed the one under her arm and added the two to the small stack beside the VCR. *"Now . . . both of you go out and play,"* she said.

Zoe followed their reluctant steps through the kitchen and watched the screen slap shut behind them then bent over the sink and splashed her face with cold water. A picture of Angus Jerguson swam before her closed eyes.

After months of avoiding the bank during her hours of work, today of all days, he had walked in, queued up in the next teller's line, then glanced her way, smiled and winked when their eyes met. Her heartbeat accelerated, remembering the excitement that had surged through her. If only, she thought. *"Yeah, if only,"* she muttered, fastening an apron around her waist.

Leaving the water on her face to air-dry, she sighed, swallowed another Tylenol, then turned toward the counter where a strip of skirt steak waited in a wash of marinade. Fajitas . . . another reminder of Robert. She grimaced. Fajitas and re-fried beans had been his favorite meal from the time they were married, and long before he had gone to prison they had become the children's favorite too.

Robert, she thought. Bitterness, fueled by years of frustration, nauseated her as memories of him between her legs futilely attempting sex, flooded her mind.

Removing the meat to a cutting board, she patted it smooth and attacked it with a cleaver.

"Robert, my dear, if you were here, I'd fix you in a minute," she sing-songed, tightening her grip on the handle. Mother of God, where did that come from? Her voice hummed to a stop. Her hands fell slack. A picture of him sprawled and bleeding through a gap in his throat sprang uncalled before her eyes. Horrified, she shuddered. The cleaver clattered to the counter. *"Murder?"* she cried, covering her face with her hands. *"No, no,"*

Forty-Seven

At the apex of a short, hand-railed bridge erected over a natural dip in the land, Marianne stopped. Beyond this point, nature had been allowed to express herself fully. Dirt trails wound through grasses and brush that had grown head-high. Clusters of towering oaks cast dark sprawling shadows.

This was as far as she had allowed herself to venture since January of the previous year. Several times, she had tried to go farther, but each time she approached this section of the park, fear had driven her back, convincing her that the trek around the ball-park and picnic areas had given her all the exercise she needed.

Stretching high, she squinted against the hot Texas sun and gazed longingly at a small lake shimmering in the distance. After discovering this spot several years earlier, sitting on its banks had been one of her favorite things to do. Quiet, alone, she could think-out problems while she cooled off and rested for the long trek back.

Karate had firmed her body for fighting if needed, but the sheer exhilaration of running and filling her lungs with the tangy, salt air of the Gulf renewed her hope, fed her courage.

Uncertain, she shrugged, sighed, and turned back to the trail that had led her to this spot. As she started down the slight wooden incline, she stopped and gazed over her shoulder at a flock of herons hanging like giant magnolias from the trees bordering the far side of the water. Beautiful, she thought. I want some pictures of that.

Stilling caution, she about-faced, re-traced her steps, and taking a deep breath, plunged into the raw, growth-covered land. There's no one here but me, she assured herself, veering onto a foot trail.

A tremor of alarm shot through her as a startled doe bolted across her path. She gasped, momentarily paused, then jogged on, her camera bouncing on her hip. She felt almost weightless as the rhythmic push and pull of her strong, pliant muscles carried her deeper and deeper into the untamed land. I've done this dozens of times, she thought, remembering her recent reluctance to venture farther than the foot of the bridge. I'm just being silly. I can take care of myself. Gradually, her apprehension vanished.

After circling the lake, she stopped, panting, and plopped down on a fallen log for a brief respite. A slight breeze lifted off the water and dried the sheen of sweat from her face. Rested, she rose, stretched and turned toward the zig-zag path she would return on. She walked a few feet, then barely into the dense over-growth, broke into a slow, easy lope. Except for stopping by a drive-in to pick up lunch, she would go directly home, eat, bathe and find something to fill the rest of the day. An unfinished book still rested on her bedside table. Perhaps she'd read. And tomorrow, she would again sit with Illyse, which had proved to be a blessing for both herself and the child. Inescapable feelings of loss remained, but hate for Loper had dimmed as she immersed herself in caring for Illyse. Now, mentally reviewing the rape, the trial, the scenes from a distance of fifteen months, she found herself almost pitying the man.

Pushing away the memory, her thoughts turned back to Illyse. If only there was a cure, she thought, praying for a miracle, again seeing the tyke's flushed cheeks, her fever-emptied eyes, remembering how panicky parents had become as news of more and more children being stricken or dying were reported.

Tomorrow, she would again relieve Illyse's mother, if the grief-sorrowed mother could bring herself to leave the child for awhile.

He tackled her from behind. Fast. Furious. Soundless.

As she fell, her head snapped back then jerked forward. Her forehead hit the straw-strewn trail with a thud. Stunned, she struggled feebly as he dragged her to a wallowed-out spot nearby, rolled her to her back and straddled her. Holding her hands with one hand, he laid a knife to her throat with the other.

Dazed, she opened her eyes and stared up at him. Maybe if I cry out, someone will hear me, she thought.

As if reading her mind, he pressed the knife harder and grinned. *"Scream,"* he said, *"and you're dead meat."*

As her brain cleared, she studied him objectively. He wasn't all that big. If she could force herself to be calm, perhaps with the strength her daily workouts had given her, she could physically outmatch him. At least, she figured, she could outrun him if she could break free of his hold. Agree with him, she thought. *"Okay, okay,"* she said. *"Just don't—"*

He grinned again. *"Just don't look at me,"* he ordered.

Obediently, she closed her eyes and felt the release of pressure on her throat. Felt the coldness of the blade lift from her skin.

Almost imperceptibly, he relaxed.

In one quick movement, she opened her eyes, snatched one hand free, brought her feet to her buttocks and thrust her torso upward.

Thrown off balance, he slid sideways. The hand holding the knife flew up. Cursing, he re-mounted her, laid his body full-length on hers and captured her flailing hands. He raised the knife and glared at her. "You bitch," he muttered. *"I outta kill you,"*

Trembling with terror, she closed her eyes.

His grip on her wrists tightened. *"Open your eyes,"* he raged. *"Damn you, I said open your eyes."*

Her eyes snapped open.

"Get a good look at this," he said, holding the knife mere inches from her nose. *"Any more tricks outta you and the next time you see it, it'll be sticking outta your throat."*

He raised the weapon above his head and plunged it into the earth beside her. Pain bit into her neck. *"That's just a sample of what you'll get,"* Yanking the knife free, he pushed the blade tight against her, fingered a pair of shoe laces from his shirt pocket and dangled them in her face. *"Looks like you're just aching for me to use these."*

Again she struggled.

He stared down at her and laughed. *"Now you just be a good little girl and hold your hands still, less, like I said, you wanna go home with a cut throat."*

'*Pretend to go along with him,*' an inner voice whispered. '*Then make your move.*'

Her breath wheezed through her constricted throat. "*Please don't tie me up,*" she begged. "*I'll be good.*"

"*You better,*" he snarled. "*Make a move and you're a goner.*"

Half-lying on top of her, he released one wrist at a time and pushed the top of her sweat-suit up and off. Momentarily removing the knife from her throat, he roughly slid its tip under her bra, turned it and cut through the silky fabric. She flinched as pain pierced her flesh. Then commanding her to lift each leg in turn, he removed her pants and panties and tossed them aside.

Tears streamed from her eyes and soaked her hair. "*Stop,*" she pleaded. "*Please stop, No . . . no, please . . .*"

The voice in her head returned. 'Wait,' it said quietly. 'You'll be all right. Calm down.'

Against the turmoil roiling through her, she closed her eyes, focused her mind on the thought and heart racing, coaxed her quivering body to relax.

Hurriedly, he rolled to his left elbow, shifted the knife to his left hand, ducked his head, slightly lifted himself and reached for his zipper.

'Now,' the voice shouted.

In one swift motion, she rammed a knee into his crotch and using her right arm and leg as leverage, rolled hard to her left and sent him sprawling to his back.

As she leaped to her feet, her attacker, now a raging bull, scrambled up and started towards her. She turned and faced him, and taking a trained fighter's stance, waited. As he rushed forward, she braced herself, aimed her foot and when he came within reach, kicked hard at his groin. The blow connected.

Groaning and cursing, he fell to his knees, staggered up and again started for her.

Avoiding his out-thrust hands, she sprang forward and delivered a chop to the side of his neck.

He went down, then pushed himself up, staggered and again hurled himself at her.

A second chop knocked him unconscious.

Panting, she looked at the blood running between her breasts, lifted a hand to her pain-filled neck and stared at the bloody smear she brought down. Blinding anger swept through her. Face set, her mind awhirl, she stared at him and the knife he'd dropped. Quickly, she looked around. A length of fishing line lay tangled in weeds a few feet away. She picked it up, tied his ankles together, rolled him to his side and brought hands and feet together at his back. He roused, struggled and cursed, but the nylon held. Calmly she cut the back out of his shirt and stuffed it in his mouth.

She cut another length of cord, knelt and yanked his pants to his knees and holding his testicles with a scrap of shirt, she tied them off and picked up the knife.

The voice from within spoke again. 'Stop,' it said. 'You've done enough,'

Sobs wracked her. You're right, she thought. He needs to die, but I don't want to be the one to kill him.

Bruised, bloody and naked, she rose and walked to the lake. Stooping, she scrubbed her hands with bottom sand, then returning to the patch of flattened grass, wiped the handle of the knife clean, laid it across the man's pelvis, then dressed, retrieved her camera and hurried to her car.

Forty-Eight

Donovan was on the Katy Freeway returning from a murder investigation when the call came through.

"*Mike,*" Captain Pierce said, "*looks like we have another case for you over at Landing Park. A woman called in and told us where to find the . . . hold on a minute.*"

Donovan pictured Pierce retrieving a smelly cigar from its bed of ashes, sucking it to life, then laying it aside to smolder off another inch or two. He chuckled. "*Would you believe the son of a bitch is one of them New York just released?*"

Donovan grunted. "*Yeah, I believe. Scum washes in here from all over. Let's see . . . Brownlee . . . right?*"

"*Right. Knight and Gainer are over there with a lab crew, but they're just filling in 'til you get there. You through in—*"

"*Yes sir,*" Donovan replied. "*A rookie could've handled it.*"

"*Where are you?*"

"*Almost to the beltway.*"

"*Well, get on over to Landon's soon's you can. He wasn't castrated, but looks like somebody might have given it some serious thought. You know how the public's gonna be up in arms when another . . . ah, let me rephrase that. You know how the men are gonna be up in arms when this news breaks.*"

Donovan harrumphed. "*I know,*" he said, remembering the outraged calls that poured in to headquarters when a prisoner had begged the court to have him castrated, the crowds of men that had gathered outside City Hall, demanding justice. He harrumphed again. Justice

191

hell, he thought. What about the kid that's lying unconscious in the hospital? What about justice for her?

He reached for the lights and siren control. "*I'll call you soon's I know something,*" he said, lightly touching the button. "*I'm on my way.*"

As traffic parted, thoughts of Jennifer crowded in. Throughout his investigation of a recently convicted rapist, he had managed to keep her buried in his subconscious, but now she emerged full-blown to his mind.

Her pinched face rose before him. He sighed. She had been such a lovely girl before the rape. Sixteen, friendly, out-going, his pick among his nieces. Then within days, she had withdrawn from all males, trusting no one but her father. At times, Donovan had felt that even he, himself, was looked on with suspicion.

What was worse, they had never caught the man who had sired such radical changes.

As news of the rape had made the rounds of Delta High, ball games, parties and dating had become things of the past for her. Even a simple look had made her shrink deeper into herself. Except for family activities, she became a recluse. Now, at twenty-two, she was a hunched, skittish, what once would have been called, old maid.

All the son of bitches ought to be castrated, Donovan thought, angrily jamming the accelerator to the floor. Hell, I could do it myself. Turning off the freeway onto Beltway 8, he roared south.

Forty-Nine

Loper opened the letter the guard handed him, read it, gulped, and read it again. He fought to keep his face straight as a familiar feelings of being watched spread through him. Nervously, he ducked his head and shot a sideways glance toward Big Richard's cell.

Richard grinned and waved. "*Hey, Lover Boy,*" he mocked. "*Letter from the wifey?*"

Unmitigated hate streamed through Loper. "*Yeah,*" he muttered, gritting his teeth.

"*Her and her gentleman friends still having at it?*" Richard threw back his head and guffawed.

Loper grunted and turned his back to Richard's cell, then stalked to his bed, lay down and faced the wall. Quickly, he tore the page into small pieces and one by one stuffed them into his mouth, chewed and swallowed.

Fifty

"*Leaving?*" Lisa said, surprise lining her voice. "*Where on earth are you going?*"

"*I don't know. I don't have any specific plans . . . I want to cover Texas, though. You know, the hill country, the Capital, The Rio Grande. East Texas. Hit all the beauty spots. I should be back in a week or two.*"

A bevy of thoughts shot through Lisa's mind. "*You going alone?*"

Marianne laughed. "*Of course. How else?*"

"*Is that smart, Marianne? You know--*"

"*Probably not, but I'll survive . . .*"

"*What can I do to help? You want to talk about it? You know I'm a good sounding-board.*"

"*I know, but I plan to pick-up where I left off years ago . . . shoot some pictures and hope they're good enough to market. I guess that's an excuse for leaving, not my primary reason.*"

Lisa visualized Marianne's shrug. "*Look,*" she said as she mentally sought to re-arrange her own schedule. "*I'm out of school for the next two weeks and I'm not going to the coast. Why don't I go with you? I can study while you work.*"

"*Thanks, Mother Hen,*" Marianne said, "*but no thanks. I really need to spend the time re-discovering who I am and just what I want to do with the rest of my life,*" She paused. "*Please understand. I'll call you when I get back.*" Without further ado, she was gone.

Fifty-One

After phoning her mother-in-law before leaving work, Zoe stopped by H.E.B. to do her weekly grocery shopping. By the time she arrived home, the sun had dipped close to the horizon and Jim and Jolanda had come trooping in from Rosa's.

"*Mom, can I turn on TV?*" Jolanda asked.

"*Not now,*" Zoe answered wearily. "*I don't feel like hearing the noise.*"

"*I won't play it loud.*"

"*No, Jolanda. I don't want to hear it. Anyway, there's nothing on but the news. Besides, you and Jimmy need to help me put away the groceries.*"

Lifting a bag of canned goods from the counter, she bent and set it on the floor beside Jimmy. "*Here, Jimmy. You put these away,*" she said, kissing his cheek. Straightening up, she turned to her daughter. Tiredly, she set another bag in front of the refrigerator, wet a dishcloth, wrung it out and handed it to Jolanda. "*Here, honey,*" she added, planting a kiss on Jolanda's smooth forehead. "*Be sure to wipe off all the containers.*"

"*I know, Mom.*"

Lately, Zoe had lost all interest in hearing the evening news. As far as she could tell, only the bad was ever reported, anyway. Never the good. Rape, murder, gang activities; these were the things that were emphasized, nightly casting additional gloom over her already gloomy day.

Currently, Israel and the Palestinians were again warring over territory, according to a Houston Chronicle headline she had glimpsed that morning on passing a news-stand. Warring, she was convinced, that had begun when the twelve tribes of Abraham were separated many thousands of years earlier and, which she was also convinced, would continue until Armageddon brought things to a flaming halt.

She sighed and crumbled ground beef into a hot skillet as her thoughts turned to her morning break at the bank.

At 10:15, she had entered the lounge where a state accountant and the bank's head bookkeeper were sitting at the small formica-covered table that centered the room, sipping coffee. She smiled and spoke, then hurried through the door to the room housing two toilet stalls and a wash basin.

On emerging minutes later, she saw that Dorothy, who cashiered next to her, was present and drawing a cup of the strong, machine-made brew.

Dorothy asked if anyone had heard about a rape that had happened the previous night. When silence met her question, she continued. *"I heard about it on the way to work this morning."* she said. Closing her eyes, she shuddered. Coffee sloshed to the floor. *"That must be a horrible experience, Killing would be too easy for him."* She minced her way to a chair, placed her cup on the table, then, as if unaware of Zoe's presence, glanced up and widened her eyes. *"Oh, Zoe,"* she said, *"I . . . didn't know you were here."*

Wordlessly, Zoe lifted her chin and left the lounge. As the door whooshed shut behind her, Dorothy's stage-whisper floated out. *"You know, her husband . . ."*

Zoe could almost see Dorothy's innocent-appearing shrug. Consider the source, she told herself. Tossing her head high, she had squared her shoulders, left the bank and strode rapidly around the block during the remaining minutes of her break.

Over tacos and beans, Zoe half-listened as the children chatted about their day, prefacing each story with, *"Know what, Mom?"* before rattling on about yet another school happening. By the time dinner was over, they were talked-out. Zoe hurried them through their baths, tucked them into bed then stumbled to the living room.

The silence of the house fell peacefully around her as she dropped into a plump, plastic-covered chair and propped her feet up on the matching hassock. Brushing aside the lingering disquiet Dorothy's remarks had brought, unbidden thoughts of Gus rose in her mind.

At noon, he had entered the bank and stopped at her window. *"Good morning, Zoe,"* he said, her name a caress on his lips. He smiled crookedly. *"Or should I say, good noonday, if there is such a term?"*

She had felt blood rush to her face and her hands had grown clammy. She centered her gaze on his hairline and forced a smile. *"Good morning, Mister Jerguson. How may I help you?"*

He laid a tan pouch on the counter and pushed it toward her. *"You know how, Zoe,"* he whispered. *"Please . . . have dinner with me. I promise, just dinner. Nothing more."*

Lowering her gaze, she unzipped the pouch and withdrew its contents. *"I can't,"* she said, her promise to Rosa racing through her mind.

Quickly, she tallied the checks, placed the deposit slip in the bag, closed it and shoved it toward him. *"Thank y-"*

"Sure I can't change your mind?" he murmured, brushing her hand with his.

A chill swept over her. Silently, she had shook her head and dropped her hands to her sides.

Rousing herself from the memory, she sighed heavily, rose and within minutes, lay in bed reading words that held no meaning as her thoughts wandered through the past. At last, she laid the book aside and fell into a restless sleep.

A muffled banging woke her. Instantly wide awake, she held her breath and listened intently. Easing out of bed, she reached for the baseball bat propped close by. Maybe she was dreaming. Maybe . . .

Barely breathing, she lifted the weapon to her shoulder. Again, the hammering, this time sharper, echoed through the house. Her heart pounded. Her throat closed. This was no dream. Someone was at the back door. But who? A robber wouldn't announce his presence.

Her mind leapt to Rosa. Was she sick? Had she sent someone to get her? That's crazy. If Rosa needed help, she would have phoned, not roused someone and sent them.

Hastily running her sweat-slicked hands down the sides of her gown, she tightened her hold on the bat and crept on weakened legs to the only window from which she would have a clear view of the back door. Surreptitiously, she pulled the curtain aside and caught her breath.

A man's silhouette loomed dark against the night. She swallowed the sudden knot in her throat. Her thoughts ran crazily. A shiver splashed across her shoulders, raced down her spine.

Afraid to take her eyes off the figure, unable to reach the phone without doing so, she numbly waited. Moments that seemed like minutes, passed, then the man again raised his hand.

The rapping became louder. *"Zoe? Zoe?"* a familiar voice called. *"Hell, I know you're in there. Open the damned door,"*

A mixture of relief and anger sped through her. At least I know my enemy, she thought. Loosening her hold on the bat, she raised the blind and stared out.

Her heart sank. *How can he be out?* she wondered, seeing her freedom melt away. *Did they release him?* Her mind flashed to a letter that had lain unopened in a drawer for the last two weeks.

"What're you doing here?" she exploded as she opened the door.

Loper grinned. *"Where in the hell else would I go?"* he said, stepping inside and holding out his arms. *"Hey, ain't you glad your old man's back home?"*

Zoe stepped back. *"Why should I be? How'd you get out?"*

"Most women ud be glad to see her man come home . . . specially when he'd been gone so long." He narrowed his eyes and stared at her. *"Less she's been getting a little on the side, that is."*

Ignoring the insinuation, Zoe tightened her jaw and glared at him. *"Can I expect the police to come tearing in here again?"*

"Hell no, They let me go. They knew I was innocent."

"Yeah. Innocent as a chainsaw murderer," she muttered, turning on her heel toward the bedroom.

He grabbed her arm. *"What was that?"*

"You heard me," she exploded, jerking free of his grasp. Turning back, she propped a hand on her hip and bent towards him. *"And don't touch me,"* Again turning away, she started for the door. *"You can sleep on the couch tonight, then I want you to get out of here,"*

As fast as a striking rattler, Loper's hand shot out and gripped her wrist. *"Like hell I will,"* he said, flipping her around and shoving her hand up between her shoulders.

Groaning, she dropped the bat.

"This ain't the same man that left here, Zoe," he thundered, forcing her to her knees. *"This go-round, I'm calling the shots,"* He bent and shoved his face closer to her's. *"Got that?"* His grip tightened. *"Got it?"*

She stared in horror at the dark, toothless gap that was his mouth.

He shook her. *"Answer me, You hear what I said?"*

Wordlessly, she glared at him.

"And get this straight. You gonna sleep with me every night, 'less I decide otherwise." He laughed, mirthlessly. *"Few little tricks I wanna teach you, anyway,"* He yanked her arm higher. *"Ya got it? Ya got it?"*

Blind with pain, her strength no match for his, she nodded silently.

Grinning wickedly, he threw her, sprawling, to the floor. *"One more thing,"* he said, oozing confidence. *"From now on, I'll be using the car if we still got one. You can ride the bus or walk to work for all I care."*

Filled with hate and revulsion, Zoe knelt before Loper's spread legs. Spasms of pain radiated from her throat where he had choked her into submission, from the back of her neck where his knotted fist had pummeled.

Wrapping a hand in her long dark hair, he yanked her forward. *"Do it,"* he snarled, forcing her head down.

She gagged and resisted.

He yanked harder. *"I said do it,"*

She cried out, then bent and lifted his flaccid penis in her trembling hands.

8 days later.

Smothering a yawn, Zoe approached the bus stop. Again this morning, Robert had waked her from a fitful sleep, noisily tromping past the couch where she slept and slammed the bedroom door. *"Bastard,"* she muttered, raw hate filling her. *"Man-handling me. Making me miss work. Forcing me to . . ."*

She gagged.

Memory of Father McAheeney's words filed like militant soldiers through her mind. *"Have patience, my child,"* he had said two days earlier when she had gone to him. *"How long has Robert been home?"*

"One week, Father," she had answered, *"and, and . . ."* Choking back tears, she pushed up her sleeves and held her pain-filled hands, palms down, toward him. *"He, he . . ."* She gulped and pulled in a fresh breath. *"My shoulders and back are even worse,"* she said, the words rushing out.

The aged priest re-settled his rimless glasses on the end of his nose and peered at her hands. *"I'm sorry, child,"* he said, clucking sympathetically, *"but the man needs time to adjust."* He squinted at her from under bristly, white brows. *"You must have more patience."*

"But Father, he's forcing me to, to . . ." Embarrassment heated her face. *"perform sickening sex acts."* she blurted. *"I can't go on."*

"Zoe," he had said, his voice quaking with age, *"I know this is a painful experience for you, but when you took your wedding vows, you knew that whatever happened, good or bad, those vows were in place for the rest of your life."* He sighed. *"You also knew that, under God's law, women must submit to their husbands."*

Scornfully dismissing the memory, Zoe lifted a hand to the effulgent light of morning and examined it. Her breath caught. The thin coat of make-up she'd applied to her wrists and hands had merely dulled, not hidden, the bruises.

Tugging her jacket sleeves lower, she thought of the previous afternoon when Rhonda Mayheu, head cashier at the bank, had phoned. *"Zoe,"* she had said. *"Can you possibly return to work tomorrow? Temporaries are simply not working out."*

Zoe stared at the discolored, over-lapping patches of bruises covering her hands and wrists. *"I can try,"* she whispered, shame washing through her.

"Over the week-end, Dorothy broke her ankle," Rhonda continued, apparently deaf to Zoe's soft words, *"and today Julie was hospitalized with a ruptured appendix."* Her voice sharpened. *"We need you."*

"I'll be there," Zoe had said.

Feelings of guilt rose in her as she stared apprehensively down at her hands. Now the lame excuse she had given when she'd called in sick a week earlier would be apparent to everyone.

Mother of God, she silently prayed. Please forgive me for lying, And please keep Robert away from me.

As a modicum of peace flowed through her, a niggling inner voice spoke up. 'How about Gus? You want him kept away, too?'

"Of course." she snapped, ignoring the absurdity of the thought.

Since their break-up, she had been careful to take her coffee breaks during times when Gus normally would be in the bank, but today she knew there'd be no escape. Tears stung her eyes.

The roar of the bus broke into her thoughts. Quickly dipping into a pocket, she withdrew her fare.

I don't know how much more of Robert's prison-spawned abuse I can take, she thought, stepping aboard. True, he's left me alone the past two nights, but how long will that last?

Unexpected visions of Jolanda and Jimmy rose between her and the broad windshield as she took a seat and stared out.

For their sake and the Church's stand, she had endured the worst hell she could imagine before Robert had finally given up on her.

That night, on the pretext of getting a glass of water, she had gone to the kitchen, turned on the faucet, eased a drawer open and slipped a cleaver under the bedclothes draped over her arm. Minutes later, settled on the fold-down couch, she tucked the instrument under her pillow and swore by all she held dear, that if he ever touched her again she would kill him.

The thought again ran through her mind.

'Forget it,' an inner voice said. 'Do that and your children lose both parents.'

Don't make me laugh. He's never been fatherly.

'But,' the voice countered. 'Given time, maybe–'

"Given time? Maybe? You're disgusting, You sound like Father McAheeney,"

'That may be true, but what alternative do you have?'

"None," she mumbled, resignation slowly moving through her.

The driver glanced to where she sat on the long seat opposite him. *"You say something, Miss? . . . Miss?"*

Momentarily pulled from her reverie, she shook her head.

As the operator turned his attention from her, she lifted a hand to the small fold of bills pinned inside her bra. Again, her anger rose. A lot of good it's done to save for a new washer, with Robert's demands draining me dry, she thought.

Fifty-Two

Loper, pretending sleep, listened to Zoe's every step as she moved quietly about the room dressing, then hurried to a window when he heard the front door shut and the bolt in the lock shoot home. Bending forward, he cautiously pulled the lacy, white curtains aside. Squinting through the fog that had risen during the night, he watched her, head thrown proudly up, back slim and straight, march down the street.

He snickered. Ain't gonna let no neighbors onto nothing, he thought, eyeing the rust-colored suit and high necked blouse she wore.

Bitch wooden uh had no bruises ta hide if she'd done like I told her to start with. He laughed. But, hell, whatta I care? Just makes the whole thing more fun. He snorted contemptuously. All that shit 'bout love, honor and obey's just a load of crap, but by god, she's gonna do what I say, like it or lump it.

Smirking, he stalked back to the bedroom and picked up his pants from the floor where he'd thrown them the night before. Bitch hadn't took so long learning I meant business, she wouldn't uh got so bruised. Reaching into a pocket, he withdrew a set of prison-made dentures, shoved them into his mouth and tongued them in place.

Most mornings, he was up and gone long before the kids were awake but this morning he'd slept late and had heard Zoe shoo them out the door. Hadn't seen 'em but twice since I been back, he thought. And that was more'n enough. Jolanda pulling back ever time I tried to hug her and that damned sniveling little Jimmy whining and clinging to his mama like a baby. Damn Zoe, anyway. She's turned 'em against me.

Even set my own mama against me. First time she seen me she got busy telling me what a good mama Zoe was, then set in on me 'bout finding work. He snorted. Same damned shit she fed me all my life. Git a job. Git a job. Git a job. Hell, I'll look for work when I'm damned good and ready and not one damn minute sooner. She might's well shut up and leave me alone, too.

Angrily, he pulled on his pants, rammed his arms through the sleeves of the faded chambray shirt he'd bought the day before from Goodwill and began buttoning it.

After fastening his trousers, he withdrew the money the state had given him upon release and counted it. She ain't found it or else she's smart enough to leave it alone. He guffawed. Bitch learns fast enough if she's got a good teacher.

He rolled his shoulders and stretched, then walked to the dresser, lifted a twenty Zoe had left for him and laughed. Traffic oughta be thinned out by now, he thought, shoving the bill into a pocket. Better get going.

In the bathroom, he turned on the hot water and picked up his razor, then looked in the mirror and smiled. Not too bad for a man just out of prison, he thought, focusing his gaze on the dark stubble covering his lower face. Still a little pale, but hell, give me a few more days and I'll be as tan as any man out there.

Shaved, he bent over the sink, and sending a shower of water splattering over the floor and walls, rinsed his face and flipped his dank hair in place with a dripping comb.

Easing the old sedan onto Highway Forty-Five, Loper pulled to the center lane and accelerated. A sense of power surged through him. Damn, it feels good to be behind the wheel of a car again, he told himself.

Again, he wandered from one old haunt to another, sitting alone far to the back of each, sucking on can after can of Red Tiger, seeing no one he knew. Happy that he didn't.

Don't wanna be bothered by any damn body, he told himself. And I shore as hell ain't wasting my money buying beer fer 'em.

He chuckled. My money? Hell yes, my money. 'fit b'longs to her, it b'longs to me.

After gulping down the contents of the can he held, he burped, plopped the container onto the scarred tabletop, rose and carefully stalked out of the Tipsy-Turvy.

He sat awhile after entering his car, letting the wooziness in his head dwindle to a dull throb, then drove to the next ice house. A picture of Marianne, followed by his thoughts, rose in his mind's eyes. He guffawed. I ain't forgot about you, Missy. You still gonna get it.

Fifty-Three

The mist that had stolen in from Galveston Bay during the night, penetrated Zoe's thin suit and flattened her hair as she tiredly waited for the Metro bus that would take her home. A watery trickle, loosening its hold on her scalp, slithered down her neck. Seething, she mopped at the water with a sodden tissue. Damn Robert, she thought. He's no nearer finding work than he was when they turned him loose. I doubt if he's even looking.

The ssshhh of airbrakes sounded. Expectantly, she looked up. "*South Houston*," she muttered, then turned her back as passengers rushed forward. As she looked away, the bank's head cashier purred by in her newest car. Here I am getting soaked while he's off doing God knows what and there's nothing I can do about it.

Scratching around in her purse, she pushed an extra set of car keys aside and grappled for another tissue.

'Don't be a fool,' the inner voice spoke up. 'There's always something you can do. Follow him. Find out where he's going, how he's spending your money.'

How? she wondered. I work all day. Ride the bus back and forth. How can I follow him?

The voice was relentless. 'There's more than one mode of transportation.'

Yeah, yeah, I know. Lemos, taxis rent-a-cars. And they're all expensive.

'Taxis cost less.'

The thought scared Zoe. I know, but I don't have money to throw around like that.

'You mean you'd rather let Robert throw it around. Is that it?'

Long after Loper had blundered into the house, Zoe lay awake see-sawing over the issue her inner self had suggested.

Within minutes after the alarm clock jolted her out of bed the next morning, she was up, had the children up dressed and out the door, and she, herself, was on her way. Feeling lighter than she had in months, she fairly danced to the bus-stop.

As the bus approached McDonald's, she pulled the cord and got off at the Stop and Go store. An empty Yellow Cab sat out front. If Robert comes this way, I'll see him, she thought, entering the store and quickly glancing around.

The driver, his tell-tale cap pushed to the back of his head, stood chewing on what she assumed was the remains of a sandwich and draining a styrofoam cup. Waiting for me, she thought, approaching him, and he just doesn't know it.

"Do you have a fare?" she asked, her eyes on the freeway.

He shook his head and swallowed hard. "*Scuse me, you caught me with my mouth full. But no Ma'am, I don't.*"

A mixture of doubt, caution and excitement spread through her. "*You do now,*" she said, turning toward the door, "*But I want to sit out front and wait awhile.*"

"*At's all right with me,*" the driver said, holding the door for her.

Minutes later, she saw the old Chevy leave the service road and come to a stop at McDonald's. Anger swept through her as Loper left the car and entered the restaurant. Seething, she waited for him to re-appear.

At last, he emerged.

"*Follow him,*" she said and sank back in the seat.

Zoe stared in disbelief and leaned forward as the cab passed a tiny park. Robert is reading a book? she wondered as Loper, who lay propped on his elbows, opened a paperback. He's never even read a newspaper.

She glanced at her watch. I'm already an hour late, she thought. Another few minutes won't matter. "*Drive back by the park,*" she told the driver.

207

On the next swing past the little patch of ground, she saw Loper lay the book aside, lift a pair of binoculars to his eyes and point them in the direction of a group of duplex apartments. She sucked in her breath. I knew it. He's watching someone. But who does he know who lives in an up-scale neighborhood like that? And why is he watching them?

Her mind in chaos, she slumped against the car seat and looked blindly out the window, trying to make sense of Loper's actions. What can I do? What can I tell tell the police if I call them? That he's in a park with binoculars and a book? She rejected the idea even as it entered her head. There's no law against that. He's not hurting anyone, at least at the moment.

Sudden dread sent icy ripples down her spine. She lifted a hand and rubbed the shoulder that at times still ached from the night Loper had returned and twisted her arm into a half-Nelson. He's up to something, she told herself. But what? Rape? Oh God, no, she pleaded. Not again. Memories of the humiliation she and the children had suffered earlier raced through her mind. Shivering, she forced herself to think of the coming day, of an excuse she'd have to come up with.

As Zoe exited the cab, Angus, who was approaching the building, broke stride and turned toward her. He smiled and tipped his hat. "*Good morning, Zoe,*" he said. "*Running late?*"

The beloved voice brought her up short. Not trusting herself to speak, she nodded and turned her back to him.

He grasped her arm. "*Hey, if you're trying to avoid me, you're . . .*" he murmured, moving to stand before her. "*My god, Zoe, what's happened? Are you all right?*"

His touch sent waves of warmth speeding through her. Tears threatened to surface. "*Yes,*" she snapped, pulling away, forcefully collecting her thoughts. "*I was just thinking.*"

Not to be deterred, he smiled teasingly. "*About having lunch with me, I hope.*"

Lighting fast, Zoe weighed her need to talk against all the reasons she had given herself for staying away from him. I can trust him, she told herself.

She smiled. "*Maybe.*"

The muted clink of china and silver heightened Zoe's already frayed nerves. She drew in a labored breath, knotted her hands in her lap and managed a smile. *"I hope I didn't mislead you when I agreed to lunch,"* she said, feeling heat rise to her face, *"but,"* the words rushed out. *"I need a friend. I need a car."*

There, it's out, she thought, watching Gus' eyes change from the soft, gentle ones of a lover to the penetrating ones of a lawyer.

Panic seized her.

Dummy, she told herself. You're doing this all wrong. He'll walk out, then . . .

His voice broke into her thoughts. *"Zoe, darling, you know I'm your friend,"* he said, bending close across the table. *"But why a car?"*

Fighting back tears, Zoe avoided his eyes. *"Robert--"*

"You're still riding the bus. Is that it?"

Zoe looked down at her hands and silently shook her head.

"Then what?" he asked, reasoning with her as if with a child, *"I can't help if you don't tell me what's wrong."*

Confusion clouded her mind. *"I need to follow Robert,"* she blurted, her embarrassment deepening. *"I know he's up to something, but until I know what it is, I can't . . ."* Tears filled her eyes. Blinking hard, she ducked her head. *"I thought if I followed him, maybe--"*

"Maybe you could intervene in whatever he's doing."

She nodded

Fifty-Four

Marianne contentedly stretched her arms above her head, wiggled her toes and gazed at the sunbeams streaming across the foot of her bed. Exuberance filled her. For months, she had wrestled with the problem of whether or not to leave Houston. No one is indispensable, she had repeatedly told herself until, at last, the words rang true. With Illese and her family moved back to Oklahoma to live with her mother's parents, she wanted to turn to something more productive, something that wouldn't be a constant reminder of her personal loss. The Haven would find other volunteers if and when they were needed.

And now that Lisa had finished school, she would soon be moving. Marianne smiled. With the courage to raise herself above prostitution, the determination to school herself in a profession that promises unlimited possibilities and a child like Coleman, Lisa has much to be proud of, she thought. Better she thinks I am ignorant of the life she's lived. A remark Lisa had made near the beginning of their renewed friendship had revealed how she earned her living. I hope her job soon comes through, she thought, turning her thoughts to her own budding career.

Pictures taken on her latest forays through Texas and Arizona had brought praise, even comparisons with Ansel Adams' work. Though stunned by the continuing kudos, she had, at last, thrust aside self-doubt and replaced it with serious thoughts of pursuing the career in photography she had put aside when she married.

Now, her plans included traveling the U.S. and getting in touch with the land; its beauty, its scars, and its inhabitants, were almost solidified.

Confidence surged through her. Mentally going over a list of last-minute things to be done before leaving, she again stretched, drank in a deep, lung-filling breath and bounced out of bed.

Except for buying the biggest bottle of Obsession I can find, and a necklace and earrings set with stones that match Lisa's eyes, it's all done, she thought. She headed for the shower.

For most of the previous day, she had packed and stacked suitcases, along with newly purchased cameras and other photographer's equipment in the trunk of her car, leaving out only two changes of clothing.

Confidently, she lifted her face to the water spilling from the shower-head. Tomorrow I'm leaving, she thought. And with the realtor regularly checking on the house and paying the utilities, I'll be free until I decide whether I want to return to it, or sell it. The thought gave her comfort.

She turned off the faucet, slicked her hair with her palms and reached for a towel.

She was ready, for now, to put Houston behind her.

Fifty-Five

Zoe, approaching the bus-stop, quelled the apprehension that had kept her awake throughout the night and haunted her all morning as a Porsche purred smoothly to a stop beside her. A flush of shame heated her face. I should never have brought you into this, she thought, as Gus reached and opened the door.

"*How are you this morning, lovely lady?*" he asked.

Quickly she got in the car, glanced at him, then driven by a sudden, uncontrollable fear that perhaps Robert, even at that moment, was watching, bent and lay her head on her knees. "*Okay,*" she murmured.

Gently, he patted her back. "*Don't be afraid, honey. No one's paying us any attention.*" He paused. "*Shall we circle the block, or--*"

Cautiously, she sat up and looked toward her house. "*No,*" she said. "*Park at the Metro lot on the corner.*"

Loper tightened his fingers on the steering wheel as he pictured Marianne cringing and begging before him. He snickered. "*Just wait, girlie,*" he muttered to himself. "*You owe me.*"

A pair of golden arches loomed ahead. Today would be his third and last time to eat there. On the two previous occasions, he'd really kicked up a racket, claiming his eggs were rotten, the toast burnt, the coffee cold and thick with grounds. He threw his head back and guffawed, remembering how he'd fooled 'em, transferring dry coffee from his shirt pocket to his cup. Set the damn fools up and they didn't even know it.

His first thought had been to find a roach, squash it, slip it under his toast, then really do some hell-raising. That woulda got their attention for sure, he thought, but his stomach hadn't felt all that strong. 'stead, I'll switch my order five or six times while one ah them dumb-assed teenagers bites their lip. Oh, yeah. They'll remember me. He smiled. Not quite as good as the roach-under-toast idea, but hell, it'll work.

Then, if the damn cops do pull me in, the kids could tell 'em I was here the whole damn time, and I'll be off the hook free and clear. He raised a hand to his smoothly-shaved face. Yeah. Damn right they'll remember me, all right. Just be a little foggy 'bout the time.

He smirked at his own cleverness.

Fifty-Six

Lisa, unable to settle anywhere for longer than a few minutes at a time, prowled from kitchen, to bedroom, to living room, then re-traced her steps, a cup of stale coffee in her hand. She sighed, plopped into a chair at the tiny dining table and gazed out as swirls of fog shifted and thickened under a bleak October sky. She pulled her sweater close.

Two weeks earlier, her classes at UH had ended. Now, her life had taken on a new twist. She stayed home.

Unaccustomed fear darted through her. Her heart plummeted. Maybe I didn't make it, after all, she worried. Her thoughts raced back to the classrooms; the test questions; the professors. Joseph Ingram, Lydi Simmons, Conroe Seidlam, and Victoria Snell, her latest journalism professor who constantly boasted about her Mayflower ancestry.

As if that matters, Lisa thought. But the facts are, if anyone failed me, it'd be her. I knew from the start that she didn't like me, but I hoped she'd be fair.

Her thoughts were as merciless as the late October cold that had sent her scurrying for blankets during the night. Anger flickered through her.

Tossing her head, she looked at the notebooks stacked on one end of the table. One day, she promised herself, when I get my life settled, you'll see. You'll all see. I'll turn Marianne's story into a blazing best seller.

The anger deserted her as quickly as it had risen. A shiver raced down her spine. Maybe I'll have to go back to . . . And Coleman will find out what I do for a living. Tears surfaced.

She wiped her eyes and heaving an impatient sigh, pushed back her chair, rose, and for the twentieth time, stalked to the door and opened it.

"*Damn,*" she railed, thrusting a hand into the mailbox and coming up empty. "*Even that damned Gulf Coast Mirror's forgotten their promise of a job.*"

She crossed to the living room, perched on the arm of an aged chair, picked up the remote from a table and punched the TV on.

Clint Eastwood, riding a dusty horse across the screen, stared dourly out. The clopping hooves annoyed her.

Impatiently, she flicked off the movie, rose and re-entered the tiny kitchen-dining area. Coffee sloshed as she dropped into a chair and pushed the half-filled cup aside. Self-doubt battered her as she idly reached for her John book that only hard-learned caution had saved from the garbage. Slowly, she began leafing through it.

Maybe I can find some diversion here, she thought, turning to the first page.

Lawrence Andran. She grimaced. He's such a bore. She leafed on.

Toby Kenton? She snorted softly and shook her head. All he ever wanted was a shoulder to cry on. I don't need that.

She flipped another page. Then another. And another. Then paused.

Randy Sutton? She laughed. Now there's a guy who really knows how to treat a woman, she thought, remembering the trip they'd made to Cancun. Maybe I'll give him a call.

A fleeting sense of guilt tainted her freedom as she quickly skipped over the page of T's where Cadance Tinsley was listed.

She sniffed and tossed the book aside, then opened the top notebook from the stack and removed a paper. A paper she'd been reluctant to assign to the trash bin.

Her eyes raced over the page. A perfect description of my life, she thought. Heaving a sigh, she began to read aloud.

> "*I'm a pawn in this thing called love.*
> *The streets are my home.*
> *Faceless lovers do not see*
> *beyond my hip-length skirts*

and four-inch heels.
They do not see
there is a soul within.
"At times, my man-worn body longs for release,
but the unknown, looming,
frightens me too much for that finality.
Instead, I send my silent cries.
I'm human.
I hurt.
I feel.
I cry.
I need.
But these thoughts are never heard.
The antennae of the faceless ones
are not attuned to me.
To them, I'm a thing to be used for an hour,
or a night,
then push aside,
forgotten as the dead butts of cigarettes
they drop on the stairs
as they leave,
their appetites assuaged.
I hurt.
I cry.
I need."

Tears filled her eyes. "No matter how hard I try, I can't seem to move beyond my past," she whispered. She reached again for her "date" book and opened it.

Grief-filled, she glanced down at the first page as the faint rattle of the mailbox sounded. Her heart leaped. Maybe, she thought, momentarily pausing and pressing her hands together. Maybe.

Bubbling with excitement, Lisa picked up the phone. After a short series of rings, Marianne's answering machine came on. *"I got it. I got it, Marianne."* she said. *"As of today, I am an honest-to-god college graduate. And the job on the Mirror came through."*

Thoughts careened wildly through her mind. Now, *to sell or give away what I don't want . . . I need to call Coleman . . .friends at the Red Wine will want to know. Bubbles.* Her thoughts slowed.

At noon, Marianne picked up her mail, hurried to Dillard's, and on to her favorite jewelers. Two hours later, she returned home.

Excitement trailed through her as she plopped into a recliner and carefully opened a thick, brown envelope that topped the mail-stack. She smiled as she removed its contents. *"Texas Nature will love these,"* she said, shuffling through close-ups of owls, of the jagged bark of a mesquite, of a bear, a coyote, a pair of stark-white, long-stalked herons she'd caught with a long-view lens at a hidden lagoon.

Her smile widened. *It's wonderful to be producing again,* she thought. *And selling.*

For a moment she sat quietly, musing over her good fortune, then punched on the television. Young Bill Cosby's antics filled the screen. Laughing, she watched him take a prat-fall, then noticed a button on the phone beside her chair was blinking red. *Lisa,* she thought, pressing the play button.

Lisa's voice, triumphant with achievement, poured out. *"Marianne? Marianne, they both came through. The job and my diploma. Can you believe it? I'm now a bonafide college graduate and, I start with The Mirror the first of January. Gosh, I'm so excited. I'm dying to talk to you. Meet me at err, err, err,"* Lisa's voice, garbled and scratchy, bled away.

After several unsuccessful attempts at retrieving the message and phoning Lisa to no avail, Marianne gave up. She smiled, checked the time, and rose. *I'll have time to pay a quick visit to my friends at the zoo, see the ancient Egyptian relics at the IMAX, and go to the exhibit at the Holocaust Museum, before I start looking for Lisa,* she thought.

When Loper again left the car, he slouched to the toilet carrying the bag he'd left the Funny Face store with. Ten minutes later, Zoe, eyes glued to the entrance of the men's restroom, watched him emerge, bearded, slouch to the old Chevy, open the door and get in. She narrowed her eyes and leaned forward. Even through the rapidly gathering dusk, there was no mistaking his familiar form and gait. *"Robert."* she muttered, convinced now, more than ever, that he was readying himself to carry out some devious plan to . . . to what? Her mind churned. Rob someone? Kill them? Meet a woman? What is he up to?

The Porsche came to life as the Chevy drove off, made the corner and turned left.

Thank God Angelina is baby-sitting the children, Zoe thought. This may take all night.

Watching the tail lights of the Chevy join the evening traffic, she re-counted the day.

Only minutes after she and Angus had parked in the Metro lot that morning, Robert had left home.

Throughout the day, they had followed him. Had watched him leave McDonald's, go to The Funny Face store in the theater district, roam from one ice house to another and finally had wind up at McGregor Park, where, after numerous trips to the restroom, he'd crawled into the back seat, apparently to sleep. Hours later, he had emerged.

Fifty-Seven

Lisa hummed as she moved about the apartment, dressing. After leaving a second message on Marianne's machine, then a third, she had finally called Bubbles as Bubbles was dressing for the night's work.

"*Oh Lisa,*" Bubbles had said, on hearing Lisa's good news. "*I'm so happy for you, but darn, I'm gonna miss you . . . who can I talk to now?*" Her voice had ended on tears.

"*Please don't,*" Lisa said, her heart torn for the child housed in the voluptuous body of a woman. "*You should have heard Coleman.*" she added, deliberately changing the subject.

"*I know he's happy.*"

"*Ecstatic's more like it. Tell you what,*" Lisa said, hoping to pull Bubbles out of the slump she'd fallen into since the last beating she'd taken. "*Why don't you and I celebrate? In a way we're both graduating . . . you're learning how to fight back, and I'm . . .*"

"*I know,*" Bubbles said, her voice happier. "*Both of us have a reason to celebrate and you know how I love a party.*" She paused. "*Might be crowded, though.*"

Lisa laughed. "*Isn't it always?*"

Bubbles giggled. "*Yeah, but tonight's different Remember that stage show begins tonight.*"

"*Oh,*" Lisa said. "*I'd forgotten about that. With all the hoopla that's been in the paper, I expect there will be a big turnout.*" She paused. "*One of us better go early and get a table--*"

"*I'll do it,*" Bubbles broke in. "*I'm almost dressed.*"

"*Okay. Be there soon as I can.*"

As Marianne emerged from the IMAX Theatre, she glanced at the bright ball hanging just above the horizon. *"It would be easier to do if Lisa were here, but . . ."* she muttered, entering her car, dreading to fulfill the promise she'd made herself.

She sighed, merged with the heavy traffic on Herman Loop, and pointed the car toward San Jacinto Boulevard.

Loper, waiting for a traffic light, saw a gleaming gray Audi, blinker on, waiting to make a left from Mc Gregor Ave. onto Golf Course Drive. Marianne immediately sprang to mind. Squinting through the fog, he recognized the car's lone occupant. Hate raced through him. *"Bitch,"* he muttered, hastily changing his plans, *"this is the night for you to die."*

Keeping a comfortable half-block behind her, he watched her cross Jacinto, crawl down Caroline and park. Where in hell's she going? he wondered.

Holding his breath, he watched her leave her car, round the corner of a building and disappear inside, then looked around for a spot where he could wait un-noticed. A cluster of oaks on the corner caught his eye. Making a quick U-turn, he eased to the curb beneath their sheltering branches and switched off the car lights and motor, reached into the glove compartment, grinned, and withdrew a hypodermic needle and a small bottle of liquid as he waited for his eyes to adjust to the deep shadows around him. Yeah, he thought. Tonight's shorely yore time to die. A picture of Old Earl back in prison rose in his mind's eye. He snickered. Thank yuh, old man fer sendin' me to 'Ain't There Williams'. Like you said, he had the goods, all right. Got 'em right off. All I had tuh do was ketch 'er at the right time and place and that's tonight. Hope to hell she ain't going home with all them damn guards they got around there. " Ain't no way that bitch can see me here.

Lifting a hand to his face, he scratched. *"Wish that bastard wudda told me this damned thing'd itch."* he muttered.

Forty minutes later, his skin stinging from glue and his blackened nails, he impatiently left the car and strolled toward the building Marianne had disappeared into.

Wipers quietly, intermittently, swished the gathering fog from the windshield. Narrowing her eyes, Zoe nervously inched forward on the car seat and leaned close to the glass. She dared not ask Angus to speed up. Not that he'd be angered, but he had volunteered to help her and she knew that staying well back, as he was doing, was the best way to avoid detection. *Yet . . . Oh, God, don't lose him. Please don't lose him.*

Memory of seeing Loper, the previous day, train binoculars onto the group of housing surged through her mind. She had tried every avenue she could think of to find out who lived in the complex, all to no avail. But she knew that whoever lived there would probably be included in whatever plans Robert had made and that those plans, once executed, would be terrible for everyone involved, especially her children.

And now, after creeping through the fog, turning this way and that, obviously following someone, here he is, parked and waiting for God only knows who or what. She shuddered.

If only the police had listened when she had called the previous day and voiced her opinion. But, they had said, Loper had been released, not paroled. Consequently, he was a free man, and they couldn't move on him unless he committed a crime.

Her thoughts ran like rats in a treadmill, echoing the same questions. *What are his plans? Robbery? Rape? Killing?*

Dread tightened her muscles.

Choking back an overwhelming need to sob, Marianne, blinded by tears, hurried from the Holocaust Museum of Houston.

By giving herself one feeble excuse after another, she had, for over two years, convinced herself that there was nothing there for her. Now, she saw the wisdom of that reluctance, as from beneath her tightly controlled memory, thoughts of her own rape-aborted child slithered like virulent vipers into her unguarded mind.

How could You allow children to suffer so? she silently railed at an unseen deity.

As she reached her car and stepped off the curb, a rock rolled beneath her foot. Her ankle turned. She fell. Intense pain shot through the pulled muscles and tendons. A flush of embarrassment stung her cheeks.

Instantly beside her, a short, heavy-bearded man bent and gripped her arm as she struggled to rise. "*Here, let me help you,*" he mumbled, his voice gruff.

Chills raced down her spine.

His hand tightened.

Words of gratitude died in her throat.

From somewhere on the fringe of a gathering crowd, a woman's voice asked. "*Shall I call an ambulance?*"

Freeing her arm from the iron grip of the man beside her, Marianne shook her head. "*No. No, please,*" she said, "*I'm all right.*"

"*Where's your car?*"

Without answering, she hobbled to her car, scrambled in and slammed the lock in place.

Advice from the spectators followed her as she buckled herself into the seat.

"*Be careful.*"

"*Is it safe for you to drive?*"

"*Better see a doctor.*"

Glancing back as they walked, the crowd scattered to their own vehicles. Watching through the rear-view mirror, Marianne saw the man who had offered his help enter a car parked directly behind her, start up, and without looking her way, pull out.

Sucking in a breath or relief, she lifted her cell-phone and dialed. Lisa didn't answer. Another dial and there were no messages on her own machine. Angry with herself, Marianne steered through the wavering, thickening mist toward The Red Wine Inn. "That was stupid, Marianne," she scolded herself. "*Utterly stupid. What did you expect to see, remnants of an ancient civilization? You should've forgotten the museum. Wasn't the zoo and the IMAX enough?*"

Fighting a rising urge to cry, she blew out a stream of air.

After parking in back of The Red Wine Inn, Marianne opened the entrance door to the discordant sound of musicians tuning their instruments.

The maitre d', menus in hand, greeted her. "*I'm sorry, Miss,*" he said, in response to her request. "*We're all filled up.*"

Glancing quickly around the room, she gestured at a few empty tables and returned her gaze to him.

"All of those are taken?"

He nodded. *"They're reserved."* His face brightened as he hastily glanced around the room. *"There's always the bar,"* he added, *"if you and--"*

"I'm alone," Marianne cut-in. I should have known they'd all be taken, she thought, again looking around the crowded room.

"I do have a table for one left."

"Show me."

The waiter craned his neck, then apparently satisfied that the table was still unoccupied, turned back to her. *"If you'll follow me, please."* he said.

"This is fine," she said as he stopped beside a tiny table partially hidden by a massive pillar and slid the table's one chair beneath her.

Squinting through the thickening fog, Zoe watched Loper jam on brakes, leap from the Chevy and apparently pacing himself to the steps of the woman he'd been tailing, follow her. *What's he up to?* she wondered.

Aiming for a better look, she opened the car door and standing with one foot on the ground, narrowed her eyes and studied the stranger through the heavy fog. There was nothing about the woman that looked familiar; her dark hair, glinting under colorful lights that ran the length of the railed gallery; the hobbling walk. *Who is she?* she asked herself.

"Zoe," Angus said, *"why don't I go in and see what's going on?"*

Guilt assailed her. *"No,"* she muttered, knowing that when the night was past she would never again see him. Shamed, she dropped to the seat and turned to face him. *"I'm sorry,"* she whispered, *"I should never have dragged you into this."*

"Zoe," he said, reaching for her hand, *"Whatever concerns you, concerns me. Don't you know that?"* His voice dropped to a whisper. *"I love you."*

She jerked her hand back. *"No."* she said, her voice raising a notch. *"You can't. I simply didn't have anyone else to turn to . Please understand. Please don't love me. Friendship--"*

"*Sorry,*" he said. "*I didn't mean to push. You made it clear when you came to me, that you came as a friend.*" His eyes darkened. Looking away, he chuckled and shook his head. "*Still. . . you can't blame a man for trying.*"

He fell silent a moment, then grasped the door handle and looked at her. "*I'm going in,*" he said.

Minutes later, Angus was back. Entering the car, he sat down and spread his hands. "*He's just sitting at the bar drinking a beer.*"

Puzzled, Zoe frowned. *Is that all?* she wondered. "*I'd like to wait, and see what . . .*"

When Emma Lanfen returned to the tiny, raised stage for a final bow and the lights were turned up, Marianne looked at her watch and gasped. "*Two-thirty.*" she muttered, leaping to her feet. "*And I'd planned an early start.*"

Turning her head, she watched the throng, pushing and jabbering their way through the two exits.

Another few minutes won't make that much difference, she scolded herself. *Now, sit down.*

As the final notes from the musicians floated out and the actress left the room, Marianne dropped to the chair and watched the musicians dismantle their instruments and pack them. Each time she glanced at Lisa's table, the bevy of celebrants surrounding it seemed to have grown, gift-wrapped packages were stacked high, and a huge cake, candles unlit, awaited the touch of a match.

She looked at her watch and rose. *Time to go*, she thought, starting toward the crowd surging through the doors, *but what will I do with these?*

After quickly glancing around the room for a waiter and seeing none, she returned to her table, dug a twenty dollar bill from her bag and approached the bar where a man, back turned, was busily polishing glasses. "*Excuse me,*" she said, clearing her throat. "*I was wondering if . . .* "

The barman paused and turned toward her. "*Yes ma'am,*" he said, smiling broadly. "*How may I help you?*"

Marianne shrugged apologetically and gestured at the packages she laid on the counter. "*It seems all the waiters have disappeared, but I* was wondering if you could get these to the corner table," she said, laying the bill next to the gifts and motioning with her head toward the table where Lisa sat laughing. "*I must leave now.*"

Through the thick fog, Zoe watched Loper exit the Inn and occasionally glancing toward the emptying parking lot, saunter down the walkway. On reaching a door standing between two yawning, black openings he halted. Puzzled, she watched him withdraw his hands from his pockets, turn his back and seconds later, swing back the door and enter.

Anger swept through her. *Is that sorry jailbird using my money to sleep off a drunk? Or wait for a woman?* Clenching her jaw, she turned to Angus. "*Gus,*" she said, thrusting a hand into her purse, "*thanks for your help, but I'll take it from here.*"

Alarm filled his eyes. "*What do you mean?*" he said, reaching toward her. "*You can't tackle him alone.*"

She avoided his hand and held up her key case. "*I'm taking the car.*" she said, getting out of the Porche.

"*Zoe.* " he said. "*Please don't confront him.*"

She bent and peered in the window. "*I, I . . . Please, Gus, forgive me and go.*"

Fifty-Eight

Softly humming the show's tunes, her thoughts on plans for the following days, Marianne paused under the bright entrance lights, surveyed the near-emptied parking lot, then drinking in a deep draft of moist air, started toward her car.

As she approached the building's corner, a door quietly opened behind her, an arm shot out and hooked around her.

A hand covered her mouth, pinched her nostrils.

Unmitigated terror raced through her. Squirming, fighting for breath, she kicked backwards, felt her foot connect with flesh.

"*Bitch.*" a voice muttered, tossing her into the room.

Fireworks exploded in her head as she staggered, slammed off a wall and fell to the floor.

Half-conscious, she felt hands drag her onto a bed and yank her skirt up, her pantyhose down.

A voice growled in her ear. "*Still feisty, huh, Missy?*"

Fuzzy memories, spurred by pain, streamed through her mind.

Her eyes sprang open.

A man, his face only inches above hers, straddled her, pinned her arms to her sides.

Frantically she pulled her feet to her buttocks and thrust her torso upward.

"*Ain't no use bucking. I gotcha.*" he said.

'*Think.*' a voice within commanded. '*Do something he's not expecting. Throw him off guard.*'

Relying on the silent instructions, she breathed deeply, gathered spittle, circled her lips and spit. The glob caught the assailant squarely between the eyes.

226

"*Whore*." he bellowed. Loosening his grip on her arms, he rose to his knees and caught her flailing hands. Shoving her arms upward, he doubled a fist and pulled back his arm.

'*Again*,' the voice whispered.

Fiercely, she rammed a knee into his groin.

Groaning, he released her, grabbed his privates and rolled to his feet.

Springing from the bed, she stood a moment fighting dizziness.

Cupping himself with one hand, he grabbed her with the other.

The gun. Clawing herself free, her eyes never leaving his, she bent to retrieve her purse.

Viciously, he slammed a fist to the back of her head. "*I said you ain't goin' nowhere.*" His straggly beard parted in a sneer, revealing yellowed teeth. "*Ain't no use hollering. Ain't nobody gonna hear ya.*"

As she fell, he pulled back a foot and kicked.

Frantically wriggling from its path, she rolled face down, jack knifed to her feet and cautiously, slowly, rose to a full stance.

'*Pretend to play his game*,' the inner voice cautioned.

Cursing, he pushed himself to his knees and reached for her.

Obeying a gut-instinct, she grabbed his beard, yanked and stared unbelievingly at the shaggy hair in her hands, then at him. "*You*," she cried, staring at the hated face.

He leaped to his feet. "*Yeah, Missy. Me.*"

Consumed with rage, she glared at him. Hate raced through her. Wary, her eyes never leaving his, she kept beyond his reach.

Inching to the dresser, he picked up an object and began to circle her. "*Y'ain't leaving alive this time,*" he said.

Allowing herself a quick glance, she saw the gleam of a hypodermic syringe.

The voice within her spoke again. Breathing heavily, she whipped around and kicking high and fast, crashed her injured foot to the side of Loper's head. Pain ricocheted through her.

Lashing wildly at her, he fell to the floor, with the needle, buried hub-deep in his thigh, emptying.

Fifty-Nine

One month later, investigation into Loper's death had broken down to that of self-destruction and Zoe had returned to work. Six months later, her children met and learned to love Angus, and just short of a year later, she and Angus were quietly married into a future bright with happiness.

Lisa, reveling in her good fortune, within a week moved to the Mississippi Gulf Coast, into the house she'd bought years earlier and she and Coleman went about their lives, her constantly thanking God for her good fortune, him shooting for manhood with every passing day. Now freed of her past, she began the novel she'd promised herself to write about Marianne's experience, then laid her pen aside. Maybe I'll tell her story later, she'd think. I can't do it now. My work at the Mirror keeps me too busy to concentrate on that, and I love my work, sooooo. Maybe someday when Coleman has taken his path in life and I'm alone I'll write it, but not now. Not just now.

As Marianne zig-zagged her way across the great southwest, she found men and women wearing what she thought of as the traditional old-west style of clothing beneath bonnets and wide-brimmed sombreros, while others dressed as if they were ready to step onto the catwalk of modern wear. Though long skirts and bonnets seemed to prevail in the hot, blistering sun, the more modern women, wearing knee-length dresses or tight-fitting pants, seemed quite comfortable despite the heat. A general mixture of the populace beckoned Marianne from one town to another before reaching California's Pacific coastline where she saw, to her horror, baby sea lions lying dead where they had been used for target practice, which reminded her of her own loss and again attacked her aching heart. She laughed at hump-backed whales leaping and cavorting in their salty home. Snapping, snapping, snapping pictures along the way: constantly on the look-out for unusual angles, eye-catching spots of light and shadow, a face where time had etched its passing; of picturesque layers of mountains where man-made machines had sliced through sediment that had taken eons of time to collect as the world spun its way into being. Her heart lightened as love of country filled her and she re-asserted being an American.

In Washington State, she turned east, and ventured into both the American and Canadian sides of Niagra Falls where she was bathed in a mist that rose hundreds of feet above her, where the rush and beauty and roar of the water beckoned, where she was one among many taking pictures of the majestic sight.

With bags of film to be processed and her need for adventure sated, she began her journey home. Down the Atlantic side of the U.S. through Virginia, the Carolinas, Georgia, on down to Key West she drove, always on the look-out for the right place, the right scene to catch with a camera. On leaving Florida, nostalgia began to nip at her. Soon she'd be entering Mississippi where she would spend a few days with Lisa and at last meet Coleman before returning to Houston. A sense of sadness enveloped her. How fortunate Lisa is, she thought, having a child.

A week later, Marianne parked in her assigned spot and sat silently surveying her home. Home again, she thought, as feelings of nostalgia raced through her. Home again and alone. Pushing the feelings aside, she shook herself out of the mood that was fast overtaking her, got out and began emptying the car. Twenty minutes later she stood in the middle of the living room surrounded by suitcases, a makeup bag and box after box of undeveloped film. Tired to the point of exhaustion, she showered and fell into bed. Within minutes, she was asleep.

Though the sleep of exhaustion had erased much of her weariness, the following morning, still feeling the effects of her long jaunt, she donned a swimsuit, grabbed a beach towel and took off for Galveston. There, she returned to a spit of land she had once discovered where peace always awaited her. Though the tide had washed over the spot during the night, the earth it left behind, under the warmth of the sun and breath of the wind, had long-since dried to the cushion of soft, lightly-gritty sand with which she was familiar. After assuring herself that she was alone, she settled her still-tired body into the complaining beach-chair she'd brought, and for a moment, closed her eyes. Except for softly- crying seagulls, it's deserted, she thought, as a feeling of serenity washed over her. Still, the wide blue gulf beckoned. Obeying her inner self, she sat up, slipped her sandals off, and as she headed for the water, felt the needle-like bite of a sandspur jab an exposed toe. Patiently, she bent, removed it, squeezed the appendage until it no longer bled, then continued on.

As she reached the shoreline, the sound of sand scrunching under her feet was drowned out by the rhythmic washing of the waves and the demanding cry of the gulls as they begged for morsels of food. Then a car door slammed, running feet sounded, and the full-bodied voice of a man invaded her private world.

"*Melody*," the voice called as Marianne's peace was shattered. "*Melody, wait.*" The voice rose. "*Wait*," it called. Intuitively, she sensed someone beside her and opened her eyes. Nearby, gazing at her through eyes as blue as the sky above her, stood a golden-haired girl, timidly stretching a hand towards her. Marianne's heart lurched. What a beautiful child, she thought. My little one would have looked like that if . . .

From a distance, a deep male voice interrupted her thoughts. "*Melody, Melody, wait . . .wait*," it called, as heavier, running footsteps came close and stopped. "*I'm sorry if she's disturbing you, Miss, but . . .*" His voice bled out. " *Her mother died shortly after she was born, and it seems she's always looking for a woman she can relate to. Over the years, I've hired several different women to care for her in our home until I could get in from work, but none of them panned out. Right now, she's in day -care, but that doesn't seem to be working out, either. And she's so darned fast on her feet, she can get away from me before I know what's happening.*" He bent, lifted Melody into his arms, kissed her, then held a hand toward Marianne. "*Sorry,*" he said. "*Please excuse my rudeness. I'm Esmond Jakes, and I guess you don't need to be introduced to Little Miss Friendly here.*" He chuckled. "*Marianne Mavin,*" she said, as she held out a hand in response to his greeting.. "*What a beautiful daughter you have.*" He smiled and nodded.

"*Yes. She is, isn't she.*" He glanced at the watch on his wrist and looked toward a pier that extended far into the sparkling Gulf waters where people were patiently feeding fish with shrimp. "*Look,*" he said. "*Why don't the three of us go over to Fisherman's Wharf for hamburgers and cokes and get better acquainted?*" He looked at Marianne and smiled. "*Sorry it can't be steak and wine, but it seems that's not one of their availables .*"

Feeling relaxed and comfortable in his presence, Marianne laughed. "*Timing's off anyway, even if they served it.*"

Twenty minutes later the three sat around a small, oilcloth-covered table at nearby Fisherman's Wharf, munching on sandwiches and sipping icy cokes as Esmond and Marianne, under the watchful eyes of Melody, became friends. A few short months later, each, starved for affection, succumbed to the pull of love and Esmond and Marianne became lovers. Within the year they quietly married and the three became the love-centered, caring family Marianne had always yearned for.

The End